The
Fall
of
Grace

By

William Holms

OTHER BOOKS BY WILLIAM HOLMS

The Killing of Faith (2020) *Faith looks back on her life and describes a mysterious - but seemingly hopeless – situation. This mystery will draw you in, as you are given clues to solving the puzzle of Faith's whereabouts, the events leading up to her current nightmare, and how a woman's simple lies plunge her into a living nightmare beyond anything you can imagine.*

The Beginning of Hope (2021) *Faith is forgotten by everyone until Hope, her youngest daughter, sets out to find her mother. She will uncover the dark truths of love, family, betrayal, and the haunting question - Who can someone really trust? Her search for the truth will put her life in danger and may destroy the Brunick family forever.*

The Fall of Grace (2022) *takes you on another twisting, turning, suspense-filled journey as it continues the unforgettable story of Ryan and Faith Brunick. With both their mother and their father gone, Hope and Grace must learn to live without them as Grace's life unravels. These beloved characters make decisions that will surprise and shock you as they navigate the challenges of life, love, and loss.*

The Rise & Fall of Ryan (2022) *takes you back to the beginning of Ryan Brunick's life and that fateful day when he met his future wife, Faith. Ryan must come face-to-face with his past as he works to get Hannah out of prison for murder. Will Ryan be able to pull out another miracle or will he lose his first case. The series concludes with even more twists and turns and another unforgettable conclusion.*

The Intruder You Know (2023) *Paige Childers, a young college student left for college ready to start all over. But leaving your past behind is seldom clean and never easy. An intruder outside her home will change her life forever, the lives of everyone around her, and leave Paige in a fight for her life.*

WHAT READERS ARE SAYING

★★★★★ Holms has done it again! The third installment of this masterfully-crafted thriller/mystery/story reminded me how good it feels to be wrapped up in a great book. Every book in this series is equally important, entering and exiting this rollercoaster of a story with ease and providing the reader with another way to interpret what's happened. Holms' ability to storytell and his perfectly-placed BOMBS of twists and turns will leave you wanting more!

---Odessa Zabala Fernandez

★★★★★ "I have just finished reading The Fall of Grace. I have to say that I didn't think the story could get any better but boy have you proved me wrong. These 3 books are some of the most incredible that I've ever read and I do hope the story doesn't end here." —Ellen Aish

★★★★★"Shocking, jaw-dropping and can't-put-down. Just a few words to describe this amazing continuation of the Killing of Faith series. This story is full of twists and turns that will keep you guessing right until the end. The characters are so well written that your heart can't help but break for them." — Christie Schneider

★★★★★ ""Once again the Brunick family characters almost jump off the page as they make their way from one complicated situation to another. Unexpected twists and turns make this another page-turner and the yell out-loud ending is unforgettable. Do yourself a favor and buy this book!"
—Deborah Jesensek

★★★★★ This book really caught me off guard as I didn't expect it to blow me away. Book has a great story premise, great writing."

—Marta Nater

– CHAPTER 1 –

When did my story begin? Was it the first day I got back from Thailand? Was it before I ever left for Thailand? Maybe it was the night when my father was killed in that car wreck over a year ago. Perhaps it was the day my mom and dad divorced and our family fell apart. The one thing I do know is my story started a long time ago…I just didn't know it at the time.

I feel like I'm searching for answers to questions that don't really matter anymore. It's not like I can go back now and change anything. Life doesn't work that way. We don't get a "do over." Still, there are those times in your life when you want answers. I need to know why things went so wrong.

It's one o'clock in the morning, and here I am lying in bed with my eyes closed, but my mind is racing a mile a minute. This has been going on for three days now. I toss, turn, and move from one position to another, but all I'm doing is making myself crazy. I'm absolutely exhausted, but I can't fall asleep to save my life.

I turn on the sound of ocean waves in the background. This always does the trick when I can't sleep, but tonight it doesn't really help at all. Just when I think I might doze off, a new thought runs through my head, and my mind is off and running all over again.

At 1:22 AM, I take two Tylenol PM's. Maybe they'll knock me out. I climb back into bed, switch to some light and easy classical music, and give it another try. Minute, after minute, after minute, slowly passes by. "Damn it," I whisper to myself after taking another quick glance at my alarm clock. *Now it's 3:02 AM.* I check my phone and see nothing but a blank screen taunting me. Not a call, not a text, not a single email.

It's pretty clear tonight won't be any different from last night, or the night before that, or the night before that. I haven't slept more than five hours since the first night I came back from Thailand three days ago. Not five hours a night, but five hours total.

At this point, I figure I might as well get up. I throw back my covers, put my robe back on, and walk down the hall to the kitchen. Our two babies are sound asleep upstairs in their beds. Our oldest daughter, Bonnie, started kindergarten this year. Our son, Wesley, is about to turn one. As far as they know, Daddy is gone on another business trip, and he'll be home any day now. They're used to Daddy's business trips. Since the day he became a CFO at DMD (a large microchip manufacturer) it's been one business trip, one late night meeting, or one unexpected emergency, after another.

Sometimes, it actually feels like we have two homes—one with the three of us going about our daily lives, and the other when Daddy's home. I'm left working, taking care of the kids, going to all the school stuff, bringing the kids to the doctor, cooking, cleaning the house, giving the kids a bath, tucking them in bed, and going to bed myself. When the teacher or day-care worker needs something, they know who to call. Basically, I'm married but living more like a single parent.

So where was I? Oh yes, I pour myself a glass of orange juice and reach for the vodka bottle on the counter. There's barely enough vodka left for one more drink. I sit down at the end of the kitchen table—the same place I sit every evening for dinner—and put my head in my hands. I massage my temples like it will actually make a difference. My eyes are so heavy, I can barely keep them open any longer. I fold my arms on the table, doing my best to make a pillow so I can rest my head. I close my eyes, and slowly feel my mind and body fade away.

With my head still in a fog, I open my eyes just enough to see over my arm. *What the heck? Where am I?* Somehow, I fell asleep while laying here at the kitchen table. *Why now? Why couldn't I fall asleep five hours ago in my soft, warm bed?*

I lay my head back down, but the *tick…tick…tick…tick* coming from the clock hanging on the wall keeps getting louder with every passing second. As much as I want to go back to sleep, the early morning sun has different plans for me. It's streaming through the kitchen window like a laser beam shooting right into my eyes.

Bonnie has to leave for school in twenty minutes. I pop my head up and say, "Oh shit."

I hurry into her room, turn on the light, and whisper, "Bonnie… Bonnie sweetie, you have to get up for school."

She's a beautiful, smart little girl who likes to dress herself, but this morning there's no time for that. I help her get dressed and quickly pull her hair back into a ponytail. I usually fix a hot breakfast and drop her off at school on my way to work, but I'm not going to work. This morning, it'll be a bowl of cold cereal and the school bus on the corner.

Anyone driving by our house right about now might think everything looks absolutely normal—even wonderful. The lawn is bright green and freshly cut; the hedges are nicely trimmed; and my car is parked safely away in the garage. I'm the beautiful wife and doctor who married the handsome, successful businessman. We have two wonderful children, a gorgeous home, and a vacation home in Aspen. To the outside world, we look like one big happy family. We're Facebook perfect, so to speak. It's a fairy-tale story—just not the one where the people live happily ever after.

Once Bonnie's out the door, and Wesley is down for his nap, the house seems so quiet again. I'm left all alone with my worries.

So far, I've been keeping everything inside—hoping, even praying, everything will turn out okay for me, but deep down inside I know nothing will ever be okay again.

I need to talk to someone. I think that's how women work—or cope with our problems. It helps to talk things through, instead of holding everything inside. It's not that I'm looking for answers, because no one I can talk to has the answers I need. More than anything else, I just want to vent.

The only person I can confide in is Hope—my little sister and best friend ever since we were kids. After my brother died, we both clung to each other and got through it together. We have no secrets, but I don't know how to tell her what's really going on in my life. Where do I even start? I wait a few seconds, take a deep breath, and give her a call.

"Hey Grace," Hope says, sounding so upbeat and happy. She's like most college students her age—busy living her life without a care in the world. When you're in college, you're living in the best of times—you just don't know it at the time. "How are you this morning?" she asks.

Still tired and exhausted, I take a deep breath and say, "Hope, we need to talk."

Showing the same heartfelt concern I've come to depend on, her tone changes. "What's wrong Grace? Are you okay?"

Trying to choke back my tears, I say, "It's Jackson, he hasn't come home."

"What? I thought he got home before you did."

"He was supposed to be home, but he's not here, and I haven't heard anything from him."

"What?"

"I know. It's been six days....*six* days. I've been waiting, hoping he'd come home. I thought he'd be back, but he's not here. He's still not here."

"We got back three days ago. You've heard nothing?" she asks.

"Nothing at all. I've called him, I've texted him, I've even emailed him. He doesn't answer."

"Oh my God, Grace."

"I know, I know."

"Do you think he was in an accident or something?"

"I don't know. If there was an accident, wouldn't you think we'd know about by now?"

"Then what?" she asks.

"I don't know. I don't know what to think. I even called all the hospitals in Austin and Denver, but…but he's not there."

"How are you holding out?" Hope asks.

"I'm not….I haven't slept since we got back. I can't eat, I can't sleep, I can't think straight."

Hope does her best to keep me calm. "Listen Grace, you need to call the police. I'm sure they'll find him."

"I just don't know. I don't want to make a big deal out of it and then it turns out to be nothing."

"If it turns out to be nothing, then it turns out to be nothing, but you need to call," she repeats.

I was hoping it wouldn't come to this. I know once I make that call, I can't go back. It's like I have this glass case around my life that reads, "IN CASE OF EMERGENCY BREAK GLASS." Once I break that glass, my life will never be the same again.

"I'll call," I say. "I'll call them as soon as we get off the phone."

"Call me back and let me know what they say."

"I will, I will."

"Grace, don't worry. Everything is going to be okay. I'm sure he's still gone on his trip, and he'll be back."

I know she means well, but something tells me everything's not going to be okay. I should have heard something by now.

"I love you, Hope."

"Love you too."

– CHAPTER 2 –

When I get off the phone, I feel the last three sleepless nights starting to take hold. *I need some coffee.* I fix a cup with plenty of French vanilla creamer, and do my best to clear my head before I finally dial 9-1-1. Halfway through my coffee, I make the call.

"9-1-1, what's your emergency?"

"It's my husband. He's been missing for three days, and I think something might have happened to him."

I lay out the basic facts about how I came home from my trip to an empty house, and how I've called everywhere with no answer. The operator taking the call, asks if I want to file a report. When I tell her I do, she lets me know she's sending someone over as soon as possible.

I grab a blanket and pillow out of the hallway closet, turn on the television, and lay down on the living room couch. I don't get through the first contestant on *The Price is Right* before I fall back asleep from exhaustion.

Next thing I know, I'm jarred awake by the front doorbell ringing and the television still playing in front of me. I'm still so groggy that I sit up, rub my eyes, and turn towards the front door, wondering what's going on. Then it all comes back to me.

"Dammit!" I say, grabbing my empty orange juice glass off the coffee table and rushing to the kitchen. "Hold on a minute," I yell as I pass by the front door. "I'll be right there."

I run into the kitchen, grab the empty vodka bottle off the counter, toss it in the trashcan, and put my glass in the sink. On my way back to the living room, I dart into the guest bathroom and take a quick look at myself in the mirror. I look terrible. I'm still in my robe, my eyes are puffy, and there's a slight smudge of mascara under each eye. My hair looks like I haven't brushed it in days, because I haven't. Only under these circumstances would I ever answer the front door looking like this. I splash a little water on my face and run my fingers through my hair until I look halfway decent.

I open the front door with a quick "good morning" and close my robe a little tighter around me. Standing on the other side of the door is a tall, slender, male investigator wearing slacks and a blue sports coat. He holds up a badge for me to examine. Beside him is a female officer in slacks and a light blue collared shirt.

"I'm Detective Stowe," the man says with a smile. He motions to the woman on his left and says, "This is my partner, Officer Fleming."

I nod at Fleming, and she smiles back.

"Thank you for coming," I say, pointing towards the living room. "Come in," I say with a smile. "Please come in." Together, we walk to the couch. Once they're settled, I offer them a cup of coffee.

"Coffee, no ma'am," Detective Stowe says, answering for both of them. "We've already had our coffee for the day. You called to report a missing person?"

I sit in the chair to their right and say, "Yes, just like I told the woman on the phone, it's my husband. He left on a business trip and was supposed to be home by now. I'm afraid something might have happened to him."

He puts his metal paper protector on the coffee table between us and takes a pen from his breast pocket. "What's your husband's full name?" he begins.

"Jackson Kennedy….Jackson Jefferson Kennedy."

"Jackson Kennedy, with DMD?" he asks.

"Yes sir. Do you know him?"

"No, I've never met him, but most people around here know who he is. Can you give me his date of birth?"

"October 12, 1984."

"Do you know his driver's license and social security number?"

"I don't," I say, scanning the room like I might have it written down somewhere. "Can I look that up and get it to you?"

"Sure," he says, waving it away like it's no big deal. "What kind of car does he drive?"

"He drives a brand-new Acura A9. It's white with tan interior."

"Would you know the license plate number?"

"I'm sorry, I don't"

"That's not a problem," he says with another wave of his hand. "I can run a check on it."

"How long has he been missing?" he asks.

"Hold on just a second," I say, getting up from the couch and walking into the bedroom. I come back with a box of tissues, sit back down on the couch and say, "I came back three days ago, and he was gone."

"You came back? Where did you go?"

I take a sip of my coffee and say, "My sister and I went to Thailand."

I take a tissue out of the box and massage it in both hands. I wipe my eyes and continue the best I can. "When I came back…when I came back…he was gone."

"Thailand? I hear that's a great place to visit," Stowe says.

"Yeah, it is. Unfortunately, I wasn't really there for pleasure."

"Why did you go then?" Fleming asks.

"We went to visit my mom's gravesite."

She looks at Fleming and asks, "Your mom died in Thailand?"

"Yes, it's a long story," I say.

"And you came back three days ago?" Stowe asks, shooting a glance at his partner.

"Yes, sir."

Detective Fleming sits back and says, "Mrs. Kennedy, he's only been gone three days. He probably just got held up."

"Well, actually it's been six days. He was supposed to return on the twenty-second. I was expecting him home before I got home."

"Where did he go?" she asks.

"He left for business. I'm not really sure where. Usually, he goes to Denver…..sometimes San Francisco, but when he goes there, he's usually gone for a few weeks. He said he'd be gone about a week, so I assume he went to Denver."

"And when was the last time you spoke to him?" Stowe asks, still taking everything down.

I pause long enough to get another tissue. My voice cracks when I say, "We last spoke the night before I left….that was the fourteenth."

"Have you tried to call his work?"

"I called, and they said they haven't heard from him either. I asked about his trip, but they wouldn't give me any information. They were really vague about everything. It's like they didn't want to talk to me. The whole conversation was kinda strange."

"Who did you speak to?" he asks.

"Arthur Bradford."

He writes the name down and asks, "Do you have his number?" After I look at my phone and give him the number, he asks, "Mrs. Kennedy, do you have any reason to believe your husband might have left, or moved out, on his own? Did he take his belongings?"

"I don't think so," I say, looking around. "Hold on just a second."

I go into the bedroom closet and search through his clothes. There's a long row of mostly white and blue dress shirts neatly hanging on a row of hangers like they always are. Beside his dress shirts are his slacks, again in a perfect row; just like you'd see hanging at the store. All his blue jeans are neatly folded and stacked on the shelf. His shoes fill up the shoe rack. Everything looks just like it always looks.

I go to the bedroom dresser and shuffle through his sock and underwear drawers. I see nothing out of place. He definitely didn't take enough clothes for a long trip.

Then I open the small drawer where we keep all our important family documents, including our passports. It's a hidden drawer at the very bottom of the shelves. No one would even know it was here unless someone told them. Again, everything is in place. His passport is sitting right on top of mine and Bonnie's. All our birth certificates are in an envelope, and our social security cards are in another envelope.

I grab a chair and pull down the shoebox on the top shelf where we keep emergency cash. Again, nothing seems touched.

I return to Mr. Stowe, shake my head, and say," It's all there. His passport…everything is where it always is."

"Do you mind if I check?" he asks.

I walk back into the bedroom with Stowe following behind. He stops for a second right inside the door and looks around the room before following me into the closet. He slides his fingers along Jackson's shirts hanging neatly together.

"You have a very nice home," he says.

"Thank you."

"You said he left his passport. May I see it?"

Our secret drawer is never supposed to be opened if anyone is present. I'm not really comfortable revealing it, but he's a police officer, and he's standing right behind me. What else can I do? I open the hidden drawer, retrieve the passports all held together by a rubber band, and hand over Jackson's passport.

"Do you mind if I take a look?" he asks, pointing to the other drawers in the closet.

"Go ahead," I say, moving out of his way.

He opens each drawer and searches inside. It doesn't look like he's finding anything important. When he's finished looking through the last drawer, he stands up and walks out the closet. Back in the bedroom, he goes to the dresser and asks, "Which are Jackson's?"

"These three," I say, pointing to the three on the right.

"May I?" he asks.

"Sure, go ahead."

He goes through each drawer, and moves things left and right, looking for I don't know what. He closes the last drawer and walks back into the living room without telling me what he found or didn't find.

"This is probably nothing," he says. "I'm sure Jackson will be home soon. I'm going to start an investigation. We need to track his last credit card charges. Do you have the credit cards he usually charges on?"

"Sure," I say as I get up and walk into the kitchen. I open my wallet from my purse and slide out the two credit cards we share. I hand him both cards and say, "We use the same cards."

He opens the metal folder still sitting on the coffee table and secures the cards to the top clip. "If you don't mind, please don't charge anything on these cards for now. We want to make sure we can trace any charges Jackson makes."

"Sure," I agree. "He also has a company card—I think an American Express—but I don't have that card. The bills go to his office, and I never see them."

Stowe looks over at Fleming and says, "I hate to ask you this, but it's important. Were you and Jackson having difficulties?"

"Difficulties?" I ask.

"Were you having marital problems?"

I shake my head and say, "Oh no…no marital problems at all. Things were really great between us."

Over the next thirty minutes, I give him all the information he wants. I hold nothing back. He writes down Jackson's phone number, cars and license plates, and all the information about our trip to Thailand.

He takes a form out of his folder and says, "Mrs. Kennedy, I wouldn't get too upset right now. He's probably just at work or something. If there was an accident, we'll learn about it any day now." He slides the paper to my side of the coffee table and says, "For now, fill out this missing person's report."

Trying to ease my concerns, Detective Fleming says, "I'm sure his car will show up at the airport or something. I'm going to run a check on his plates and follow up at his work."

I take a fresh tissue from the box and wipe my eyes. "I'm just worried," I say. "It's not like him to not answer his phone. He always calls me back."

Stowe and Fleming stand up from the couch. Stowe taps his hands on his knees, and with a firm handshake says, "I think we have everything we need for now."

I set my tissue down on the coffee table and walk them to the front door. Mr. Stowe hands me his business card and says, "Here's my number. Call me if you hear anything…anything at all…and make sure you let me know if he returns."

"Thank you so much," I say, holding my robe closed.

"We'll be back in touch," Detective Stowe says with a smile.

After they walk out, I open the curtains just enough to see outside. They walk out to a black Ford sedan and stand there talking for a while. I can't make out what they're saying, but it looks like they're going over the things we were just talking about for the past hour. Stowe does most of the talking, while Fleming nods her head now and then. After about fifteen minutes, they get in their car and drive away.

I go back into our bedroom and look at myself in the mirror. I need a shower. *Maybe it will help clear my head.* I always take hot showers, but this time it's *boil*ing. As the hot water pours over my head and burns my back, the whole thing runs through my mind—especially the last few weeks we were together.

When I told the police my marriage was great, it wasn't the whole truth. Over the past two years, our marriage has been under a lot of stress. Hope was admitted to rehab, Bonnie almost drowned in my dad's swimming pool, and then we found out everything about our mom dying in prison.

From the day I moved to Dallas until Hope found that damn watch in my dad's closet, my dad and I spoke just about every day. He became the person I leaned on the most during tough times, and he was such a big help with Bonnie. He loved her as much as I do. He'd drive up to Dallas to see us every chance he could, and she spent a month at his house every summer. It was during one of those summer visits, that he taught her to swim. When I needed advice, he always seemed to know the right thing to say.

Jackson and I were growing apart. He was never home, and I was becoming more and more unhappy in my marriage. Several times, I talked with my dad about divorce. He begged me to stick it out and don't give up. At one point, he drove to Dallas and talked to Jackson and me together. My whole life I hated disappointing my dad, so for his sake I put all my efforts into saving my marriage.

Then my world came crashing down when I found out my dad was behind the whole thing with my mom. At first, I was in denial. I couldn't believe the father I knew would ever do something like that. Then, when I couldn't deny it any longer, I was so angry. I don't know if I was angrier about what he did to my mom, or about what he did to me. I knew our relationship would never be the same.

Then, just when I thought things couldn't get any worse, my dad was killed in that car wreck. The news floored me. I had such a hard time making sense of it all. For the first few months, I was paralyzed. I really didn't think I could go on without him. It felt like the weight of the world was crushing me. Night after night, I dreamed of my dad's Mercedes going over that cliff and crashing into an inferno down below.

I couldn't help but blame myself for it all. My dad loved us unconditionally, and when he needed it the most, I didn't give him my unconditional love in return. His death is something I'll have to live with for the rest of my life.

I remember the best of my dad—not the person at the end. He had so much good in him, and he loved his kids so much. Despite everything he did, my dad didn't deserve to die.

Jackson disagreed. He thought my dad got exactly what he deserved. *Lots of people cheat. What he did was unforgiveable.* I resented him for saying such things about my dad. By this time Jackson had been gone so much, he was no longer the man I could lean on. I pretty much withdrew from him and everyone else.

I was falling apart, but the world kept on spinning without me. Jackson kept working more than ever, which I resented, so I focused all my energy on my babies. Bonnie still had to go to school, and Wesley still needed a mommy. Little by little, the pain that crippled me began to loosen its grip. I slowly picked myself up and got back on my feet.

Then I went to Thailand. When Hope first suggested we visit our mom's gravesite, I wasn't thrilled with the idea. I came up with every excuse imaginable to get out of it—I can't take off work, Bonnie has school, Jackson has work, I don't want to leave Wesley while he's so young, I'm just too busy.

Why was I so against it? I'm not really sure. Maybe down deep, I blamed my mom for how our family wound up. We once had this All-American family, but she broke it up. After the divorce, things were so crazy. I never really got over our life with her. Did she love us? Maybe she did, but I always felt like we came third. She loved herself the most, and she loved the latest guy she was dating second. It felt like we came in a distant third.

But Hope was determined to go. She brought it up again and again. When I finally made it clear, I couldn't or wouldn't go; she said she was going with or without me. Well, now she was the only family I had left, and there was no way I was going to let her go back to Thailand all by herself.

So, what did I do? I came up with this great idea. Jackson was always gone, and I was so busy at the hospital that we spent little quality time together. Our last vacation was a year ago at this private resort in Mexico; and it didn't go too well. He spent half our time at the resort leaving for work; which led to more arguments and ruined our vacation.

Since our anniversary was only two months away, I figured we could celebrate in Thailand. Spending a week relaxing on a beautiful beach seemed exactly what we needed. With a little—well a lot—of convincing, Jackson eventually agreed to go.

I wanted everything to be special. My best friend agreed to keep our kids for as long as we needed. I planned out everything like I always do. I've always been this romantic, so I found an amazing resort with its own private beach. I bought tickets for a couple of city tours, arranged two-day trips, and made reservations at the best restaurants I could find. I even bought him an expensive watch in a fancy box to surprise him. I wanted to have another baby and thought this would be a good time to start.

I was so excited to go. I thought Jackson was excited too. Then two weeks before our trip, he called me from work to break the bad news—he was dealing with another emergency at work and couldn't make it. Again and again, he tried to explain how I have no idea what it's like to run a large company.

Jackson and I didn't argue a lot, and when we did, it was usually civil. But this one was different. By the time he got home, I was so upset; more like furious. I'd heard these same excuses too many times, and this was one excuse too many. We went round and round, but nothing changed his mind. In the end, he couldn't go, and nothing I said made any difference. Really, I should have seen it coming. It seemed like his job was one big emergency after another.

In the end, I went without him. I returned the watch and changed all our plans, so we could take the kids. It wasn't the wonderful, romantic vacation I had planned, but I was determined to make the best of it.

By the time we left, Jackson and I were no longer talking. We walked around the house like two strangers with nothing to say to one another. When we passed in the hall, we looked the other way. My anger was plain to see. If Jackson smiled; I gave a blank stare. If he tried to talk; I had nothing to say.

On the day I left, things were cold as ice. He kissed the kids goodbye and looked at me like he wanted to apologize or something. When he moved in to kiss me goodbye, I turned away and walked off. I drove off without so much as a hello, goodbye, or go to hell. We didn't talk, text, or email the entire time I was in Thailand.

It feels like I've been in the shower for over an hour. It definitely made me feel physically better, but it doesn't last. I put back on my robe and sit on the edge of our bed. I almost call Hope again, but I decide to call Jackson one more time.

By now, I've called, texted, and messaged Jackson so many times. I've called his office and his friends. Still, I feel like I should call again. This time, my call goes straight to voicemail.

"Jackson, it's me. I'm so worried about you. Please, please, please…….just call me back. I love you so much.

– CHAPTER 3 –

If you draw a line across the State of Texas from Laredo to Corpus Christi, you find what some people call the "cactus curtain." It divides the Mexican Texas from the Anglo Texas. Most of the area below the line looks more like Mexico than the United States. The landscape consists of a lot of dirt, sand, pebbles, and boulders. The one hundred ten-degree summers are scorching hot, leaving the soil dry and cracked. The whole place is covered in a white calcium carbonate called "caliche."

Back in 1888, the San Antonio and Aransas Pass Railroad established a train depot forty miles west of Corpus Christi, where US Highway 281 and state highways 44 and 359 intersect. They named the depot Bandana; and it became a thriving point for shipping cattle. Over time, more and more people moved to the area and a small town sprung up around the depot. They wanted to name the town Kleberg, after Robert Justus Kleberg who was a war hero who fought in the Battle of San Jacinto, supported the Confederacy, and raised a militia when the Civil War broke out. Kleberg was taken, so they named the town Alice after his wife.

By 1896, Alice had a population of 885 people. It had one hotel, two saloons, two general stores, a library, a bank, a Methodist Church, and an

Episcopal Church. Not much ever happened there. No one living in Alice, Texas at the time would have dreamed their little south Texas town would one day change the county, the State of Texas, the United States of America, and history as we know it.

Next to Jim Wells County lies another little county called Duval County. People usually drive through Duval County on their way to somewhere else. Again, not much to see there. Someone once wrote, "There is not a thing to do in this lonely land but drink and fornicate." But this small, desolate place would be the location of the greatest, and most powerful, dynasty in the history of the United States. Duval County is where our story begins.

Back in the early 1900s, the Mexican Americans (children born in America to Mexican parents) dominated the population of little Duval County. Like most places, however, it was the white landowners who wielded all the power. The Mexican Americans worked the land and the whites pretty much treated them like ignorant servants to be used and disposed of. Mexican Americans weren't welcome around town, couldn't go to the local school, or get a normal, decent job. They had no voice in local or state government.

Everything in Duval County changed when a white man named Archie Parr came along. Parr grew up pretty poor. He dropped out of school in the third grade to wrangle horses; he'd walk cattle to market on foot! He later became a schoolteacher and a boss on the Chisholm Trail cattle drive. He eventually moved to Duval County to run the Sweden Ranch.

Parr was kind, charismatic, and understood the Hispanic culture. He learned perfect Spanish from his time working alongside Mexicans as a ranch hand and his job as a teacher. Unlike most whites, he came to realize the value of these hard-working people.

Parr rose to prominence during an election that divided the county. Most whites were on one side of the issue, and the Mexican Americans were on the other. Things got so heated, that three Mexican American men were gunned down right in front of the Duval County Courthouse in broad daylight because they wanted to vote. The massacre terrified the local community, who armed themselves for battle and were ready for a shootout. Parr arrived, eased the tension, and urged everyone to stick together and not respond with violence.

From there, Archie Parr earned the love and respect of all the local Mexican Americans and became their voice. For over a decade, starting in 1896, he was elected and re-elected as a county commissioner. He then served two more decades as a Texas State Senator.

Over time, Parr wielded most of the power in the county, but he did have his opposition. It went on like this until his chief rival was shot in the back with buckshot and killed while eating in a local café. This gave Parr complete control over the entire county. By 1908, every elected official was chosen by Parr. Parr became known around the county as "El Patrón," or "the boss." He wielded absolute power, and you know what they say— power corrupts and absolute power corrupts absolutely.

When Parr became a County Commissioner, he began using the county treasury, the Water District funds, and the local school district funds as his own little piggy bank to benefit himself and all of his friends. He controlled everything—including everyone sitting on the Duval County Commissioners Court, all the members of the Duval County Water District, the trustee at the San Diego Independent School Board, and the officers who wrote checks to fictitious persons. He owned the construction company that was paid for work that was never performed. The bank he owned, cashed the checks with forged endorsements or no endorsements at all. The Duval County books showed new roads that were supposed to be built, and projects that were supposed to be completed. But if you drove around Duval County, you mostly found the same hot, dry ground covered with that white caliche, and nothing else.

It wasn't just the county funds that made Parr rich. If you were a contractor and wanted to work on a county project, or you wanted a permit to build something, or you wanted to do any other business in the county, you had to get the approval of Mr. Parr. No job could be completed (or not completed) unless Parr got his cut of the action. The Parr's were partners in virtually every business venture within the county.

While Archie Parr was amassing an incredible fortune, he made sure he took care of his constituents. Some say he became a modern-day Robin Hood. Unfortunately for the taxpayers, it takes a lot of money to run a county and become rich at the same time. The big oil companies and rich landowners (many of them absentee) paid the highest tax rates in the state. Most of the Mexican American landowners, however, never paid their tax bill at all and the county never tried to collect.

As a reporter once wrote: "In Duval County, Archie Parr was king. No one got a job without Archie's approval. No one got elected without Archie's endorsement. Senator Parr treated the Duval County budget as his own personal bank account, but a lot of the money trickled back to Parr's faithful Mexican friends. Parr ran a one-man welfare department, and anyone who needed money for food, or clothing, or a doctor's bill could get it, with no strings attached."

Parr doled out dollars like Santa Claus on Christmas Eve. Just like the good Lord, when they were hungry, he fed them; when they were jobless, he found them work; and when their wives and babies fell sick, he paid the doctor's bills. If you couldn't afford your child's tuition, Parr might put your kid through college.

Parr's favor went far beyond just cash handouts. For the first time, Mexican-Americans felt at home in this little county. They owned many of the Mexican-style homes, held most county jobs, were elected to local offices, and their children went to the same schools as the white kids. Mexican Americans in Duval County possessed a sense of self-worth they couldn't find anywhere else in the State. As time went on, most of the tenant farmers and ranch workers in the county were Mexican-Americans while the white, educated population just about disappeared.

If you drove through Duval County and needed directions, sat down at the café for a bite to eat, or stopped at a gas station to fill up your car with gas, you might want to brush up on your Spanish. That's pretty much all anyone spoke there. It's probably the only place in the United States where

Anglos actually assimilated into the Mexican culture rather than the other way around.

To the Mexican Americans, Parr was a hero. They saw him as one of their own. It was only natural his people voted just as he wanted them to vote. At that time, the Democrats in Texas controlled the state and Parr controlled the south Texas Democratic vote. This meant more wealth and more power. He became known around the state as the "Duke of Duval" because of the complete control he had over Duval County. If you wanted to run for governor, lieutenant governor, senator, or any other statewide office, your first move was to come down to little Duval County and eat some enchiladas, rice, and beans with Archie Parr.

Parr's power did have its challenges, but most were stomped out with either a gold coin or a silver bullet. The biggest threat to his dynasty came in 1914, after Parr was elected governor of Duval County. Unable to stop him politically, his enemies turned to the courts. A group of local farmers alleged that $24,000 was paid by the county for work that was never performed. They demanded an audit of the county's financial records. Parr refused to allow anyone near the county records. Parr was asked in court if he would allow an examination of the books.

"No, we are not going to let you see them," Parr answered, like the question was ridiculous.

"We will have some difficulty in obtaining proof, probably, Mr. Parr, won't we?"

"It sorta' looks like it," he quipped.

Well, a preliminary audit was ordered, and it revealed all kinds of illegal activity, including the massive amount of money taken by Parr. Parr's enemies finally had the evidence they needed to send Parr to prison for a long time and end his grip on the county. The case eventually made its way to trial, where Parr would have his day in court.

Fortunately for Mr. Parr, on August 11, 1914, a mysterious fire destroyed the whole damn courthouse, including all the documents, records, and evidence that were about to be used against him at trial. Luckily for the county, right before the fire, all birth records and other county documents were moved to a fireproof vault and kept safe.

All charges against Parr were dismissed. There were a few remaining charges against other people involved in the scheme to defraud the county, but they were all dismissed a little later for a lack of evidence. Archie Parr's legal problems disappeared. The Parr dynasty would continue for many years. Oh….and Duval County got a brand-new courthouse.

By the time of his death, Parr had amassed a fortune. The Parr dynasty grew from Duval County to neighboring Jim Wells County, and his influence stretched throughout the whole Rio Grande Valley including Jim Hogg County, Nueces County, Brooks County, Starr County, Cameron County, Hidalgo County, Webb County, Willacy County, and Zapata County.

Archie Parr made sure he surrounded himself with loyal followers—people who could burn down a whole courthouse when you need it. Back when he was boss on the Chisholm Trail, he became friends with a young man named Robert Flint. Flint was tall, thin, and pretty wiry. He had to quit school in the tenth grade to help support the family. By the time he was seventeen, he could outride, outgun, and outfight any man on the trail. He was tough, worked hard, and eventually became Parr's right-hand man. When Parr left to run the Sweden Ranch, he knew he would need someone who would always have his back, so he brought Flint with him. Flint would spend the rest of his life protecting the powerful Parr family.

– CHAPTER 4 –

The next weeks are so hard for me. I can't eat, sleep, laugh, or cry. I just feel numb. I keep waiting for someone—a police officer, or sheriff, or constable, or whoever does this kind of thing—to show up at my door and tell me the bad news. When that eventually happens, my life will be over. Every day that passes, only makes me worry more. I take time off work while I figure out what to do next.

On Wednesday morning, just as I get back from dropping Bonnie off at school, I get the call I've been waiting for.

"Mrs. Kennedy, it's Detective Stowe. Do you have a moment?"

"Detective Stowe, did you find my husband?"

"Do you mind coming down to the station?" he asks.

I'm not sure why he wants me to come to the station. *Why not talk to me here? Why not tell me the bad news now?*

"Sure," I agree. "I'll come right down."

"I tell you what," Stowe says, sounds like he's wanting to be helpful, "I'll send a car to come pick you up."

"It's okay," I assure him. "I need to make sure my neighbor can watch my little boy. I'm fine driving myself."

Now, sounding a little more determined, he says, "I'd rather have someone pick you up. He'll be there in a few minutes."

A Dallas police car arrives at my house just as I leave my neighbor's house. Stowe must have sent the car before he even called me. A police officer comes to my door, and I follow him to his patrol car. I start to get in the front seat, but he opens the back door and helps me in.

Once we arrive at the police station, we go in through a side door. It feels a little strange. He escorts me to a small, white room with a desk, three chairs, and a large mirror against one of the walls.

"Can I get you anything?" the officer asks.

"I'm fine," I say, so he walks out the door.

Once he's gone, I'm left all by myself. It's so cold in here, and I didn't bring a sweater. I look around and notice a camera hanging in the corner. I need to go to the bathroom, but when I reach over and turn the doorknob, it's locked. I sit back down in the chair and wait…and wait…and wait. I keep looking at my watch, as five minutes becomes ten minutes, and then becomes fifteen minutes. At this point, I get a weird feeling inside. I start to wonder if everything's okay.

When I look back up at the camera, I realize for the first time exactly where I am. I've seen enough of those missing person shows on television to know this is an interrogation room. This is not what I was expecting at all. Never, never, never would I have thought I'd be in a place like this. *Am I in trouble? Do I need a lawyer?*

Never in my life have I felt like I needed my dad more than I do right now. I've never been too religious. After leaving home, I stopped going to church. Still, I take a deep breath and say a little prayer.

With my head still down in prayer, Detective Stowe comes in. Now, he's holding a file filled with papers. "Mrs. Kennedy, how are you today?" he asks, without so much as a smile.

"I don't know," I say shivering. "It's freezing in here."

Ignoring what I just said, he takes out a large notebook pad, like a lawyer might use, and a pen. Something tells me this can't be good.

"Why are we in here?" I ask. "Why couldn't we just meet at my house again?"

"We just need some more information." he says. He seems much harder than he was the first time we met.

Unable to hide my fear, I ask, "Did you find Jackson?"

Without addressing my question, he says, "First, I need to read you your rights."

"My rights? Why do I need—"

"You have the right to remain silent," he interrupts. "If you choose to talk, anything you say can and will be used against you in a court of law. You have the right to an attorney at trial or during questioning. If you cannot afford an attorney, one will be appointed for you. Do you understand these rights?"

"Did you find my husband?" I ask again.

Gone is the friendly detective who came to my house a few weeks back. Now he's all business. "Do you understand your rights as I've explained them to you?" he repeats.

"I understand my rights," I say. "Have you found him?"

"Do you wish to waive your rights and talk to us?" he continues.

At this point, I don't know what to do. Everything is so confusing. So many times, I've watched these shows and said to myself, "Just leave; walk out; don't talk; don't say anything," but my stomach is in knots. Instead of leaving, I simply say, "Sure."

Once we get that out of the way, he says, "No ma'am, we haven't found your husband, but we do have some concerns. We need more information from you."

"I don't understand—what kind of concerns? Is Jackson okay?"

"We don't know, Mrs. Kennedy. Have you heard from him?"

"I've heard nothing," I respond.

"Mrs. Kennedy, were y'all having financial troubles before you left for Thailand?" he asks, writing everything I say down on his pad.

"No, like I told you before, we both work. I'm a doctor and he works for DMD. We do just fine. Why?"

"We don't know right now. Just trying to clear a few things up."

I feel like he's intentionally keeping me in the dark. "What kind of things?" I ask.

"Mrs. Kennedy, we spoke to Arthur Bradford at DMD. Were you aware of the financial situation at your husband's business?"

I don't understand why he's asking these financial questions. "I don't know much about his business."

"Well, I don't really know how to say this. Your husband was being investigated by his company. It appears they did an audit of the company records, and it revealed some improprieties."

"Improprieties….what kind of improprieties?"

"They won't say more until they speak to their lawyers. They're supposed to get back to us. All we know at this point, is there were some financial problems after an audit of the books and a formal investigation."

I put my hand over my mouth, shake my head, and say, "I knew nothing about this."

Suddenly, everything changes, when he asks, "How would you describe your marriage?"

"My marriage? Why are you asking about my marriage?"

"It's nothing really," he says. "It's just a formality."

The way this is going, I know I should just shut up, but I don't. "Like I said, my marriage is fine. My marriage is great."

He drops his pen and asks, "So, you weren't having any marital problems?"

"Not at all," I insist, doing my best to make it sound true. "We had a pretty normal marriage."

"What do you consider normal?" he asks.

I shrug my shoulders and say, "I don't know…I would say our marriage was better than normal."

I know the spouse is always the first suspect when someone is missing. I'm afraid to tell the truth. If I say we argue from time to time and lately we've argued more than usual, he'll turn the focus on me.

Stowe continues. "This can remain confidential, but I have to ask. Have you been seeing anyone else?"

This takes me by surprise. Actually, it shocks me. "Absolutely not," I snap.

"What about your husband? Do you have any reason to believe he's been seeing someone else?"

"Not at all," I insist, starting to tremble. "Jackson would never do something like that."

He picks up his pen and returns to writing. I stop him and ask, "Am I a suspect? Am I being accused of something?"

"Right now, your husband is missing. These are the usual questions we ask in situations like this."

"So is my husband okay?" I ask again.

"At this point, we don't know. He hasn't been to work in quite some time. and no one there knows where he is. As far as—"

"What?" I ask, showing a flash of confusion. "So, he never went to work?" I interrupt.

"No ma'am. They haven't seen him in months. As far as we can tell, you're the last person to see him."

"I can't be the last one to see him," I say, shaking my head. "I told you, I was in Thailand. That was a month ago."

"Yeah, we know about your trip to Thailand."

I thought I was coming down for *them* to give *me* information—not the other way around. I was supposed to be the one asking all the questions, but I'm doing all the answering. For the first time, I feel like I might be in trouble. I pull my phone closer and touch the side button to light up the screen. I thought I was coming for a quick sit down—an update. Now I've been here for over an hour, and it feels like we're just getting started.

I look up to the far corner of the room and see the light on the camera blinking on and off. Each time I glance at the mirror, all I see is my own reflection. I'm sure someone is standing on the other side looking in. At one point when he's gone, I feel the urge to knock on the mirror and ask if I can go to the bathroom, or get something to drink, but I just stay sitting here.

"I don't know what's going on here," I say, a little testy. "Am I in trouble? Do I need to hire an attorney?

Every time I feel like walking out and ending this whole thing, he switches to something easier and less confrontational.

"Mrs. Kennedy, are you aware of any other credit cards your husband might charge on?"

"Just the ones I gave you," I say, before reminding him. "Like I said, Jackson had an American Express credit card he'd use for business."

"Had?" Stowe asks.

Where did this guy get his training…at the KGB? How can one little word be so important? Everything I say is being twisted, and he takes everything the wrong way.

"Yes, *had* it," I say. "He *had* it the last time I saw him. I'm sure he still has it."

"We're aware of that card," he continues. "Were there any other cards?

"Other cards?"

"A CitiSelect card?" he asks.

"A CitiSelect card? I've never heard of it. Is this a card he uses for business?"

"No, this isn't a card associated with DMD. Are you aware of a CitiSelect Card?"

"No sir, I've never seen any other cards. He's pretty busy. Maybe they gave him another card I didn't know about."

"So, he never charges on this other card—maybe at a restaurant or buying things at the store?"

"This is crazy!" I say, throwing up my hands and leaning back in my chair. "What's going on here? You're asking me a lot of questions, and I have no idea what's going on."

Suddenly, he changes the subject. "Have you ever heard of a Hannah Overton?"

"Who?"

"Hannah Overton...or Hannah Jackson....do you know her?"

"Hannah Jackson? No, I've never heard that name before."

"You've never spoken to her?"

"Never," I say.

Why would I know this woman? Why is he asking about her...my marriage...about affairs? Sometimes, my dad would talk about his cases and say, "The police never ask anything for no reason." *Are these really just normal questions?* Something tells me they aren't.

When we started, I was sharp and wide-awake. Two hours....two hours I've been here. I'm cold, I'm tired, and I'm hungry. I know I have rights. I know I can end all this questioning. All I have to do is ask for a lawyer, but for some reason I don't—or I can't. I don't know what to do. I don't even know if I can walk out of the room if I want to. If I walk out or stop cooperating, they'll think I'm hiding something and what then? Will I be arrested? Instead of leaving, I stay while the questions keep coming.

When did I last talk to Jackson?

Was he upset?

Did we argue?

When did I plan my trip?

Why did we go alone?

Where did we stay?

Why didn't I call while in Thailand?

Can my sister confirm everything?

What did the house look like when I returned?

Why did I wait three days to call the police?

He leaves for a week or two at a time and you don't even know where he goes?

How can I know so little about his business?

I make it sound like Jackson and I have the best marriage in the history of marriages, but I don't think he believes me.

How often do you argue?

When was your last argument?

Why did you go weeks without talking?

Three hours into the questioning, Stowe pulls out a paper and looks it over. "Mrs. Kennedy, we know you bought a two-million-dollar life insurance policy on your husband."

"No…." I say, and then ask, "I what?"

"A two-million-dollar life insurance policy," he repeats and then turns the paper around. He hands it to me, and asks, "Is this your signature?"

I take a second to look over the paper. Sure enough, it's the life insurance policy on Jackson's life. We increased the amount two years ago after Jackson started making more money.

"It looks like my signature," I say, handing the paper back.

He looks up from his pad as if to say, *Here we go again.* "So, you do have a life insurance policy," he says like he's chastising me. "How can you forget a two-million-dollar policy?"

"Oh my God," I say. "It's not like you're making it sound. Jackson bought that policy. It was all his decision. He bought a policy for both of us over a year ago."

"Why so much?"

"I don't know why he bought so much."

He turns the paper back around to me and asks, "But this is your signature right here?"

"Yes, but he did it. All I did was sign the papers."

"Why didn't you just say this when I asked?"

"I don't know," I say with shrug. "I'm tired and I need to eat."

"So, it looks like you'll be paid two million dollars, won't you?"

I put my head on the table and ask, "Are you saying he's gone?"

"Why don't *you* tell *us*?" he says looking right at me. When I don't answer, he says, "We don't know if he's gone. We're trying to figure out where he went."

I've seen this kind of questioning on television so many times. He pounces on my words again and again. He twists everything around to mean something I never intended. Next thing, I'm even second-guessing myself.

I remember a time when my dad was working on this big murder case. Some guy finally confessed after fifteen hours of constant questioning. One evening at the dinner table, my dad went on and on about police interrogations. "They're ruthless! Why in the world do these people sit there talking? Don't they know the police are trained at what they do? The tactics they use will eventually break you down and make you confess, even if you're innocent. Just ask for a lawyer. All you have to do is ask for a lawyer."

So why don't I just ask for a lawyer? It sounds pretty simple, right? I don't really know why. I feel like it'll be suspicious if I refuse to answer their questions and I don't want to look guilty. Plus, who would I call? It's not like I have a criminal lawyer on my speed dial who will rush in and save me from myself. The only lawyer I knew is gone. Mostly, I don't want it to go the legal route. I don't want to be arrested. I just want it all to end. If I give them everything they want, surely, they'll believe I'm innocent.

We've been here four hours and I keep thinking we're almost done, so I can go back home to my family. I told my neighbor I'd be back shortly, but I've been here such a long time. It's hard to believe they have so many questions…or keep asking the same questions over and over again, like my answers will change if he asks just one more time. As the hours go by, I get exhausted from it all.

The questions keep coming and coming. I feel like I'm in the middle of this weird battle I cannot win. Each time he leaves the room, I'm left all alone knowing that I'm being watched. I'm not sure what Detective Stowe does out there, but he always comes back refreshed and ready to go on. He knows what he's doing. At times, I want to ask for a lawyer, but he keeps asking questions, and I keep answering. He has this way about him that keeps me talking.

Between his latest questions about our vacation house, I look down at my watch. We've been here for five hours now. A terrible feeling sweeps over me like wind blowing through the leaves of a tree. My stomach aches, and my whole body starts shaking. I lay my head down on the desk in front of me and start bawling uncontrollably. Detective Stowe reaches in the desk, pulls out a box of tissues, and sets the box down beside me without showing the least bit of compassion or sympathy. Maybe he thinks I'm just about to crack.

I lift my head with my face covered in tears, and cry, "I swear…I swear I had nothing to do with this."

"Mrs. Kennedy, just tell us the truth. We're wanting to find out what happened to Jackson. That's it."

"But I want the same thing," I say, wiping my eyes.

Right then, Fleming comes in and says, "Hi, Mrs. Kennedy."

"Hello," I say, blowing my runny nose with the tissue.

She takes the chair closest to me and hands me another tissue out of the box. She leans towards me and puts her hand on my arm. For the first time since I got here, I feel like someone believes me.

Sounding so understanding, like she's on my side all the way, she says, "Grace….can I call you Grace?"

"Sure."

"Grace, why don't you tell us what happened. Did you have an argument?"

"Nothing happened," I cry. "I'm telling you the truth."

"You just had a baby, right?"

I nod my head.

"Your husband works a lot of hours?"

I nod again.

"I know that can be hard on a new mom. You're taking care of a baby and….what's your little girl's name?"

"Bonnie," I answer.

"And your little boy?"

"Wesley."

"Yes, Bonnie and Wesley," she says, like she's known them for years. "You're busy taking care of little Bonnie and Wesley all by yourself all day. I know what it's like. I have a little boy too. Sometimes it can really stress you out."

"No," I say.

"We want to help you," Fleming says. "We can't help you unless you tell us what happened."

This can't be happening. I close my eyes and shake my head. By now, I know there's nothing I can say to change what they already believe. Their minds are made up. Maybe I should admit that I lied—tell them we were arguing when he left and for the year or so before he left. I'm pretty sure I'm going to jail, anyway. Perhaps if I just tell them what they want to hear, they'll stop and leave me alone. I'll hire a lawyer to straighten everything out later. No one who knows me would ever believe I would hurt Jackson.

I want my dad. Oh God, how I want my dad.

All my talking, all my answering, all my crying, doesn't seem to make a bit of difference. "Am I going to jail?" I ask, afraid to hear the answer.

"Do you have a reason to go to jail?" Stowe asks, like he's taunting me for some reason.

I grab another tissue from the box and try to dry my eyes, but the tears keep coming. "It's just…my…my neighbor is watching my baby and my daughter will be home from school soon. I don't want her to come home, and there's no one there. Can I please call someone? I need to make arrangements for them."

Fleming looks at Stowe and back to me again. "Right now, you're not under arrest. We're just trying to get to the truth."

I nod my head, still wiping my nose with the tissue. "But I had nothing to do with it. You have to believe me," I plead. "I had nothing to do with any of this."

"I think we're about finished here, Mrs. Kennedy," Stowe says, gathering his things.

Stowe looks at the mirror and gives a subtle nod; then he and Fleming stand up from their chairs. "I thank you for cooperating," he says, reaching for the door. "We may have more questions for you later, so please don't leave the county."

"Yes sir," I cry. "I have nowhere else to go."

Grace Kennedy,
— Day 22

– CHAPTER 5 –

I came to the police station wanting answers. In the end, they asked all the questions and told me nothing. I'm walking out of the police station; glad I get to go home at all. There was a point when I was sure I would be arrested. Stowe offers to have an officer take me back home, but I'd rather crawl home on my hands and knees than spend another day with them.

By the time my ride arrives and I get home, there are two police cars parked in my driveway. I have to park on the street. I get out of my car and go up to my front door, but a police officer is standing in the doorway. He extends his arm to block my entry.

"Mrs. Kennedy?"

"Yes," I say, trying to understand what's going on. "I live here. This is my home."

"You can't come in right now. We have a warrant to search your house. We'll be finished shortly."

I sit outside waiting for them to finish whatever it is they're doing in there. Forty-five minutes later, an officer walks out carrying our family computer and Jackson's personal laptop. Another officer comes walking out with a large cardboard box and puts it in the back of a police van. I watch as the officers go inside our house and come back out with more and more boxes. I have no idea what's inside them all.

When it appears they're done taking things out of our house, I go back to the man standing guard in front of my door and ask, "Can I go in now?"

"Yes ma'am," he says, stepping out of my way.

When I first walk into the house, things don't look so bad. The kitchen is another story. Most of the cabinets and drawers are hanging open, and one of our cabinet doors has papers falling out onto the counter. At first, I'm not sure what they were after. This cabinet is just full of cookbooks, instructions manuals, warranties to our appliances, and other household papers. Then I realize what's missing. They took all my day planners from the past four years.

We have an office to the right of the front entry, where we keep most of our bills and records. When I go inside, it looks like a tornado blew through here. You'd think we were robbed or something. Papers are scattered all over the place, our computer is gone, and desk drawers are all hanging open or sitting on the floor. The drawers to our file cabinet are also sitting open. You can tell they searched through everything. When I look inside the file cabinet where all our financial documents are kept, all our bank statements, tax returns, receipts, and other important documents are gone.

I go back to our bedroom hoping our personal belongings were spared their search. Our dresser has clothes sticking out of the closed drawers—a few items are now on the floor. When I open each drawer, I can tell someone went through everything. My panties, which are usually neatly folded, are now in one big ball. The other drawers are all the same—clothes that were once folded and in order, are now stuffed back in the drawers like someone purposefully tore through them.

Our closet looks even worse. Jackson's shirts, that were hanging so orderly this morning, are now pushed all the way to the left. Everything that was once folded neatly on the shelves is now strung across the floor. They took the shoebox full of money, along with a couple of other boxes on the top shelf. Our secret drawer, that just a few days ago held all our passports and other important documents, is now hanging open and everything in it is gone; including all our family passports, birth certificates, and social security cards.

It makes me so angry. I cooperated. I did everything they asked. They never would have found this drawer except I showed it to Stowe. Now he used my help against me. They took all our important family records.

I cannot believe what I'm looking at. My bedroom—my most private and personal place—is in disarray. Strangers went through my bras, my panties, and my lingerie. My shoes and most of my clothes are in a pile on the floor. They even went through my jewelry box. Isn't it enough that I lost my husband? Now they have laid my whole life bare?

I take two steps backward until I'm leaning against the wall. I slowly slide down to the floor and fold my knees in front of my face. Laying there feeling helpless, I lay my arms on my knees and lower my head to shut out everything around me. As I sit here on my closet floor, hearing nothing but the beating of my own heart, I feel so alone and afraid. I'm not sure what to do next.

So many questions run through my head. *Who was he? Who was this man I was married to all these years? Where is this all going to end?* I'm not sure what's going on. With my head still resting on my knees, all the questions from Stowe replays in my mind. I'm finally jarred back to the present by the ringing of my cell. It's Hope calling.

"Hope," I cry.

"Grace, what's wrong? What happened?"

"They….they…they took me," I get out.

"Who? Who took you?"

"The police…the police took me to the station. They put me in this interrogation room and questioned me."

"God no," Hope says. "Is Jackson….is Jackson dead?"

"I don't know. They don't know. No one knows what happened to him. He never went to work after we left."

"What? Where has he been?"

"I don't know," I say, still choked up. "It seems I was the last one to see him."

"What are you talking about?" Hope asks.

"I don't know. The detectives started asking me all kinds of questions."

"About what?"

"Jackson, our marriage, his business……everything. I don't know what the hell is going on. It was like something you see on television. I don't think they believed me. They said Jackson was being investigated at his work."

"Investigated? For what?"

"I'm not totally sure. Some kind of fraud or theft. They asked me what I knew about it. They wanted to know about his business…how we were doing financially."

"How you were doing financially? You didn't have financial problems, did you?"

"Not at all. Our paychecks went straight into our bank account. I would look at it from time to time. We made enough money to pay our bills and put some money away each month. If money was coming in from somewhere else, I would have known about it. There was nothing…nothing at all."

"Wow," she says.

"It went on and on and on. They'd ask me the same question over and over, like they were trying to catch me lying or something."

"Oh my god, Grace, this is crazy."

"It's all crazy. They asked about some woman….some woman named Hannah."

"What about her?"

"I don't know. They wouldn't say. I don't know if she was in on whatever was going on at his office or what."

"Do you think Jackson could have been seeing her?" Hope asks.

I don't answer her question, so she continues.

"There's no way Jackson would cheat on you. Look at you—you're beautiful, you're fun, you have it all. Why would anyone cheat on you?"

"I can't even think about it. Just the thought of it makes me sick."

"I just don't believe Jackson would do that," she repeats.

"They asked if I was seeing someone else." Just thinking about all these questions causes tears to fill my eyes.

"Jackson's missing. Maybe these are all just normal questions," Hope says.

"That's what he said. He said it was just routine, but I don't think so. Remember Dad? He always said the police ask everything for a reason. It felt like he knew something.....something he wasn't telling me."

Hope exhales and says, "Jesus."

"When I came back, they were searching my house."

"What?"

"They went through everything—our office, our bedroom, our closet...everything. They just threw things all over the floor."

"Can they do that?" Hope asks.

"They had a search warrant. There was nothing I could do. They blocked the door to my own house. They carried out boxes and boxes of stuff."

"Grace, there has to be an explanation for everything. Jackson's going to show up and explain everything."

"I don't know. I hope so."

Any problems in my marriage I've kept to myself. My dad and mom divorced, and I was determined to be different—to make it work. I loved Jackson, and I didn't want people to know things weren't as rosy on the inside as it seemed on the outside. So, I told no one, because I wanted no one to know we failed—or I failed.

I decide to tell Hope, for the first time, what was really going on. "Hope, things have not been so good between Jackson and me. It's like we've grown apart over the last few years. He was always gone. It seems like all he does is work all the time."

"I know he works a lot," Hope says.

"Then we faced so many problems. It seemed like it was one thing after another. It all started after his mom and dad died. Then everything with you in the hospital and then going to rehab. It really got me down. Then Bonnie nearly drowned in the pool. I was so busy taking her to all her doctor's appointments and I was still dealing with my pregnancy. Then you came back from Thailand and told me our mom was dead. It was all just too much."

"I know," Hope whispers.

"Then just when I thought it couldn't get any worse, Dad was killed," I say, fighting back tears. "It hurt so bad. I was so depressed, I could barely function. I was living in this funk…this funk I couldn't get out of. I was too sad and Jackson was always gone. I don't think I had anything left to give to anyone."

"Of course," Hope says. "Who wouldn't?"

"Hope, I don't know what to do. I need Dad. He'd know what to do."

As soon as I get the words out, I can't hold my tears back any longer. Hope and I have never directly discussed everything about Dad. I already know we see things differently. It's been a very touchy subject. She just sits here, not saying much.

"I miss him so much. I feel like it's all my fault. Dad and I were always so close. He needed someone, but everyone turned against him. I should have been that someone. I should have let him know that I still loved him, but I didn't, and now it's too late. He's gone…he's gone, and he's never coming back."

"It's not your fault," Hope says. "You can't blame yourself. He's responsible for what he did."

I ponder this for a second. Not wanting to start an argument, I whisper, "I wish it were that simple,"

"It's pretty simple," Hope counters like everything is black-and-white. She's so hard. That's why we never talk about this.

"We'll never agree on this," I concede with a deep breath. "You just don't know. You don't know what it's like to be married…to love someone so much…to build your whole life around them and find out they're lying and cheating on you."

"What are you saying?" Hope asks.

I wipe my eyes, and say, *"It destroys you."*

"Fine," she agrees, "but you divorce them. You don't kill them."

"He didn't kill her," I say.

"Yes, he did," she insists.

This is not going well. I calm down a bit and say, "What I mean is, I don't think he meant to kill her. I think he loved her. I think he always loved her. I really believe he just wanted to get his kids back, and it all went wrong."

"That's not love," Hope insists. "If you love someone, you don't put them in prison. You go to court….you don't kill them."

"It's a thin line between love and hate," I say.

"What?" she asks.

"You love Blake, right?"

"I do."

"But if you were with someone you didn't love and found out they were cheating on you…you wouldn't really care, would you?"

"I guess not," she says.

"But what if it were Blake? What if you spent ten years married to Blake and had kids, and then you found out he'd been cheating on you for years?"

"Grace, stop!" Hope says, not backing down an inch. "I don't want to talk about this."

"Then on top of it all, he takes your kids and your house, and you have to pay him every month."

"Grace, I don't know what I'd do…okay?" Hope says, sounding frustrated. "I guess I'd go to court!"

"And what if you found out your judge always gives the kids to the father?"

She doesn't respond.

"I'm sorry," I say, trying to reason with her. "What if it were Bonnie? What if someone tried to take Bonnie away?" I sit for a moment and then continue, "I couldn't imagine going two weeks without seeing her."

"Me either," Hope says, finally easing up a bit.

"I don't know what I would have done if it were Bonnie, but I wouldn't have sat there and done nothing. I would have done whatever it takes. I'm not saying mom got what she deserved, but she wasn't the angel you think she was."

"Obviously, she was no angel," Hope says, finally backing down.

Hope is the only family I have left, and I hate to argue with her. At the same time, I feel like the truth has gotten lost. "Look at dad," I continue. "He was always there for us. He always put us first. Kate didn't care about us—he was going to take everything. She and Ben were going to kick us out and take everything Dad worked for all his life. Dad would rather die than let that happen."

"Kate wouldn't have done that," Hope whispers, like she doesn't even believe it herself.

"Really?" I ask, trying to remind her how heartless Kate was. "And where is she? Where is she now? We haven't heard a word from her since she left."

"You never really loved Kate," Hope says.

"It's not that I didn't love her," I say, biting my lip. "There was just something about her. I could never put my finger on it, but there was something about her that I didn't trust. Honestly, I always wondered if she was only there for dad's money. Dad always said, 'In tough times, you find out who really loves you. In the end, family is all that matters.' Well, in the end, she left. I guess dad was right."

Hope finally says, "I just wish none of this ever happened. I miss Dad too. Sometimes I wish I never started digging. If anyone is to blame for what happened, it's me."

Ever since she found that watch in the closet, Hope has been so mad and unforgiving. This is the first time she's softened towards Dad—even just a little. Suddenly, the temperature turns down about a hundred degrees.

"It's not your fault," I say, trying to console her. "It was all a bad deal, and now Mom is gone, Dad is gone, and Colt is gone. All we have now is each other. We have to stick together."

"Of course, we'll stick together—always."

This has been a day I'll never forget. First, I was torn apart like I'm a criminal and now my home is torn apart. I would have thought they'd be careful executing a search warrant, but obviously not. I have a long day ahead of me.

"Hope, I've got to let you go. This house is a wreck. I want to straighten up the best I can before Bonnie gets home."

Hope pauses just a second and says, "Grace, I'm coming there. I'm coming to see you."

"It's okay," I say, "I'll be alright."

"It's not okay. Your husband is missing, and you need someone to be there. I want to be there with you."

Another time, and I would have tried to stop her, but this isn't like any other time. I'm in trouble and I'm scared. If I get arrested, I don't want my kids taken by Child Protective Services. I'll need Hope here to take care of Bonnie and Wesley.

Feeling so grateful, I say, "I don't know how to thank you."

"Grace, you're my sister. We're family. I want to be there with you. I want to make sure you're okay. I'll leave when Jackson comes back."

Thank you so much," I say.

– CHAPTER 6 –

After Archer Parr's death on October 18, 1942, his son, George Parr, inherited the Parr dynasty. The locals called him "El Patrón," just as they did his father.

George Parr continued his powerful political machine and delivered a solid block of Hispanic voters. How did it work? In Texas, like many other southern states, you had to pay a poll tax if you wanted to vote. Most Tejanos (Texans from Mexican descent) were working as farmers, ranchers, or day laborers, and either couldn't, or didn't want to pay a poll tax. Their "patrones" (or bosses) would pay the poll tax for them—as long as they voted for a Democrat. The ballots were all in English. To make sure no one "accidentally" cast a vote for the wrong candidate, sheriffs (or deputy sheriffs) handed out ballots that were already filled out and ready to be deposited safely into the local ballot box.

This is how the system worked, and, for the most part, elections went exactly as Parr wanted. But, every now and then, Parr "resorted to fraud and coercion to control elections. Techniques included marked ballots, having armed guards patrol the polling places to intimidate voters, and altering election returns. One thing for sure, Parr's minions knew how to stuff a ballot box."

Most kids who left Duval County to get an education, moved away so they didn't have to worry about the Parr dynasty. But after World War II, a bunch of college kids came back from war and wanted to change the old way of doing things. They founded the Freedom Party, ran new candidates for office, and started stirring up trouble for old Parr. But real change is often met with real bullets, and George Parr made sure these troublemakers were either run out of town or killed.

Parr's hold on South Texas politics got national attention in 1948, when a young and upcoming congressman by the name of Lyndon Baines Johnson decided he'd run for the United States Senate against Coke Stevenson.

Coke Stevenson looked like he'd surely win the race. He was once a very popular Texas governor, and he beat Johnson by over 70,000 votes in the previous primary election. Johnson barely received enough votes in that primary race to force a runoff. Fortunately for Johnson, there was bad blood between Stevenson and Parr. Because of their past, Parr supported Lyndon Johnson in the race.

On election night, the first vote tallies showed Stevenson winning by 20,000 votes, with more votes still coming in. When the votes came in from San Antonio, Stevenson's lead was reduced from 20,000 to 10,000 votes. This was a little surprising, since Stevenson won this county in the primary. After the votes came in from the Rio Grande, Stevenson's lead was cut to 854 votes.

After all the votes were counted, you might think the race was over, but you'd be wrong. It was 1948, and this was south Texas politics—the fun was just beginning. Over the next few days, one Rio Grande County after another called in corrections, recounts, and questionable shifting of votes. In the end, Lyndon Johnson closed the gap to only 150 votes. It was close, but Stevenson was the winner.

But as the State (and the entire nation) was about to name Coke Stevenson the next Senator from Texas, something incredible happened. Six days after the election, officials in Jim Wells County announced they just discovered a ballot box in Alice, Texas—that still hadn't been counted. This became known as the famous Ballot Box 13.

When Ballot Box 13, was opened, there were 202 votes cast. Johnson received 200 of the votes and Stevenson received only 2. Johnson now led Stevenson by 97 votes out of almost one million votes cast. Thanks to Alice, Texas, Lyndon Johnson won the Texas Senate seat by less than one one-hundredth of one percent!

Well, Stevenson wasn't about to take this whole thing lying down. He showed up in Alice, Texas with Frank Hamer—the legendary Texas Ranger who led the posse that ambushed and killed Bonnie and Clyde on the side of that dusty Louisiana backroad.

Stevenson and Hamer demanded to see the tally sheet from Ballot Box 13. After a brief scuffle, they were allowed to see, but not copy, the tally sheet. It revealed something really amazing. The last 202 voters all voted in alphabetical order, they all signed in the same color ink, and they all had the exact same handwriting!

Stevenson and Hamer next interviewed some of these new voters on the list. Some people who voted claimed they didn't even know there was an election that day!

Equipped with his newly discovered evidence, Stevenson challenged the results in court, and asked the judge to throw out all votes from Precinct 13. When Box 13 was opened in court, however, the tally sheet Stevenson once held in his hands was missing. The case went all the way to the United States Supreme Court. The Court eventually ruled that the federal government has no authority over state elections. With that, Lyndon Baines Johnson was named the official winner of the Texas Senate race.

If not for the help of George Parr—and a little town in south Texas called Alice—this would have been Johnson's second Senate loss and would have doomed his political career. Instead, history would change forever. Johnson would become John F. Kennedy's vice president and the 36th President of the United States after Kennedy's unfortunate shooting in Dallas, Texas. Three days after the shooting, reports would surface, connecting Parr to the conspiracy to kill Kennedy.

As president, LBJ launched "The Great Society" and his "War on Poverty". He would give America, among other things, Medicare, Medicaid, the Older Americans Act, Elementary and Secondary Education Act, Water Quality Act, Clean Air Act, Endangered Species Act, the Motor Vehicle and the Pollution Control Act, and the Civil Rights Act of 1964. He would also escalate the Vietnam War that would change America and the world forever.

While Johnson was busy being President, the Parr dynasty continued from 1906 through 1975. Robert Flint continued to work as George Parr's right-hand man until he died in 1971. Robert's oldest son, Tom, took over after his father died.

Tom Flint was a lot like his father—the apple didn't fall far from the tree. The two were inseparable. Tom's grades weren't great, but his father didn't really care. Tom was an All-District linebacker for his high school football team, and his dad showed up for every game. He might have gotten a scholarship offer, except his grades, his reputation for cheap shots, and his reputation for partying on the weekends made him too high a risk.

When Lyndon Johnson began escalating the Vietnam War, Tom's dad pulled every string imaginable to keep his son out of the draft. Against his dad's wishes, Tom turned eighteen, joined the army, and spent three years in the jungles of Vietnam "shooting anything and everything that moved."

At that time, America thought winning the war was fairly simple. The Viet Cong would eventually surrender if the Americans simply killed more enemy soldiers than the Vietnamese could replace. Well, this suited Flint just fine, because he actually enjoyed killing. You would always find Tom Flint's name on the top of the "kill boards" which earned him more days off, a couple packs of cigarettes, or an extra case of beer. He volunteered for every dangerous mission and always made sure he included all his civilian corpses in his tally of slain enemies.

Tom Flint was eager to serve another term, but he was discharged from duty after he threatened to kill two fellow soldiers at gunpoint. His Sargent wrote in his report, "There's something wrong with the boy. He's the kind of soldier you want in a bunker, but not the kind of guy you want to have a drink with afterwards."

When Tom Flint returned home from war, he followed in his father's footsteps until his father died of lung cancer. Officially, he was on the payroll at the Duval County Sheriff's Department. Unofficially, he served behind the scenes as the right-hand man for George Parr. If Parr needed someone investigated or someone just needed a *good talkin' to*, Tom Flint was the man for the job. He was suspected in several mysterious deaths in Duval and Jim Wells County, but usually there was never any evidence other than gossip and a bunch of rumors that went nowhere. A young teenager accused him of raping her in the back of his car, but she dropped all charges after some guy named Jesse paid her a visit.

There was one case, however, that wouldn't, or couldn't, simply disappear. Tom Flint was "allegedly" involved in the killing of a young kid named Brian, for which he was indicted and tried for murder.

Brian's father was one of the original founders of the Freedom Party. While Flint was busy serving his country over in Vietnam, Brian was at some big college getting his fancy Liberal Arts degree. Brian's father offered him a cushy job at some oil company in Houston, but Brian had other plans. He wanted to make a difference in the world. After graduation, he returned to Duval County, ready to establish the next Freedom Party and finish what his father started long ago.

Exactly what happened back then really wasn't in dispute. Brian and his buddies were protesting something or another, so Flint gave him a good talkin' to. Then he gave him another—but this one was very specific. He urged this kid to move somewhere far, far away—maybe take his daddy's job in Houston. When the warning didn't work, Tom Flint stopped Brian just outside the city limits with a broken taillight. One thing led to another, and Brian was shot and killed.

The evidence in the case was pretty damning. Seems the car's tail light was scattered along the highway right where Brian was stopped. To make matters worse, Brian was shot in the back of the head at close range, while kneeling between his car and Flint's vehicle. Another vehicle just happened to drive by, and the driver of that vehicle testified that he saw Flint standing over this boy with something that looked like a pistol pointing right at his head. He never saw Brian struggle or resist. The case appeared open and shut.

Throughout the weeklong trial, Flint never seemed the least bit concerned. He kept smiling at the jury and talking to onlookers and the press like this was a lot to do about nothing. His attorney called one witness, who testified how dangerous it is for cops working the streets. The jury was out for twenty minutes before finding Flint not guilty of all charges. The reporters couldn't figure out how the jury could read the judge's instructions and elect a jury foreman in that time—much less consider the evidence and vote on a verdict in the case.

Before leaving the courtroom, each juror personally thanked Flint for his long and brave service to Duval County—especially his service to George Parr. As he stepped out of the Duval County courthouse, Flint paused just long enough to stop in front of a microphone and say, "I wanna thank the good Lord and the good fellers of this county. No finer folk ever lived anywhere in the world. Now I'm gonna get back to doing the people's business around here."

He was never tried again for anything.

People might have thought a life-or-death trial like that might have calmed Flint down just a bit. They would be dead wrong. The trial just emboldened him. Flint himself once said he was "mean as all get out." He once told a Texas Ranger who was poking his head around "where it din't belong" that "I'm mighty wiry. You better pack a big lunch if you wanna square off with me." He pulled a gun on the Ranger and there was almost a shootout.

In 1974, George Parr was finally brought down by an unlikely event. The IRS conducted a routine audit of an Austin contractor who did business in Duval County. When they examined this contractor's company books, they discovered checks worth more than $350,000.00 written to cash. The contractor eventually confessed that the money was a bribe to do work for the county.

In 1974, Parr went on trial in federal court in Corpus Christi for tax evasion. The trial exposed the incredible amount of money taken from the county. The evidence was overwhelming.

In 1945, George Parr "borrowed" (and never paid back) over a half a million dollars from the Duval County Road Bond Account to buy a ranch. Paid for by the water district and delivered to the Parr ranch, were one hundred thousand tons of fertilizer, $166,000 for an irrigation system, five caterpillar tractors worth over $50,000.00 each, and a $21,925 aluminum pipe. Parr was also paid a $5,000 salary every month from the water district for doing God knows what. The school district paid $410,000 for gasoline, fuel, and maintenance. Duval County paid for Parr's Thunderbird, and $1,900 a month went to a gas station owned by Parr's family.

A jury found George Parr guilty on all eight counts and sentenced him to ten years in prison. Parr was previously convicted of tax evasion and served nine months, for which he was later granted a pardon by President Harry Truman. He had no intention of returning to prison. On March 31, 1975, at the ripe age of 74, Parr went around town with an AR-15 ready to kill his political enemies. Luckily for them, they were all tipped off.

When he failed to appear before Judge Owen Cox for sentencing, a team that included FBI agents, US marshals, the Sheriff and his deputies, and a Texas Department of Public Safety helicopter, went searching for Parr to arrest him. They eventually found him in his dark blue Chrysler Imperial at his favorite spot on the Parr family ranch, where he frequently went to relax and meditate. The FBI agent described what he found:

"I walked up to the car. The car engine was running. I went to the passenger's side, looked in, and I could see Mr. Parr slumped to his right side. There was a bullet hole on the right side of his head with an exit wound on the left side."

After Parr's death, the Duval Grand Jury issued a flood of indictments against the many people involved in the scheme to defraud the Duval County Treasury. Some were convicted, while others fled the county before they could be arrested for their own crimes.

Two days after George Parr put that bullet through his head, Tom Flint disappeared. He didn't even bother selling his four-bedroom house and the five acres it sat on just outside the city limits before heading out. The infamous Ballot Box 13, along with the tally sheet, also disappeared. Some said the Ballot Box was stashed in a meat locker, burned somewhere, or thrown into the Rio Grande. Some were sure Tom Flint took the Ballot Box (and other political documents that would embarrass politicians all over the state) with him as insurance if he ever needed it.

Where he went, or what he did, was anyone's guess. Most people were sure he was well taken care of thanks to all that money from Water District and the Benavides Independent School District.

Some thought Flint was surely dead—payback now that he was no longer protected by Parr's umbrella—until he popped up again in Austin, Texas exactly one month after the Statute of Limitations ran on any possible criminal charges he might face. He came back sporting a dark tan and speaking perfect Spanish.

Flint started offering his many years of law enforcement experience as a professional investigator for a hefty price. His office was small and not much to look at. For the most part, it was empty except for photos of Flint and dozens of Democratic big-shots hanging on the wall behind his desk; including one with the great LBJ. Flint was most proud of the photo of him and ole George Parr standing arm-in-arm. It was taken right before Parr's real troubles began.

Flint advertises all kinds of services, but the few clients he has know good and well not to bother him with "the baby stuff." You need to serve some papers, run a credit check, or want to investigate your cheating spouse? Don't call Flint. Does an unpleasant situation need fixed; someone needs a good talkin' to; or something or someone needs to disappear? Flint is the man for the job.

Tom Flint came from an era long gone. The world at that time looked like a much different place. Men called all the shots. As far as Flint was concerned, women knew where they stood in the world and a couple of marches or a million burnt bras couldn't change that. Whites didn't have to share no drinking fountains, or toilets, or lunch counters. There was no need for good, God-fearing men to hide behind some silly bed sheets. Flint could never imagine a black, or Mexican, or woman ever being elected president of this great country. Before that ever happened, the magnificent statue of General Lee sitting on his horse, Traveler, sitting in the middle of Lee Park in Charlottesville, would come alive and lead the south in another Civil War.

If you wanted justice, you didn't go to no courthouse. Trials were always decided before they ever started. Real justice was found out on the streets. There were shoot-outs back then that made the Wild West look tame.

Archie Parr died in 1942. Robert Flint died in 1971. LBJ died in 1972. George Parr and Coke Stevenson died in 1975. Tom Flint is still alive and well, and his story is far from over.

Ryan Brunick and Faith Brunick are two names he'll never forget.

– CHAPTER 7 –

As if my life wasn't crazy enough, the story of Jackson's disappearance first breaks on all the local news stations before turning into a national media story. If you turn on Fox News, CNN, or MSNBC, it's all they're talking about.

"BREAKING NEWS"

"EXECUTIVE AT LARGE CHIP MANUFACTURER

MYSTERIOUSLY DISAPPEARS."

They cover every single angle imaginable.

Who is Jackson Kennedy?

What was his position at DMD?

Why is he missing?

Who is the wife?

Who were we as a family?

Did his wife kill him?

I don't have to turn on my television to find a reporter, because they're all camped right outside my house in vans and news trucks. It's like some kind of circus.

Stowe comes on the television saying they're doing everything possible to find Jackson. He keeps telling the reporters he'll find Jackson….it's just a matter of time.

A reporter shouts out, "It's being reported his wife was out of the country during this time. Have you eliminated her as a suspect yet?"

Stowe shakes his head and says, "We haven't eliminated anyone yet. Our investigation is still ongoing."

"Detective Stowe, Detective Stowe," another reporter shouts, trying to get his attention over all the other reporters. "So, is Jackson Kennedy's wife a suspect in his disappearance?"

"I cannot comment on the specific evidence we have in the case," he says, pointing to the next reporter.

"So, do you have evidence against her?"

"No comment."

"Is his wife cooperating?" another reporter asks.

"She came in and gave a statement," Stowe answers.

Came in and gave a statement? This is how he portrays me—like I came in and dropped off a paper saying what happened? Why doesn't he tell the truth? Why not say, "*Mrs. Kennedy came in and was interrogated for five long, excruciating hours. We treated her like a criminal. I practically slapped her around the room. She could have walked out. She could have asked for a lawyer, but she didn't. She stayed to the very end. Has she cooperated…hell yes, she's cooperated. We owe her a debt of gratitude. Let's take a minute of silence in her honor.*"

Instead, Stowe says, "Thank you. That's all we have at this time." He walks away from the microphone while the reporters are still trying to ask questions.

"Shit," I say, listening to all this crap. "I hate you."

This news conference sets the reporters into a frenzy. Now I'm all the focus. Each time I walk out of my house, I'm met with a mob of reporters pointing their cameras my way and sticking a microphone in my face. They want an interview or at least a comment. My comment is always the same, "I have no comment. Please move out of my way."

Now when I turn on the news, I see one commentator after another explain to the entire world how the spouse, meaning me, is always the prime suspect in a disappearance like this. These reporters have never met me. They've never even talked to me. Now everyone's connecting dots I didn't even know existed. Watching the reports, you'd be convinced I had something to do with Jackson's disappearance even though I was on the other side of the world.

I'm not a real public person. I never wanted to be in the spotlight. That's why I chose to be a doctor instead of an attorney. Now I turn on the television and see my picture all over the place. I'm not sure how they even got some of the photos. They must have come from my Instagram page.

They have a close-up of my face everywhere I go. They show videos of Bonnie and me getting in my Mercedes and then getting out again at her school. The school has to hire a police officer to keep the reporters at bay.

There aren't any videos of me at the grocery store, sitting at the park, or eating at a restaurant, because I don't do those things anymore.

Finally, to my shock, a reporter reveals that I'll be paid a large amount of money from Jackson's life insurance policy. This story runs all across the country for two days. I'm not sure how they found out about the life insurance. It had to be Detective Stowe who leaked it to the press.

They make it sound like I went to the insurance company right before Jackson disappeared and bought the policy. No one reports that it was Jackson who actually chose the policy and paid for it.

The whole story about Jackson's disappearance goes on and on for weeks until there's a new political scandal. It appears they caught our married Senator sending naked photos of himself to one of his young interns. By morning, every news van and reporter disappear from outside my home.

All the news stories and reporters do nothing to find Jackson. I still want answers more than ever, but everywhere and everything I would search through is gone. The police took all the documents and records I want to look through. *Where's the phone bill for this other cell phone? Where's the credit card bills for the credit card I know nothing about? Who is this Hannah woman?*

I came to the police wanting help. Instead of helping, they turned the whole thing against me. Now I never want to see a police officer again. I'd rather die than spend another five hours locked in a room with Stowe and

Fleming. I promise myself that I'll never—NEVER—talk to the police again. Next time I'll demand a lawyer.

All I have left is my laptop. Lucky for me, it was in my car during the search of my home. Hope and I spend weeks going online searching through our credit card statements for the past three years. All we find is a bunch of charges I already know all about. We search our bank records, but the only deposits into our account are our monthly paychecks. I look at every check written, but not one check raises any suspicions. If Jackson was hiding something, you'd never know it by looking through our financial records.

Hope and I review months and months of Jackson's cell phone bills. I call one strange number after another hoping to find a call, or a text, or anything to a Hannah. Every road is a dead end.

I go online and look at Jackson's Facebook page. He was never really big at social media, but he would post something every now and then. He doesn't have a single new post in the last five months. There's nothing to give me any idea where he went before or after we left for Thailand. We go to his list of friends looking for a "Hannah." There's nothing there.

I get on my phone and read through all my text messages to and from Jackson. It brings back the arguments we had about all the hours he worked away from home. If Stowe gets his hand on some of these texts, he'll know things weren't as lovely between us as I let on. It makes me wish I didn't make things seem so great between us. I should have admitted we argue, and lately we've been arguing a lot. I know good and well he'll use these texts against me like he does everything else.

Nothing in our texts, emails, and other records gives me any idea what, if anything, has been going on with Jackson. If he was having an affair, it wasn't on his phone. If he was stealing from his company, I sure didn't get any of the money.

After driving myself crazy for weeks, I come to a new conclusion. One thing I know is that the police can lie. They say anything they want, regardless of the truth. They'll claim they have DNA evidence or that they have proof you did something when they have nothing at all.

How do I know anything Stowe said is even true? I feel like I've fallen down a rabbit hole or something, and now up is down, right is wrong, and nothing makes sense.

I only know one thing for sure. My husband is gone—and the police are no help to me at all. Even worse, I'm their prime suspect.

– CHAPTER 8 –

Tom Flint rarely goes to his office, and when he does, it's usually to meet with a client. He's more comfortable driving around in his Ford F250 pickup truck with a gun rack hanging in the rear window and a spotlight secured right outside his driver's side window. His truck leads many drivers to think he's a DPS trooper, which isn't by accident. Some drivers pull over to the side of the road or abruptly hit their brakes when he comes up from behind, which suits him just fine.

He has no more right to pull someone over or make an arrest than an eighty-year-old grandma out for a Sunday drive after church, but he still has his Sheriff's badge and handcuffs from long ago. Both have come in real handy on more than one occasion.

Flint is really picky about who he works for and what cases he takes. In his line of work, you have to be careful. Most of his work comes from a handful of important attorneys around town. It gives him as much work as he can handle. Now that one of those lawyers is gone, he has more time on his hands. At his age, he should be retiring anyway. *Maybe I'll go fishing more. Maybe I'll go back to Duval County and see some old buddies. I should get back to hunting again.*

Flint got an unusual call this morning from a man who seemed real upset. He was willing to pay "whatever it costs" for some important investigation work. As much as Flint pressed for more information, the man was pretty vague on the phone. He only wanted to talk in person. When Flint said he'd need a twenty-thousand-dollar retainer, the man didn't flinch, so Flint agreed to meet him after lunch.

Flint arrives at one-fifteen for this mysterious appointment. When he pulls up, the driveway is empty because his receptionist still hasn't returned from lunch. Just as he gets out of his truck and grabs his coffee, a black Suburban drives up, turns in, and parks directly behind Flint's pickup. It must be his future client arriving early as well. A tall man in a sports coat and jeans gets out of his car, meets him at the door, and introduces himself.

"Mr. Flint," he says, extending his hand.

"Yes sir," Flint answers, drawing out the words with his own firm handshake.

"How are you today?" the man asks.

"Oh…busy as all get–out," Flint answers.

The man keeps his grip on Flint's hand, which strikes Flint as odd until the whole scene changes. Two men come from around each side of his little office, and two more unmarked Suburbans with their lights flashing bright blue and red drive up on each side of the grass, blocking any exit from the driveway. A few seconds later, two more police cars with sirens come to an abrupt stop, blocking all access up and down the street. Before Flint can unlock the door to his office, he's surrounded by six more officers.

"What the hell is going on here?" Flint demands to know.

The officer to Flint's right grabs the coffee cup out of his hand and tosses it onto the grass. The other officer gives him a completely unnecessary shove against the front door and says, "Mr. Thomas Flint, I have a warrant for your arrest. Put your hands behind your back."

When they try to click the cuffs on his wrist, Flint pulls away and yells, "Is that really necessary?"

The two officers twist Flint's left arm behind his back, circle the handcuffs around his wrist, and click them tight.

"What am I being arrested for?" Flint demands to know.

Ignoring his question, the officer says, "You have the right to remain silent. If you refuse that right to remain silent, anything you say can and will be used against you in a court of law."

"I know my goddamn rights," Flint barks. "Now what in the name of God am I being arrested for?"

"You have the right to an attorney and to have an attorney present during questioning. If you cannot afford an attorney, one will be appointed for you."

Flint spits on the ground and yells, "What in Sam hell is this all about? What am I being arrested for?"

"Murder," the officer answers, turning Flint around.

"This is a bunch of horseshit, and you know it," Flint roars. "Who the hell am I accused of murdering?"

"Zachary Bell," the officer says, escorting him to one of the patrol cars parked on the grass.

This is the first time Flint has ever been handcuffed. In his previous arrest, he surrendered at the police station and never spent so much as a minute in jail. They dispensed with all the formalities of a photo and fingerprints, and Flint was brought before a Duval County judge. He was immediately released without spending a night in jail.

Flint has a hunch it won't go so easy on him this time around. He doesn't say a word the whole ride to the jail. He knows none of these officers, and talking will do him no good. Under his breath, however, he says plenty. "Ryan Brunick….you sum bitch."

When they arrive at the jail, Flint isn't given any of the courtesies he'd expect from his fellow law enforcement officers. No, he's booked like any common criminal. After sitting there handcuffed against the wall for almost an hour, he's fingerprinted, photographed, and put in a cell with the same kind of "trash" he once arrested day in and day out over the years.

Several times, he tries to explain who he is and how long he's been serving in law enforcement. The officer in charge of his booking doesn't seem to care. Another officer arrives who knows exactly who Flint is, and he's well aware of his reputation in South Texas. It seems to carry no weight whatsoever.

The next day, he appears before a magistrate. He has no more pull with this judge than he did with any of the police who treated him like a murderer or anyone else they might bring in. After reading the charges against him, the judge denied any bail without discussion or argument. Flint will be stuck in this disgusting jail until his trial.

Grace Kennedy,
— Day 102

– CHAPTER 9 –

Nobody tells me anything about Jackson. As much as I want him found, I'm helpless to do anything to help. There's no way I'll ever go back and talk to the police again, so I sit and wait, day after day, week after week, month after month.

When I first left the police station, I actually thought I did okay. Now, as time goes by, I can't even remember everything I said that day. *What was I thinking? Why didn't I ask for an attorney?* I was tired, hungry, and cold. Now I know the truth isn't as black and white as most people think. Words can be twisted and taken out of context. I said some things that bent the truth—even if just a little. A couple of things I told them were completely false. Even when I was telling the truth, they made it sound like I was lying half the time. The only thing I know for sure is I made a lot of mistakes.

Three months have gone by with no word at all. As much as I want life to go on as usual, it doesn't. I almost never go outside, I keep my blinds closed, my curtains drawn, and I never answer the phone unless I know who's calling. It feels like I've become a prisoner in my own home.

Bonnie keeps asking me when her daddy's coming home. Mostly, I live with this fear of the unknown. I'm so afraid the police will come one day and take *me* to jail.

Hope and I are sitting at home feeding Wesley his breakfast when my phone rings. It's Detective Stowe. I ignore his call, so it goes to voicemail. He calls again and again, but each time I ignore it, and each time he leaves the same message.

"This is Detective Stowe. I need to speak with you. Can you please call me back?"

"This is Detective Stowe again. Please call me back."

"Mrs. Kennedy, it's Detective Stowe….we need to talk."

Wesley is down for a nap and I'm cleaning the kitchen when the front doorbell rings. Hope and I look through the side window and see the man I almost hate at this point. It's Detective Stowe back with Detective Fleming. I feel myself go limp. *They're here to arrest me.*

"What do I do?" I ask Hope.

"Nothing….just hide," she says looking around for a hiding spot. "Go in the bedroom and hide. I'll tell him you're not here."

"I can't. I can't stay in this house forever. If they want to arrest me, they will."

"Who is it?" I yell through the door.

"It's Detective Stowe."

"Show me a warrant."

"There's no warrant," he says. "Can we speak for a few minutes?"

I open the door but cannot speak. My mouth is dry and my body is trembling with fear.

"Can we come in?" Fleming asks.

I step to the side, and motion him in. Once inside the door, I turn to Hope and say, "This is Hope, my sister."

After they shake hands, we return to the living room and take our place back on the couch—except this time I have Hope sitting next to me for support. They won't be able to lower the temperature in the room to freeze me out. There won't be hours and hours of questioning until I'm so tired I can't think straight. When he questions everything I say, or twists my words, I'll order him out of my house. Once he sits on the couch, I look for a sign—something to tell me what's going on.

"Mrs. Kennedy, I want to thank you for meeting with us," Stowe begins. Now he sounds more like the old detective—the one who met with me the first day. He talks with a smile, like he's back on my side again.

"What's going on?" I ask putting my guard down. "Did you find Jackson?"

"This will be difficult for you to hear," he continues.

Now I'm visibly shaken and I start to cry. "What is it?"

"Mrs. Kennedy, we have everyone in the world searching for your husband—the APD, the Sheriff's Department, DPS, the FBI, the CIA, — everyone."

"Then why are you here? What's happened?"

"We ran a check on your husband's credit card—the card we talked about last time."

"So, there is another card?"

"Yes ma'am, the CitiSelect card I told you about. We also tracked his cell phone calls. He has another cell phone that you're probably not aware of."

"What?" I ask, trying to understand everything.

"I'm sorry, Mrs. Kennedy, but I don't know how to say this. It appears your husband has been living a lie for some time now."

"A lie?" I ask. "What kind of lie?"

"He has another phone, another credit card, another car—everything. He has a whole other life."

I shake my head and say, "This can't be. What about his job?"

"Like I said before, hadn't worked for DMD for three months. When the company started questioning him, he just stopped coming in. After he left, they hired an outside company to do an audit of the company's financials and discovered he was embezzling money from the company—a lot of money."

I get up from the couch and put my hand over my forehead in disbelief. "No, no, no….this can't be happening."

Stowe continues. "Mrs. Kennedy, that's only the beginning. Your husband…your husband has another house in Denver. He goes—"

"That's our vacation house!" I clarify. "It's just outside of Aspen. I told you all about it."

"Not your vacation house," Stowe continues. "We know about your vacation home. He has another house in Denver where he lives when he's not here in Texas."

"Noooo," I say, shaking my head in disbelief, "You must be mistaken. You've got it all wrong."

Stowe looks over at Fleming, at Hope, and then back at me again. "Mrs. Kennedy….Mrs. Kennedy, I don't know how to say this except to come right out with it. Your husband has another wife."

I jerk my head back and shout, "Another wife?" With my lips trembling, I say, "I'm his wife." Hope comes up and puts her arm on my shoulder. I fall into her arms.

"Mrs. Kennedy, you're not his only wife. They live in Denver. They got married eight months ago—right after they found out she was pregnant. His wife just had the baby three months ago."

My hands start shaking and my legs can no longer hold me. I sit back on the couch, slump over, and bury my head to hide my tears. "STOP!" I shout. "This can't be true. He can't be….can't be," I can't even get the word out. "He can't be married."

"I'm sorry Mrs. Kennedy but—"

"Don't you think I'd know?" I ask, still choking back my tears. "I'd know if he was married to someone else."

Stowe glances over at Fleming with a helpless look. He turns back to me and says, "We found all the evidence about the money. The proof is on his office computer. With that, I got an arrest warrant and went to Denver, hoping to find him. Mrs. Fleming, I saw his house. I spoke to his wife— his other woman. He has a new driver's license, new bank account…everything."

"Where the hell is he?" I demand to know.

"We don't know. We have warrants issued for his arrest for felony theft. We're doing everything to find him. The company audit revealed all the missing money. We think he left town….he probably even left the country. More indictments are coming down."

"Then find him," I say as my hurt turns to anger. "Find the son of a bitch."

"That's why we're here," Fleming jumps in. "Can you be any help in finding him?"

"I have no idea," I say. "I've looked through everything trying to find out what's going on, but I found nothing. I don't know. If I knew I'd tell you."

"We believe you," Stowe says.

Detective Fleming looks at Hope and me and says, "Listen, Grace, the story is about to break wide open. By tonight it will be on every news station across the country. We didn't want you to find out that way. We wanted to let you know in advance."

I sit on the couch and try to catch my breath. I think about all the long hours Jackson worked, the "sudden emergency calls" he'd receive, and the constant trips that lasted days and sometimes weeks. Barely able to talk, I look up and whisper, "How long has this been going on?"

Stowe closes his eyes and slowly shakes his head. "It appears he started seeing this woman a little over two years ago. About six months later, he bought the house in Denver and they moved in together. Like I said…when they found out she was pregnant about a year ago, they got married."

"So, they've been living together for…..for—"

"Over a year," he says.

"Does she know about me?"

"I don't think so. She was just as surprised to hear from us as you are."

I sit up and regain my thoughts. "I don't believe it. How could she not know? How could she be married to someone who has another family—two kids—and not know? She had to know."

"I really don't think so. Somehow, he balanced going back and forth, staying just long enough before leaving again."

Hope jumps in and says, "But now he's gone. Maybe she found out about everything. Maybe it was her. How do you know it wasn't her—maybe she killed him?"

Detective Stowe shrugs his shoulders and says, "At this time, there's no reason to believe there's been a homicide. Right now, we believe he left. We're searching every flight, every train, and every bus station to find him. We're monitoring his bank accounts, his credit cards, and his phone records. I assure you; we want to find him. We're investigating everyone and everything. We have a nationwide warrant for his arrest. If he shows up again, he'll be taken in."

Unable to breathe, I get up from the couch again. "I need some water. Can I get you something to drink—some coffee or something?"

They both stand up, and at the same time, they say, "No thank you."

I walk into the kitchen and lean against the counter, with tears running down my nose and falling in front of me. I pour a glass of water and drink most of it down, before it slips out of my hand and shatters on the floor.

I'm standing here in silence, trying to understand it all. Hope comes in and puts her hand on my shoulder.

"I'm so sorry," she says.

I turn around and lay my head on her shoulder. "I can't believe this," I repeat again and again.

I reach over, grab the kitchen towel, and wipe my tears away. "What do I do?" I whisper.

Hope bends down and picks up the pieces of glass all over the floor. "I don't know," she answers.

When we walk back into the living room, Stowe and Fleming are standing by the front door. I walk up and Stowe asks, "Mrs. Kennedy, can we call anyone for you?"

"There's no one to call. Everyone is gone. The only person I have left is already here."

Fleming steps forward and says, "Like we said, we'll be looking for him. If he gets on a plane or tries to leave the country, he'll be stopped. As far as we can tell, you were the last person to see him when you left to go to Thailand. He's had plenty of time to get his affairs in order and leave the country."

"But I looked through his closet and didn't see anything missing. If he left, he didn't take much with him." Suddenly, I stop myself and throw my hands up. "Hell….I don't even know anymore. Maybe he took everything from his other home."

"I don't think so," Stowe says. "She never heard from him. She was actually expecting him, but he never showed up."

"And you believe her?" Hope interjects. "I don't believe a thing this woman says."

Stowe shrugs his shoulders and says, "The Denver police questioned her for an hour."

Only one hour?

"We're keeping an eye on her too," Fleming advises. "If she flies anywhere or tries to leave the country, we'll know."

"What about me?" I ask. "Are you watching me too?"

"Stowe looks at Fleming and says, "Let's just say we'd like to remain in contact. I'd appreciate it if you'd let us know if you leave the county for any reason."

I look at him in disbelief. "So, *I'm* a suspect?"

"No, not at all," Fleming says. "We want the same thing you want. We want to find Jackson."

"Well, I assure you, I don't know where he is."

"No one thinks you do," Fleming says.

"Mrs. Kennedy, I'm really sorry. I know this has been a lot for you to take in. We'll keep you informed about everything. When we find him….and we will find him….you'll be the first to know. If you hear from him, please contact us right away."

– CHAPTER 10 –

After Stowe and Fleming walk out the door, I go back into the kitchen with Hope following right behind me. She sits down at the table, and I go over to the counter and sweep up the broken glass. Then I unload the dishwasher without saying a word. Hope just sits there, like she's not sure what to say. She watches as I wipe off the sink, the counters, load the dishwasher, and wipe off the stove. Just when it appears I may never stop cleaning, Hope walks up beside me and asks, "You okay?"

Looking out the window, I feel an emotion sweep over me like I've never felt before. It's a combination of sadness, hurt, rage, and hate. I'm not sure if there's a name for it.

"Am I okay?" I repeat, with the muscles in my jaw twitching and my eyes burning with anger. "I don't know what the hell I am. All this time I've been worried sick—worried he's dead. Now I find out the whole time he's been fuc—." I can't even bring myself to say it. I make a fist and slam it down on the counter.

Hope puts her head on my back and says, "I don't know what to say."

I stand there for a second then say, "And what? He's been stealing from his company? Oh, that's just great."

"I'm so sorry," Hope says, leaning against my back and wrapping her arms around me.

"You know," I say, shaking my head in disbelief, "I actually felt sorry for him. I thought he was working all these long hours. 'Poor Jackson's leaving for another business trip.' Another business trip, my ass. The whole time I'm here killing myself, he's playing daddy with his new family. How could I be so stupid?"

"How could you have known?" Hope asks, squeezing my hand.

"Come on….how do you keep something like this a secret for what….two years?"

"Because you trusted him?"

Furious, I shake my head and say, "I should have listened to my gut. You know how many times he'd say, 'you don't trust me' or he'd ask 'why don't you believe me,' like I'm the one at fault."

"How was he when you last saw him?" she asks.

"I told you something wasn't right…I KNEW IT!" I yell. "I planned this whole trip to Thailand, and he decides he's not going? How was he doing? I don't know how he was doing. I wasn't talking to him anymore. I was so pissed." I stop for a second and shout, "God I'm such an idiot."

"You're not an idiot," she says.

I calm down, shake my head, and say, "No, I'm pretty damn stupid."

Hope hugs me tight and says, "I'm here for you. We're gonna get through this."

I put my head down and whisper, "I don't know….I don't know what to think."

Hope pulls away and says, "I hope he burns…him and this Hannah woman. I don't think these cops know what the hell they're doing. I think she's involved in it all."

"I don't know what to think. They said she didn't know anything."

We both sit at the table and Hope says, "She's just as guilty as he is. She married a married man. We know she's a liar—can you imagine all the work it took to keep this whole life secret? And, surprise, surprise, now he disappears. She knows exactly where he is. She probably helped him get out of the country, and now they're going to run away with millions of dollars?"

This is all too much to process right now. I put my head down and say, "I can't believe he'd do this to me, to our kids."

"They questioned her for an hour…one hour! They questioned you for five hours. What's that tell you?"

I get up from the table and look out the kitchen window. Without turning back, I say, "You know what I want? I want to meet her. I want to talk to her."

– CHAPTER 11 –

Flint has been locked up for two months at the Travis County Correctional Complex in Del Valle, Texas. Del Valle is a little town just down the road from Austin. If you don't get out on bail, this is where you stay until your case is tried or you plead out. The biggest event of the week in Del Valle is the high school football games on Friday nights.

To Flint, jail is a place for the Blacks, the Mexicans, and the white trash who can't afford a good lawyer—not for a guy like him. He keeps his head down and stays to himself the best he can. He has to be careful. If anyone finds out who he really is, he might be stabbed in the gut by some feller he knew from the good old days.

When he was working for the Sheriff's office, Flint would throw someone in jail just because they mouthed off or had a bad attitude. They might sit there for a week or so before being released. All the officers would walk by and have a good laugh at their expense. It feels a lot different now that he's the one on the other side of the steel bars.

Days feel like months, and weeks feel like an eternity. The food is terrible. Flint didn't eat for two days, until he finally broke down and ate the slop they call food. The only visitor who comes to visit him is the lawyer he recently hired to handle his case.

It takes over two months before Flint finds out anything more about the charges against him. Two months, walking around in a clown outfit with flip-flops that stick to his feet. He's got to get out of this place. He can't do anything sitting in a tiny cell without so much as a clock on the wall. No one tells him anything. All he knows is he's charged with murdering that idiot, Zachary Bell, and he's damn sure it was Ryan F'n Brunick who got him caught.

Flint finally shows up at the Travis County District Court for his initial appearance, wearing his prison uniform and shackles on his ankles and wrists. This is the day he'll officially hear the charges against him and receive the initial discovery in his case.

Waiting for him in front of the judge is Whitney Fanning, the best lawyer he knows in the entire county. He was once the second-best lawyer, until the best lawyer got drunk and drove his damn car off that cliff. They already met twice at the jail, where he paid a fifty-thousand-dollar retainer and discussed the facts of his case. Flint swore he was completely innocent— framed by God knows who.

When Flint walks in through the side door, Fanning turns away from the prosecutor, holding a handful of documents. It's the discovery they've been waiting for. It's not much yet, but it lays out the evidence used for the arrest.

Fanning skims through the documents, before turning to Flint. "You're not going to believe this. It appears this Zachary Bell got an anonymous call two days before the shooting warning him what was coming. Bell wrote a letter explaining how you were threatening to kill him, and you're responsible if anything happens to him. He left the letter with his co-worker to be handed over to the police in the event of his death. Well, he handed it over. The letter is in the file."

Flint scoffs at it all. "Well, ain't that the damnedest thing I've ever heard my whole life. See what I told you? It sounds like someone is trying to set me up."

The truth is, Flint knows exactly who tipped Zachary off. In his last conversation with Ryan Brunick, he explained how he put a tracker on Zachary's car and bugged his home after he found out that sum bitch was talking to Ryan's daughter, Hope. Despite a firm warning, Zach was still calling Hope, still crying to his wife, and still telling the whole sordid affair to one of his friends at work. Then Flint learned Zach bought a ticket to Los Angeles and was planning on meeting with Hope. He knew good and well what the meeting was all about.

At the time, everything was getting out of hand. Flint was going to make sure Bell never got on that plane to California to spill his guts. Flint hired his guy to "shut him up once and for all" and he went to Ryan's office to get the twenty thousand dollars to pay for it.

Ryan wanted no part of it. The conversation went round and round with a lot of yelling going on.

"Enough!" Ryan finally yelled over Flint's constant badgering. "There's too much blood already. I won't let you do it."

"Do you want to go to some goddam prison for the rest of your life?" Flint barked.

Ryan sat back in his chair and regained his composure. Shaking his head, he said, "I'll cross that bridge when I come to it, but you're not going to kill Zach."

Flint wasn't going down like that. He clenched his fist and brought it down so hard on Ryan's desk it caused a *boom* throughout the office. Debbie, Ryan's secretary who sat right outside the door, peeked her head inside and asked, "Is everything okay in here, Mr. Brunick?"

Ryan closed his eyes and gave her a quick nod of his head. Debbie returned to her desk.

Still going strong, Flint shouted, "I'm not crossing any goddamn bridge, and I'm not going to prison. This is on you—you and that pretty little wife you wanted to get rid of. Well, what'd you think was gonna happen? You thought everything would go back like nothing ever happened? Well, partner, it never works like that. You lie down with dogs, you're gonna wake up with fleas—plain and simple." Flint pointed his finger at Ryan and said, "Well, this kid ain't the first and he probably won't be the last."

Ryan worked with Flint for years but never knew him—not really. This is insanity, and Ryan was out of the insanity business. "I'm warning you Flint—" Ryan yelled.

"Listen to me," Flint interrupted. "You don't warn me of anything. You pulled me into this. I once took care of a Texas Ranger and I can damn sure take care of you. One way or another, I'm getting us out of this, and I never want to hear from you again."

"I never want to hear from you again" was the best thing Ryan could hear.

Before Ryan could say anything more, Flint walked out and slammed the door behind him. Flint made one last call, and put the whole plan in motion.

Now, all this time later, Flint finds out it was Ryan Brunick, that no good double-crosser, who actually called Zach to warn him. *How in the world could he be so stupid?*

Once Flint finishes discussing the discovery documents, Fanning puts everything in his briefcase and clips it shut. The first order of business is to ask the court for bail in the case. It's a tall task in most murder cases, but Fanning thinks he has a good shot at having bail granted.

Fanning knows the judge in his case—he knows all the judges. This might not be Duval County, but it's still Texas, and judges still have to get re-elected. A campaign costs a lot of money, and Fanning is happy to help judges on both sides of the political aisle. Most judges also like hunting, or fishing, or golfing at a country club, so Fanning has memberships to hunt and golf. He also has a big fancy boat if fishing is their thing.

Each time the judge calls someone's case, some poor sucker goes up to the bench and cries about needing a lawyer. The next guy in front of the judge just got charged with smacking his wife around after coming home from a hard day's work. Flint remembers the good ole' days when police officers would consider it a "domestic disturbance" and go on their merry way. Now you look at a woman wrong and they send you to San Quentin.

The guy pleads not guilty and gets a lawyer appointed who looks like he just graduated from high school.

"He's still got pimples on his face for God's sake," Flint says to his lawyer.

As soon as the kid opens his mouth to say "Yes, your honor," Flint can tell he don't know the difference between his ass and his elbow. Flint shakes his head. It won't be like that for him.

When the judge calls out his case number and announces that the case is "The State of Texas versus Defendant, Thomas Wayne Flint," Flint walks right up to the bench with Fanning at his side–skipping any formality of talking from that table so far away. The judge turns to Fanning and says, "Good morning, counselor. How nice to see you today."

"Nice to see you too, Henry—I mean, Your Honor."

Motioning him to come approach the bench, the judge says, "I understand you have a motion for the court to hear."

"Yes sir, Your Honor," Fanning says with a smile. "My client, Thomas Flint, is asking the court to set a reasonable amount of bail in the case, or to release him on his own personal recognizance pending the trial or dismissal of this case."

The judge turns to the prosecutor and asks, "What's the State's position regarding bail?"

The prosecutor present today, recently moved up from the County Attorney's office. He won't get close to the trial of the case or even handle the important pre-trial matters, but he's certainly capable of handling a simple bail matter—especially given the fact that bail is almost never granted in a murder case.

"Your Honor, the state is opposed to bail in this case. This is a murder case, and the state expects there will be a charge of capital murder. The defendant poses a flight—"

"Your Honor," Fanning loudly interrupts, causing everyone in the courtroom to look up. "This defendant poses no flight risk. My client has lived in Texas his entire life. He's a law enforcement officer, for God's sake."

The prosecutor, a little shaken but wanting to continue where he left off, says, "Your Honor, the state believes….the state believes—"

"Excuse me, judge," Fanning breaks in again with the same intensity. He shoots a hard look at the prosecutor and says, "I wasn't finished talking, if you don't mind."

"Go on, Mr. Fanning," the judge says with a smile.

"The Defendant was born and raised in Texas. His father was born and raised in Texas, and he has two brothers born and raised in Texas. All his children live in Texas. He lives in this county, and his business is right here in Austin. He's not going anywhere."

"Is he willing to surrender his passport to the court?" the judge asks.

"Of course, he will, Your Honor."

Feeling things starting to slip away, the prosecutor jumps back into the ring. "Your Honor! The Defendant is charged with murder for hire. The victim was shot in the head. Before the victim was killed, he was actually warned by a third party that the Defendant was threatening to kill him. The victim then wrote a letter naming the Defendant in the event anything happened to him. Sure enough, the victim was shot in the head. This is cold-blooded murder. It's one of the strongest cases I've ever seen."

The judge raises his hand at the prosecutor, and with a slight chuckle says, "Calm down there, counselor. I know you're excited to be here in the big league, but there's no jury here. You'll get your trial, but this is a simple bail hearing."

The judge's attempt at humor causes others waiting in the courtroom to laugh along. When you're the District Judge, everyone laughs at your attempts at humor like you're a stand-up comedian.

The prosecutor takes a step back and says, "Yes sir, I apologize. All I'm saying is this is a strong case. The state—"

"A strong case?" Fanning laughs, shaking his head in disbelief. "This was a suicide, plain and simple. The initial autopsy found as much. They got no witnesses other than the victim who, unfortunately, is no longer with us. This alleged tipster he's talking about? That tipster is Ryan Brunick. This doesn't even pass the smell test. Mr. Brunick was an upstanding member of the Texas Bar. I'm sure he would have gone directly to the police station if he thought for a second there was a murder plot to kill someone. We'll never know, Your Honor. As you're aware, Ryan Brunick was killed in a car accident six months ago."

The judge looks at the prosecutor and asks, "Is this true counselor? Did the initial autopsy list the cause of death as suicide?"

"Well, yes, Your Honor….but that was before the—"

"And are your only witnesses deceased?"

"I wouldn't say that," the prosecutor says, like he's not sure what else to say. "We anticipate additional evidence in the case."

Fanning is on a roll and has no intention of taking his boot off the prosecutor's neck. "Your Honor, we anticipate this case will be dismissed. My client has no criminal record whatsoever, and he's no flight risk. We ask that he be released on bond."

The prosecutor tries to regain his footing. "He has no *convictions,* Your Honor, but he was previously tried for murder in—"

"OBJECTION JUDGE!" Fanning shouts. The whole courtroom waits to find out what got Fanning so worked up. "This is completely improper. My client was acquitted of all charges against him. The prosecutor is just trying to slander the good name of a law enforcement officer, and I won't sit here and listen to it."

The judge bangs his gavel before chastising the prosecutor. "Counselor, I know you're new to this court, but you should know better. If he was acquitted, he was acquitted—end of story. Now let's stay focused here."

The prosecutor hangs his head and mumbles, "Yes, sir."

The judge returns to Fanning with a smile and asks, "What amount of bail would you propose, counselor?"

"Judge, we believe a PR bond is appropriate."

"Very well," the judge says before returning to the prosecutor. "And what amount of bail does the state feel is appropriate to secure the defendant's presence at trial?"

"Uh…Judge….the State opposes any bail at all."

Appearing to lose his patience, the judge drops his pen on his desk in a theatrical fashion. "I already heard your position, counselor," he grumbles. "Didn't we move past that? I thought I ruled on that. What amount of bail do you propose, counselor?"

Now that it's clear bail will be granted, the prosecutor says, "If the court is inclined to grant bail…if the court grants bail…I guess we'd ask bail be set in the amount of five million dol—"

"Five million dollars!" Fanning breaks in like he can't believe his own ears. By the look on his face, the judge appears to be in complete agreement. "My client is Tom Flint—not Bill Gates or Donald Trump! He's a lowly public servant who lives on a public servant's salary. The only point of bail is to make sure my client shows up for trial. Anything above twenty-five thousand dollars is, in effect, the same as a denial of bail."

The prosecutor wastes no time to jump back in. He turns to Fanning, ready to go toe-to-toe after a rough first start. "Are you kidding me, judge? Twenty-five thousand dollars? The state would ask for at least a million-dollar bond, that the Defendant surrender his passport, and he turn over all his guns."

"Why don't we make him turn over his first-born son while we're at it?" Fanning asks.

The judge, and everyone in the courtroom, get a good laugh out of that one. The judge bangs his gavel on his bench a few times and says, "Counselors….counselors….let's all calm down for a minute. I think I've heard enough."

Once the courtroom quiets down, the judge removes the docket sheet from the file, and writes something down before proceeding. Once he has the attention of everyone, he says, "Given the facts of the case, the defendant's criminal record, or lack thereof, his background as an upstanding police officer, and his ties to the community, the court is inclined to grant bail in this case."

Flint takes an enormous sigh of relief.

"Bail is hereby set at $100,000 by cash, cashier's check, or a surety bond."

The judge takes a few minutes to write more down on the docket sheet before talking directly to Flint. "Now Mr. Flint, I'm well aware you worked for the Duval County Sheriff's Department for many years, and I respect your service. Mr. Parr was a fine public servant. I don't want to take away your guns because I know you like to hunt here and there…am I right?"

"Yes sir," Flint answers. "I hunt and fish."

"Well, no one's gonna take your fishing pole away, either."

Everyone gets another cheap laugh.

"Mr. Fanning has agreed to surrender your passport, so I'll enter that order. You know how it all works, Mr. Flint. Keep your nose clean. If you get in any trouble, I'll revoke your bail and lock you up until trial. Do you understand?"

"Yes sir," Flint says.

"Very well," the judge says with another smile.

Flint can't hide his elation. He clasps his hand on his attorney's shoulder and gives him a smile. They walk over to the corner of the courtroom where

Flint, with a laugh that turns a few heads, says, "Holy shit, for a minute I thought he was gonna grant that PR bond."

"Sorry about that," Fanning says. "I did my best."

"Hell yes, you did your best," Flint says, shaking his shoulder. "You did good, son."

"I have a bondsman who will bond you out. You'll need to come up with maybe ten or twenty thousand dollars."

"Ten thousand dollars? Hell no!" Flint says. "I'm not about to just throw my money away. That judge didn't get elected because of his good looks. We're gonna get this case dismissed. I'll post that hundred-thousand-dollar bond myself.....cash....so I can get it all back. You just file your motions and keep greasing that judge."

Flint is left sitting in a chair against the wall waiting to be taken back to his cell so he can post his cash bond and get out of here. The longer he sits there thinking about the documents, and the tip Zach received, the more he fumes. Sitting in his chair, he starts plotting and planning. Not about his case. That will take care of itself soon enough. He has other things to take care of.

You see, it had taken everyone by surprise when the news broke that Ryan Brunick was killed in a car wreck. The more Flint heard, the harder it was to believe. How could Ryan go off the road so close to his own home in a single car collision?

Now that he's out on bail, Flint will be free to discover the truth. If he has to dig up Ryan's body with his own two hands, he'll get to the bottom of this. One way or another, he'll find the truth. If Ryan's good and dead, then that suits Flint just fine. If he's alive out there, Flint will make damn sure he ain't alive for long.

-102-

You don't double cross Tom Flint. If it's the last thing I do….if it's the last thing I do before I die, I'll find that sum bitch. I'll find him and show him what real justice looks like—just like I showed that smart-ass kid back in Alice who mouthed off one too many times and wound up with a bullet in the back of his head.

Grace Kennedy,
— Day 174

– CHAPTER 12 –

Hope starts taking classes at SMU so she can stay nearby. It's not Stanford, but I couldn't convince her to return to California right now if I tried. She flies back from time to time to see Blake, and he comes to Dallas all the time. He's at my house so often, he's like one of the family.

On Sunday night, right after kissing him goodbye at the door, Hope comes into my bedroom with a giddy smile and her face practically glowing

"What?" I ask, when she hops up on the bed beside me.

"He's just so sweet. I love him so much."

"Right…," I say more as a question, still wondering where this is going."

"Well, we talked about getting married."

Not wanting to rain on her parade, I raise my eyebrows and say, "Oh, great," with the best smile I can muster.

"He asked where I'd like to get married, where we'd live, all about kids…everything. He wants to marry me."

I think Blake is a great guy, and I know Hope's a great girl. I want to be happy for her—I do. It's the whole marriage thing that scares me now. I'm not sure I believe in marriage any longer. But that's not fair to Hope. I open my arms and say, "That's great…I'm so happy for you."

Every couple of days, I call Detective Stowe or drop by the police station to see if there's any news about my husband—or whoever's husband he is. I can feel the exacerbation in his voice each time I come by. I've become that pest who won't go away.

The answer is always the same. There's no sign of him anywhere. There hasn't been a charge on his credit cards, or a call on his cell phone, and he hasn't been seen in Denver or anywhere else. He practically tells me, *"Don't call me, I'll call you."*

Each time we talk, he swears, "Don't worry. We're going to find him. It's just a matter of time."

Grace Kennedy,
— Day 193

– CHAPTER 13 –

By the time I graduated from high school, I knew I wanted to be a doctor. I graduated valedictorian of my high school; I made great grades in college; and I was accepted into one of the best medical schools in the country.

To me, life was simple. It's not really complicated. All you have to do is work hard, live an honest life, and don't do anything stupid. In America, you can be whatever you want to be. The people who don't make it have no one but themselves to blame.

Now I know better. Everyone doesn't start at the same starting point. I was lucky enough to be born into a wealthy, supportive family. Life isn't this simple, straight line, always pointing forward. It's more of a series of ups and downs, successes and failures, usually moving three steps forward and two steps back. You shouldn't congratulate yourself too much for your successes, or beat yourself up too much for your failures. Even if you make all the right choices, and do all the right things, everything can still go horribly wrong. Something can (and probably will) come along that you never expected and cause all your best hopes and dreams to come crashing down.

I'm so glad to have Hope with me, because my whole life is about to fall apart. I was so relieved when the police cleared me of all charges—at least I'm not going to prison—but my troubles are just beginning. Now I find myself in the middle of this nightmare, and it's a nightmare I'm not going to wake up from any time soon.

First, I have no money coming in. Of course, Jackson's company stopped his paycheck when he stopped going to work. It's not like he resigned, he just stopped going in.

It became pretty obvious that I must end my little vacation before I run out of money, so I sit down with my supervisor to let her know I'm ready to return to the hospital. This is when I learn there's a difference between no longer being a suspect and being cleared of all charges.

I've always believed you don't spread your family's dirty secrets all over town. As far as anyone knew, our marriage was perfect. Now my family, my neighbors, Bonnie's teachers, and anyone who has a television set or internet access, knows the whole sordid affair. There's still a cloud of suspicion hanging over me. Most people believe I'm the jilted wife who killed her husband. With the media circus everywhere I go, my supervisor tells me the hospital doesn't want that distraction. She suggests I take an indefinite leave from work.

The truth is, I know it's for the best. My face has been all over the news, so I can only imagine what a patient coming into the hospital might think. I'm in no condition to be treating patients anyway, and with their father missing, my kids need me more now than ever.

Luckily, I've been paying for one of those disability policies for the last eight years for an emergency like this. This money should last me until everything blows over. I get all the documents they require to make a claim, and fill out all the paperwork. First, I learn that I haven't been off work long enough yet. When I later file all the paperwork, the insurance company denies my claim because "my husband is missing" doesn't qualify as a disability.

Next, I turn to that two-million-dollar life insurance policy Stowe was in such a tizzy about. Needless to say, two million dollars will solve all my financial problems and allow me to move forward with my life.

I spend two days filling out all their forms, doing my best to explain how Jackson is gone. I send everything in and cross my fingers. A month later, I receive a letter from the insurance company explaining in a whole bunch of legal mumbo jumbo how I won't be receiving a single penny. Until there's proof of Jackson's death—preferably a dead body and a death certificate—the policy will never pay.

Before Jackson took off, we put together a little savings that I've been living off of for the past five months. Our savings is running out and will be gone in two, maybe three, months. After that I'm at a loss.

So, things look pretty rough…right? Well, my problems are just beginning. Six months after Jackson disappeared, with my savings running out, I'm approached by a constable who, with a smile, serves me with the first of several lawsuits.

The first lawsuit is brought by DMD. They want all the money back that Jackson stole, as well as a couple of paychecks he didn't earn. Just asking for their money back isn't enough. They actually filed an injunction, freezing all my accounts—including my savings that I need to live on. I'm not sure how I'm expected to live until this stupid lawsuit is resolved.

Like they say, when it rains, it pours. It seems people have to pay taxes on their income—even when they steal that income. I receive letters and notices from the IRS regarding the eight million dollars Jackson embezzled. They want all the back taxes owed plus interest and penalties. It seems from the letters, they can put a lien on our house if I don't pay!

Sitting at the same desk where Jackson and I would review our finances and rejoice over our savings that kept climbing, I'm staring at a pile of bills. I'm drowning in bills and notices. Reading these letters and the different lawsuits, you'd think I was the one who stole all that money. At one of the hearings, the lawyer for DMD said, "Frankly, DMD doesn't care who stole the money; they just want it back."

When my dad died, he put the money for us into a trust. Per my dad's will, none of us can have it until we turn thirty-five years old. The trust provides money for normal living expenses, and education, and we can request more money in case of an "unexpected emergency." Well, this is an unexpected emergency.

With all my bank accounts frozen, I have only one way to pay my bills. I need the money my dad left Hope, Bonnie, and me. My dad took care of me all the way through medical school. Now here I am, thirty-three years old, and going back to my daddy for money.

My dad named his best friend, Ted Wood, as the trustee of his estate. They went to law school together, and their law firms worked together on different cases. I've known Mr. Wood for years, but not on a personal basis. All I know is, he's my dad's friend, and he always seemed like a nice guy.

The idea that someone else—especially someone who's not even a family member—will decide what money we can or cannot have didn't seem right. but as time goes by, I come to realize how smart it was on the part of my dad. The money is safe.

Hope is given more than enough money each month to pay her bills and to live on. If she needs money for school, books, clothes, or anything else, he never says no. Four months ago, Hope wanted to buy a used, dependable car to drive. Mr. Wood returned two days later with the title to a brand-new BMW he located and paid in full. Any time she wants to fly back to California, he always buys her a first-class ticket. Six months ago, she wanted to take a vacation with Blake, so Wood reclassified everything as an "emergency expense" and paid for the whole vacation—even Blake's ticket. They stayed at some luxury resort where everything, including drinks, were included.

Because the money is in a trust, it's protected. Debt collectors can't seize the money. If it had been given to me outright, it would have been frozen like everything else. Thanks to my dad, the trust pays my bills and gives me enough money to make sure Bonnie and Wesley get the things they need. Now I can breathe again.

– CHAPTER 14 –

Tracking someone down has never been a problem for Flint. Most people on the run aren't real smart about it. Lots of people commit a crime and flee to Mexico or South America to avoid criminal charges. After a few months, they get sloppy and go around town without a care in the world.

As a private investigator, many attorneys have hired Flint to track down bail jumpers. He has tracked down criminals as far south as the poorest slums of Nicaragua and as far north as Vancouver. In twenty-five years of working for law enforcement, there hasn't been a single person, not one, who's escaped his grasp. It might take a little time and a lot of work, but if you're out there, Flint will find you.

Being charged with first-degree murder has done nothing to help Flint's investigation business. The same lawyers who once paid out the nose for his expertise now want nothing to do with him. Flint has nothing but time on his hands. If Ryan's out there, you can bet your bottom dollar Flint will find him.

So where to begin? One thing's for sure, Ryan's not so stupid, and he won't act stupid. Flint is well aware of Ryan's reputation of turning lemons into lemonade. When a case seemed hopeless, he always found a way to turn it around. Finding him (if he doesn't want to be found) won't be easy.

When you want to find someone, you start with the people who know him best—family. Usually family members are tight mouthed, but an ex-wife….that's a horse of different color. Ex-husbands and ex-wives are usually a treasure trove of information. Hell hath no fury as a woman scorned, right? Well, Flint has a good hunch there's one woman out there where the fires of hell are burning bright. Getting her to talk should be no problem at all.

It takes Flint only a few computer strokes to find out Kate Brunick is living and working in Waco, Texas. She's living in some little apartment with her only son, while working at a small insurance company. Located just an hour north of Austin, Flint drives his Ford F150 pickup truck up north to have a little chat.

Flint has driven through Waco many times, but only stopped there once in his life. When you drive through the city, you can't miss Baylor University sitting right off the interstate. It's a beautiful school with red bricks and a bright gold dome roof. Otherwise, there's not a whole lot to do in Waco other than go to the zoo, spend a few hours at Cameron Park, or go out to the lake. Somehow, the high-tech boom that made Austin the next Silicon Valley always seems to turn its back on Waco, Texas.

There are a couple of things Flint might do before leaving town. If he has time, he might jump over to the Dr. Pepper Museum to learn all about his favorite soda pop.

Charles Alderton, a Waco pharmacist who worked at Morrison's Old Corner Drug Store, invented Dr. Pepper in 1885. He tried one recipe after another before mixing twenty-three different flavors together to arrive at a taste he liked. He thought he had a hit. It was first served at the pharmacy. Patrons who wanted to order the drink would simply say "shoot me a Waco." Dr. Pepper was later introduced to almost 20 million people at the 1904 World's Fair Exposition in St. Louis, and the rest is history. It went national one year before Coca-Cola. It's said the recipe is kept as two halves in safe deposit boxes in two different banks.

Waco also holds the Texas Ranger Museum. Flint's never been a big fan of the Texas Rangers. It all started back in Duval County when he had a run-in with a Ranger that damn near ended in a fistfight—or a gunfight. Still, Flint has been fascinated with Bonnie and Clyde because, as a young boy, he went to a carnival and got a good look at the bullet-ridden Deluxe automobile they were killed in. He even stuck his finger right in one of the bullet holes. The museum holds some of the guns, photos, newspaper reports, and other artifacts from Bonnie and Clyde's crime spree across Texas and the Bible belt.

For now, Flint follows his navigation off the highway to a street that has more than its fair share of potholes. When he stops at the first traffic light, a group of panhandlers are gathered at every corner. One fella comes over holding a cardboard sign with something scribbled on it about being a hungry vet. To Flint, these guys should all be arrested. As the beggar comes a little closer, Flint looks down at his phone until the light turns green and he can move on without being bothered.

The streets ahead aren't any better. They're full of houses with dead grass, weeds that won't stop growing, and broke down cars. It's obvious this isn't the best part of town.

Flint turns into the apartment complex he's been looking for. It looks old and outdated, with none of the frills you might find in a modern apartment complex. The place could stand to be painted, and the parking lot is in need of repair. It's full of cracks and potholes, with a few reserved parking spots along the side fence where the canopy is about to fall down. Most cars have to hunt for an empty parking space that's hard to come by. The pool appears to be temporarily out of service with the gate chained shut to keep everyone out.

After circling around the parking lot twice, Flint finally finds a space after another car pulls out. He parks right next to a dumpster in the back with two mattresses leaning on their side and an old beat-up dresser behind it. He gets out of his pickup, not sure if it will still be there when he returns. Before walking off, he opens the back door, takes his rifle off his gun rack, and slides it under the back seat.

Walking back around to Building 12, a group of teenage kids are sitting in the shade of one of the few trees, obviously trying to get out of the scorching Texas heat. Their bikes are scattered all around them with a basketball laying nearby. It looks like they were just playing basketball on the court with a rim but no net.

When Flint walks past, one of the black kids and a taller white kid stand up and walk over to the sidewalk, blocking him from walking by. Flint can walk across the grass, or through the parking lot, but the day will never come when he lets a bunch of punks tell him what to do.

"Yo' grandpa," the white kid says, as Flint gets closer.

"Gotta pay the toll to cross these tracks." the black kid says, looking square into Flint's eyes.

"Yo' that's church there…know what I'm sayin'," the white kid says fist bumping the other kid.

Flint ignores these punks and tries to walk between them, but both kids squeeze together and block his path. The white kid looks about sixteen or seventeen, but he's just as tall as Flint. "Yo' grandpa," he says, "my main man gave you the juice…know what I'm sayin'?"

"Throw down some cabbage," the black kid says.

Flint isn't backing down, and he don't give a good damn about any cabbage. He looks first at the white kid, then at the black kid, and asks, "What's your names?"

"Still Bill," the black kid says. "What's it to ya'?"

Flint looks at the other kid. "And you?"

This kid raises both arms and says, "Catfish…grandpa." He jerks forward like he might head-butt Flint. All the kids in the group break out laughing, but Flint doesn't even blink.

"Well, Still Bill…and Mr. Catfish," Flint says with a grin, "I have business here. You punks better get back to your little basketball game, or I'm gonna pop a knot on your heads. You know what *I'm* saying?"

"Now you buggin", Catfish says, reaching out and poking Flint on the chest. "Why you buggin?"

All the kids sitting on the grass have stayed back until now. They stand to their feet and start laughing and whooping it up as they circle behind Flint. One yells, "Dude needs to get a grip!"

"Kick his ass, Catfish," someone laughs.

"Bust a cap in that nigga'," another yells.

Catfish looks over at Still Bill, ready to make his move. "I gotcha' bro," Still Bill says.

Flint moves his jacket just enough to reveal the badge he has clipped to his waist and the gun on his side. Catfish jumps back and says, , "Yo, yo, yo….he's the po-po."

"Ah, that's sick," a kid behind Flint says, turning around and running to his bike.

"Let's bounce to the crib," someone shouts, also heading to his bike.

"Chill bro," Still Bill says, moving to the left so Flint has plenty of room to pass by.

Catfish steps back and throws up both hands like he's trying to surrender or something. When Flint walks by, Catfish says, "That's dope, grandpa… know what I'm sayin'."

Today is these kid's lucky day. There was a time when Flint would have rounded them all up and taken them downtown. Attempted robbery, disorderly conduct, criminal trespass, and obstructing a sidewalk all come to mind. Flint and Ryan, however, have a date with destiny, and Flint can't be distracted by a bunch of disrespectful punks. He continues on his way down the sidewalk.

When Flint hits the stairs, he moves slowly, using the rail to help him up. Kate's apartment is only on the second floor, but he's about out of breath when he arrives. He has a good idea what Kate looks like. Every time he went to Ryan's law office (usually to pick up cash) there was a large family portrait hanging in the waiting room. Ryan also kept a photo on his desk of the two of them looking like honeymooners at their latest vacation spot.

Flint even met Kate once about a decade ago at the Travis County Las Vegas Night Gala. Back in the day, this was the yearly event everyone looked forward to. It cost a thousand dollars a ticket, or you could pay ten thousand dollars to reserve a table for twelve.

The money went to some charity that benefited the poor. Everyone who's anyone in Austin (and many other places around the state) attended the party, and Ryan was one of the biggest lawyers in Texas. He paid for a table big enough for his entire office and donated another twenty-five thousand dollars to the cause.

Ryan showed up sporting a black tux, a gold Rolex watch, and his new young wife by his side. She was wearing a metallic gold dress that fit her perfect figure like a glove. If her young, perfectly shaped breasts didn't hold your attention, the four-carat emerald necklace hanging between them, surrounded by 3.5 carat diamonds, would almost hypnotize you. Queen Elizabeth would have been proud to wear that necklace.

Ryan and Kate looked like the perfect couple, and she couldn't get enough of him. Everywhere he went, she was by his side. When he stopped to talk to someone, sat at the table, or gave a few words at the front podium, she was close by, admiring her handsome new husband with a smile on her face bigger than Texas. It was easy to see the love she felt for him.

Flint knocks on the door, waits a minute, and knocks again. The door opens until it catches on the chain. Kate looks through the opening and asks, "May I help you?"

Flint is wearing his usual cowboy hat, light blue collared shirt, blue jeans, and boots. "Yes, ma'am, my name is Tom Flint. Can I ask you a few questions?"

"Is this about Jackson Kennedy?" she asks. "I'm not a member of that family anymore, and I know nothing about it. Please leave me alone."

Just as she starts to shut the door, Flint puts his boot in the opening. "No ma'am, I'm not here about Jackson Kennedy. I want to talk with you about Ryan Brunick."

Looking down at Flint's boot blocking the entry, Kate asks, "Who are you with?"

Flint removes the badge from his belt and holds it up just long enough for it to be seen, but not studied. Kate slides the chain off the door, opens it just enough to see outside, and asks, "What is it you want to know?"

She's barefoot, and has on a white spaghetti strap cotton shirt dotted with tiny red roses, and blue jeans shorts that rise well below her bellybutton. They give you just a peek at her still firm and tan stomach. Flint knows from his research that she's thirty-six. She's still quite attractive, but that gorgeous face that once turned every head at the gala, is beginning to show the wear and tear caused by a full-time job, a willful teenage son, sleepless nights, too many tears, and constant cigarette smoke blowing in front of her face. It gives Flint a good idea what money can do for a woman. Long gone are the fancy gym memberships, five-hundred-dollar haircuts, face massages and chemical peels, Botox injections at all the right spots, and the best makeup money can buy.

Flint tips his hat and asks, "You mind if I step in, ma'am? It's hotter than the Dickens out here."

Kate shuts the door, releases the chain, and opens the door again. "Come on in," she says. "Can I get you something to drink?"

"You got a soda…maybe a Dr. Pepper?"

Kate's a little surprised by this request and says, "No…no soda."

"How bout' a glass of sweet tea, pretty lady?"

"No sweet tea either," she answers.

"Lemonade?"

When Kate shakes her head, Flints says, "Some water would tickle me pink."

Kate walks over to the small kitchen and comes back with a glass of water in a Baylor Bears plastic cup. She sits on the couch, lights a cigarette, and asks, "Who are you again?"

"Flint…Tom Flint."

The name sounds familiar, but Kate doesn't know why. She can't even remember that she identified Tom Flint by name a while back when she filled out the divorce papers and the affidavit she presented to Ryan. "Tom Flint," she says, blowing smoke at the ceiling. "Have we met? Did you work for my ex-husband?"

"No ma'am," Flint lies, "but I am interested in knowing more about Ryan Brunick. Are y'all divorced?"

"Three months ago," she says, showing her naked marital ring finger. "I'm back to my maiden name, Flowers."

"Mrs. Brunick….I mean Flowers, I'm investigating Ryan's death. I have some questions about it all, and I thought you might be able to fill in a few details."

"What about it?"

"I want to find out more about the circumstances that led to the crash that night."

"Mr. Flint, if you're wanting to know if he really died, you're barking up the wrong tree. Trust me….I've asked. I didn't want to believe Ryan would drive his car off a road he's been down hundreds of times. The police closed the case, and the Sheriff's office won't even look at it. My lawyer thought the whole idea was ridiculous."

"Yeah, but those folks are about as useful as tits on boar," Flint says. "Something about it never smelled right to me, and when I get a scent, I can be like an ole' hound dog sniffing a hot trail. Maybe there's nothing to see here, but I want to be sure."

"Why?" Kate asks tapping her cigarette on an empty Diet Dr. Pepper can sitting on the coffee table. "What do you care?"

"Let's just say there's some unfinished business that needs taken care of."

Flint pulls out a small notebook and asks, "I understand he drove off that ravine coming home from work?"

"No sir," Kate says, lifting her index finger in protest. "I had just filed for divorce. He was no longer living there. He wasn't coming home. I have no idea what he was doing that night."

For the next twenty minutes, Kate lays out everything that led up to her filing for divorce. She explains how Ryan's first wife went to prison in Thailand, like she's breaking some unbelievable news. "It was Ryan's daughter, Hope, who started searching for her mom and discovered the truth. Ryan set up the whole thing."

Flint listens closely, like he's hearing this same old story for the first time. Kate continues talking—how Faith died in that hellhole and Zach killed himself because of his part in the murder.

Flint never knew Kate found out about everything. Now he understands why she filed for divorce.

"You know, you live with someone for thirteen years and you think you know them," Kate continues. "Then you find out you don't know them at all. What kind of person could do something so horrible to the mother of your children? A monster…that's who."

"Yes ma'am," Flint says, shaking his head in disgust. "A real monster."

So, Kate filed for divorce? Big deal. This doesn't explain why Ryan would kill himself. Ryan knows more than anyone how to handle a divorce.

"Did you and Ryan have a prenup?" he asks.

"Oh yeah," Kate says, blowing smoke. "I was young and stupid. What can I say? I loved him, so I signed it. I thought we would be married forever. You know, I would have signed anything he put in front of me."

This is even more reason why Ryan would have been fine. It makes no sense at all. Was Ryan in love? Was he heartbroken? Flint doesn't think so. Ryan had been around the block once or twice, and it only takes one nasty divorce to break you. Nah, by now Ryan knew better than anyone that love is a young man's folly.

"So, what happened?" Flint asks.

"You know, Mr. Flint, Ryan offered to give me everything if I'd just give him the house. I should have done it, but my lawyer wanted it all. It was all his idea. He told me to do it."

"Do what?"

"Everything! I gave him a list of all our property, and he told me I could take it all. I met with Ryan. I told him to give me everything, or I'd tell everyone what he did to Faith. He'd lose his law license and go to prison. I even recorded him. I called him and recorded him admitting what he did. My lawyer was thrilled. He said Ryan was finished. Within a few weeks of me giving him the papers, he was killed in that car wreck, and I got nothing."

Flint can't believe what he just heard. "You got nothing?"

"Not a damn thing. Under the prenup, if we divorced, I got one hundred thousand dollars for each year we were married, but when Ryan died, his will determined everything. Well, under his will, the kids got everything. You know what I got?"

Flint just waits while she continues. He's learning plenty by simply shutting up and letting her vent. "Ryan wasn't gone three days before I got a letter from his best friend—now the administrator of his will—giving me seven days to get the hell out of the house—the house I furnished, I decorated, and I put together with my blood, sweat, and tears. His friend was at the house with a constable on the day I left looking over everything I took. If I'd known they'd be there, maybe I could have taken things out beforehand. He made sure I took nothing except my personal stuff. He treated me like a burglar in my own house. What'd I get? I got jack shit. That's what I got."

Now it all makes sense.

"Mrs. Brunick, something about Ryan's death just don't add up. I just wanna make sure. I wanna exhume his body and make sure it's actually Ryan down there."

"You can't," Kate says.

"Oh yes we can," Flint nods. "All we have to do is get a court order."

"He was cremated. Under his will, he was to be cremated within forty-eight hours. No autopsy, no burial….nothing. The ashes were turned over to his kids."

"Of course, he was cremated," Flint says, shaking his head. "Let me ask you…when was that will signed?"

"He went to some hot-shot lawyer right after I gave him the divorce papers and changed his will."

Flint looks up and says, "I'll be damned! I knew it." He slaps his leg and repeats, "I knew it."

"But he was in the car. They carried his body out of that wreck," Kate explains.

"Bull-butter," Flint says with a wicked smile.

"What?"

"I said bull-butter. Hell, all you need is the right connections and you can buy a cadaver for a couple thousand dollars. Fill that car with gas, add some accelerant, and drop it off a cliff in the middle of the night. By morning some rent-a-cop investigator won't be able to tell the difference between come here and sick-em'."

"I knew it!" Kate yells, brushing her hair back over her ears. "I knew Ryan wouldn't drive over that cliff. Mr. Flint, I got to ask you. Ryan had a large life insurance policy. I was the beneficiary. He paid on it for ten years. Then, right before he died, he cancelled the policy. Why would he do that? Why would he throw all that money away if he was about to stage his own death? Why not just name his kids as the new beneficiaries?"

A smile spreads across Flint's face. "Brilliant…..just brilliant."

Kate looks on, unable to understand. "What?" she asks.

"You see, faking your own death ain't no crime. There's nothing illegal about disappearing. If you haven't committed a crime, no one's going to send out a posse looking for you. Ryan would be free as a bird."

"I'm still not following you," Kate says.

"Insurance fraud, now that's a crime. The police care a lot about that. More important, the insurance company who pays out the money cares a lot about it. How much insurance did he have?"

"Five million dollars," Kate says.

Flint gives a long, loud whistle and repeats, "Five million dollars! That's a hell of a lot of money. The insurance company would have to pay it. They wouldn't have a choice. But they ain't no fool. If you think the police will search for someone, well you ain't seen nothin'. They'll hire the best damn investigators money can buy and track him down to the ends of the earth. He'll have to hide out forever. He'd never get a good night's sleep. This way….this way nobody gives a damn. No one's looking for Ryan. He can take it easy for a while, live wherever he wants to live, and come back any time he pleases. He just needed to get the divorce finalized. I wouldn't be surprised if he did this whole thing, so you'd finish your divorce and be done with it. He is one brilliant sum bitch."

"I can't believe this," Kate says. "Our divorce is over. I went to court a few weeks ago and finished everything. I just wanted this whole thing behind me."

Flint puts his hand on her shoulder to console her and says, "I understand."

"I woulda' got over a million bucks, but now I got nothing. The order gave me my car, my jewelry, and all my personal belongings, and that's it. That damn trustee sat there in my home with a constable, watching everything I took out."

For the first time, Flint sees tears welling up in Kate's eyes, but he feels no sympathy for her whatsoever. He went through his own ugly divorce fifteen years ago, and his wife took everything. She knew too many of his old secrets—knew where the bodies were buried, so to speak. She threatened him the same way Kate threatened Ryan. The problem? Flint's wife had already filed for divorce, and Flint knew he'd be the prime suspect if she popped up dead somewhere. In the end, he gave her the home, most of the family property, and their children.

Actually, the whole thing only makes Flint admire Ryan more. Kate could have been well taken care of, but greed got the best of her. Well, she played the game, and she lost. Thought she could record him? She was playing checkers and Ryan was playing chess, and now it's checkmate—game…set…match. As far as he's concerned, she's a fool….and a fool and her money will eventually part ways.

"I'm mighty sorry for everything you've been through, Kate. Do you mind if I call you Kate?"

"Sure," Kate says, looking towards the window as her neighbor passes by.

Flint leans closer, puts his hand on Kate's bare leg, and gives it an easy squeeze. It's been a long time since he's held a young woman's leg. It feels soft and smooth under his old, wrinkled hand.

"Look at me now," Kate says, picking up a towel off the floor and wiping her runny nose. "I was stupid. I lost everything. I sold my jewelry and everything of value I had. My ring….I know damn good and well my wedding ring cost Ryan sixty thousand dollars. You know what I got for it?"

Flint raises his eyebrows and waits for her to continue.

"Ten thousand dollars for my wedding ring, my diamond and emerald necklace, and the matching bracelet and earrings."

Flint looks down and shakes his head in disbelief. He wants to appear sympathetic, but all he's really thinking is, *"A fool and her money will eventually part ways."*

Kate stands up and waves her hand around the apartment like she's a model on *The Price Is Right,* showing off the next prize for the contestants to bid on. "I was living in a million-dollar house. Now look at this place."

"It's not so bad," Flint lies. "I think you have it dressed up pretty darn nice."

Kate leans back against the kitchen counter and looks around. Even she can't believe her new life. "Now I'm making fifteen dollars an hour, and I can't even pay my bills. I went to the AG's office to get child support, but that will take months. Can you help me get it started?"

"I sure would, but that's not what I do. If you already had the order, I could help enforce it."

"No, that's the problem," Kate says, looking down. "I need to get an order."

Kate puts both hands on the counter behind her, looks up at the ceiling, and squeezes her eyes shut, which causes a tear to fall down her cheek. "What the hell am I gonna do?" she whispers.

Flint, seeing how vulnerable Kate is, stands up, walks over, and pulls her close. He holds her in his arms, gently stroking her hair. As Kate remains there in his arms, Flint's mind starts wandering to a dark place. She's been single for a spell now. He actually convinces himself she might want him as much as he wants her.

Flint's been here before. So many sexy women speeding through Duval County would break down in tears; willing to do just about anything to avoid an outstanding warrant, or even some silly speeding ticket. He was more than happy to drive somewhere private and work out a payment plan. To Flint, it was the best part of his job.

Kate feels soft and warm as her breasts press against him. Her hair smells like cheap strawberry shampoo. The memory of this classy woman standing next to Ryan at the gala so long-ago flashes through his mind. For half an hour, Flint stood at a distance watching everything they did. At one point, he made a promise to God, or the devil, or anyone who'd listen, that he'd give anything to have a woman like that. Now here he is, holding this gorgeous woman crying in his arms. It's like God looked down and answered his prayers.

Even when he was a young man, Flint wasn't known for his good looks, and his better days are long behind him now. Nothing has really changed. He's still twenty-five years older than Kate, and maybe a hundred pounds heavier, but he'd still give anything—or risk everything—to have her.

Flint pulls Kate even closer and strokes her back, feeling the clasp of her bra against his hand. That's all it takes to get him aroused. He lowers his right hand down her cotton shirt until he finds the soft, warm skin of her back, right above the top of her tiny shorts.

Feeling Flint's fingers going inside the waist of her shorts startles Kate. She looks up, wipes away her tears, and says, "I'm sorry, Mr. Flint. I don't know what got into me."

"Nothing to be sorry about, pretty lady," Flint says, staring right into her eyes. He slides his hand a little higher up her back, causing her shirt to pull up with his hand. As he moves his other hand towards her breast, Kate realizes, for the first time, the fix she's put herself in. Flint is so much bigger than her, and she's now caught in his grasp, like a fly in a spider's web. It may be too late for her to do anything about it.

The second he puts his hand over the cup of her bra, Kate screams as loud as she can, before he puts his other hand over her mouth, muffling the sound. She pushes hard against his hand and pulls away with all her might. It doesn't do a bit of good; she can feel his large hand tighten over her mouth. Suddenly, Kate fears he might suffocate her.

"It's okay, little darling," Flint says, kissing her forehead, reeking of cigarette smoke and cheap cologne. He removes his hand from her mouth and moves his lips to hers—pushing down hard. All she can hear is the sound of him breathing loud against her face. His old gray mustache scratches her lips. Practically gagging from his stench and his cold, cracked lips against hers, she immediately turns her face away with a look of absolute disgust.

It doesn't deter Flint a bit. He moves his hand down her stomach until he reaches the button on her jean shorts. He fumbles with the button until he feels them pop open. Kate grabs his wrist and tries to pull his hand back up, but he's way too strong. "Don't fight it honey," Flint says, pushing her against the wall and sliding his hand deeper inside her open shorts. Moaning just a bit, he says, "Take it easy…. just take it easy."

Kate's best friend growing up was molested by her step-father for years until they moved away when she was fourteen. She had another friend in college who was raped at a fraternity party by two guys. When she heard these stories, she wondered afterwards why they let it happen. She told herself she would have done something, anything, to stop it if the same thing happened to her. Now the same thing is happening to her, and she has no idea what the hell to do.

Unsure how to get out of this, Kate does the only thing that comes to her mind right now—she'll swing her knee straight up to kick him between the legs. She builds up her courage and kicks as hard as she can; but it doesn't go the way she saw it in her mind. Flint moves to the right just in time to avoid her clumsy, off-balance attempt, and she hits his upper thigh instead.

Thinking Flint will be furious, Kate covers her face. It doesn't seem to upset Flint at all. In fact, it seems to turn him on even more. He pushes Kate to the floor, and whispers in her ear, "Relax honey…. just relax."

It's obvious screaming and fighting will do her no good, so she goes limp and pleads to Flint's better nature. "Please don't do this," she cries. "You don't have to do this."

As many women before Kate have already learned, Flint doesn't have a better nature. He pulls up her cotton shirt along with her tan bra, exposing her beautiful breast.

Kate tries her best to wiggle free, but it's impossible. "Get off me," she screams one last time.

Flint puts his mouth on her breast, right as the front door swings open, bringing a burst of sunlight into the apartment. The door stops with a *bang* when it catches against the chain. Ben yells through the small opening, "Mom, open the door."

Flint releases his hold on Kate and jumps to his feet. He picks up his cowboy hat that fell to the floor and quickly tucks his shirt back into his jeans. Still protected from Ben's prying eyes, he gives Kate a look that scares the hell out of her. He puts one finger to his lips, and whispers, "Shhhhh".

Kate sits up, puts her bra back in place, and buttons her shorts. She hurries to the door before Flint can react. She slams the door closed, slides the chain off, and pulls it open again. Ben takes a step inside, looks over at Flint, and then looks back at his mom, who's obviously shaken. He can see she's been crying. "What's wrong?" he asks.

"Nothing…nothing's wrong," Kate says, holding back her tears. Kate steps back from the door to give Flint plenty of room to pass by without touching her. Keeping plenty of distance, she says, "He was just leaving."

"Thank you, ma'am," Flint says with a tip of his cowboy hat. He reaches in his breast pocket, pulls out a business card, and hands it to her. "Call me if you think of anything else."

The thought of reaching out for his card disgusts her—even scares her. "Get out," she says, practically hiding behind the door.

With a quick, "Have a nice day," Flint leaves his card on the counter and walks outside. Kate flinches when he comes close.

Once he's gone, Kate secures the chain and locks the deadbolt. She watches through the curtains as he wobbles down the stairs. For a minute, she feels like she might actually throw up. She walks over to the counter and examines the card without picking it up. Even the thought of touching it repulses her. Finally, she grabs the card, crumples it, and throws it in the trash.

Back in his pickup truck, Flint looks in the rearview mirror at his rough, sunburnt face. He shakes his head and whispers, "You're such a shit."

Ben, ignoring everything he just saw, heads to his room to play video games like he does every evening until he falls asleep. "Ben, do your homework," Kate says, almost crying before Ben can close the door.

"I just got home!" he shouts with the same disrespect and anger Kate has learned to live with. "I'll do it later."

Kate never had to be the disciplinarian. Ryan had a way of handling Ben that demanded respect. She'd rather walk through fire than deal with her teenage boy with an attitude. "Now," Kate shouts.

Ben slams the door so hard it shakes the whole apartment. "God," he screams through the door, "leave me the fuck alone."

While Flint fastens his seatbelt, not caring a bit about the damage he left behind, Kate sits back down on the couch and reaches for a cigarette. Her hands are shaking so badly, she has to steady herself just to light it. As she leans back on the couch, the memory of Flint forcing his hand down her shorts sickens her. Feeling like she's about to throw up, she gets up, goes into the bathroom, and leans over the toilet. When the urge to vomit dies down, she takes off all her clothes and turns on a hot shower to wash his filth away.

Standing under the hot water, she's unable to process what just happened. It all unfolded so fast. Before she knew what was happening, Flint had her pinned against the wall. Standing under the hot shower, she takes a deep breath as it sinks in how differently things would have ended for her if Ben hadn't walked in the door when he did.

The more the whole thing runs through her mind, the more she wants to vomit. Trying to burn his stink off of her, she turns the shower even hotter, causing the steam to fill the bathroom and fog the mirrors. The water burns her skin and her chest. Her stomach turns bright red.

Ryan would have killed him. I was his angel and he would have killed any man who put his hands on me.

With the hot water beating against her chest, she can remember the foul smell of Flint's breath as he pressed his lips against hers. He reeked of coffee, cigarette smoke, and the smell of a man who hadn't brushed his teeth in months. Just the memory of it all causes her to gag. Kate's only been with two men, and the thought of Flint being the third causes her to gag again and vomit all over herself. To forever extinguish Flint's smell from her nostrils, she turns the shower even further to the left and moves her face under the burning hot water.

Part of her blames herself for inviting Flint inside her apartment in the first place. *What was I thinking?* Angry at herself and hating Flint, she grabs her face scrub, turns the shower handle all the way to the left, and drops down in the tub. Desperately hoping to remove any trace of Flint from her body, she frantically scrubs her face, her chest, her stomach, and between her legs while the scalding water pours over her. She cries so hard while she scrubs and scrubs, until her skin is so red, swollen, and blistered that there's no feeling left. As hard as she tries, the intense pain can't erase the memory that will stay with her for the rest of her life.

Kate stays there scrubbing until the hot water turns warm, and then cold. She gets out of the shower and tries to wrap a towel around her tender body, but the pain is too intense. She gets out of the tub and clears the bathroom mirror with a towel. She stares into the mirror at the woman in front of her. It makes her cry all over again.

Kate is so shaken up, she lies in a ball on the bed, just as helpless as a newborn baby. Still feeling the sting from the scalding water, her mind goes back to her younger days.

She was nineteen years old, and in her first year of college to become a veterinarian, when she found out she was pregnant. Young and naïve, she dropped out of college and married her boyfriend. It was always her plan to return to her studies one day. Two years after giving birth to their only son, Ben, her husband told her he wanted a divorce. She soon found out he'd been carrying on with some girl for over six months. Twenty-one years old with a young baby, she never returned to school and never became a veterinarian.

A year later, she met Ryan, and her whole life turned around. No more bills, working long hours, barely scraping by, and raising a child as a single parent. Ben really took to Ryan, and Ryan treated him like his own son— the son he lost in that terrible car wreck. Life seemed perfect. She should have known it wouldn't last.

For the next thirteen years, she was treated like royalty. She always hosted the nicest neighborhood lunches and dinner parties. Every time she entered Ryan's law office, the staff treated her like she owned the place. At the restaurants where they ate, it was always "yes ma'am," and "no ma'am," and "may I get you anything else ma'am?" The boys at the country club opened her door, parked her car, carried in her bags, and made sure she had everything she needed before a professional masseuse pampered her for the next couple of hours. She had the most magnificent garden that was her pride. Ryan had two wonderful children she adored.

She'll never forget that day she met Ryan at the hotel to give him the divorce agreement. She watched from the window across the street as he walked in. She made him wait, and wait, and wait, for her to arrive. Without showing an ounce of fear, she told him what she wanted and slid the envelope across the table, knowing it would infuriate him. When he offered her everything—everything except the house—she knew she should take it, but as hard as it was, she stuck with the plan.

For some reason that she can't begin to understand now, she actually thought she could beat the man who never loses. It didn't matter if it was a court case, the stock market, a weekend at a Vegas casino, or a game show on television, Ryan always seemed to come out on top. His mind just worked like that. Even as she passed him the envelope, she had this feeling deep down inside that something would go horribly wrong. Somehow….someway, it had to go wrong.

She knew things had gone way too far when her lawyer recorded her private conversation with Ryan. She told him she didn't want to make Ryan mad, but again and again he kept saying, "Trust me…just trust me." Then, without telling her anything about it, her lawyer sent the recording to Ryan.

She thinks about those days all the time—it's all she ever thinks about. Ryan was once the love of her life and now, now he's gone. What she'd give to go back and do things differently. She wants to start all over again, but it's too late for that now. It's too late for sorries, too late for forgiveness, and too late for please hold me one more time.

They say what doesn't kill you makes you stronger; but now, after crying oceans of tears, Kate knows better. Some things break you into a million pieces, and you can never be strong....or whole...or happy ....ever again.

– CHAPTER 15 –

It's been eight months since I came back from Thailand, and I know no more today than I did the day Jackson left. So far, I've been patient, waiting for the police to do their thing. After eight months, my patience is running thin. Hope and I storm into Stowe's office demanding answers.

"Mrs. Kennedy, please try to calm down," he says.

"I have been calm. Week after week I come in here wanting to know where the hell my husband is, and week after week you tell me the same thing—sorry, we know nothing. Are you hiding something? Do you know more than you're letting on?"

"No ma'am," he insists. "I told you I'd keep you updated. You know everything that I know."

Irritated, I ask, "Then where is he?"

"I wish I knew. He's out there. I'm sure he's out there somewhere. Like I keep telling you, he will pop up. Eventually he's going to try to come back to the US, or he'll commit a crime as simple as speeding, or he'll try to contact his brother. He's going to mess up. He'll put his guard down and we'll be all over him. We have so many agents looking for him. No matter what we have to do or how long it takes, we *will* find him."

Hope leans closer and says, "Look, I've got to level with you. This Hannah girl—I don't trust her. How do you know she didn't find out about Grace? Maybe she found out he has two kids and another wife. It could happen. It could drive someone to do something terrible."

"The problem with what you're saying is that there's no evidence he traveled to Denver, or anywhere else, after you left."

"They found his car at the airport!" I say.

"His car was found *near* the airport," he clarifies, "but he never got on a flight to Denver or anywhere else."

"Maybe he used a different name."

"That's possible if he was wanting to disappear—which we think he did—but not if he was killed. If he flew to Denver and was killed, he'd have no reason to travel under a fake name or a fake passport."

Hope clenches her fists and says, "I don't trust her! Get her…put her in a freezing cold room like you did Grace."

Stowe turns to me, wanting to calm everything down. Turning to me, he says, "Mrs. Kennedy, we questioned her just like we questioned you."

"For one hour!" Hope says. She points at me and says, "You questioned her for five hours."

He rubs his forehead with his hands and says, "She asked for a lawyer."

"What?"

"She asked for a lawyer. We had to stop the interrogation."

"I can't believe what I'm hearing," Hope says with a fake laugh. "Of course, she did it! Don't you see? She had to be involved. If she was innocent, then tell me…why would she ask for a lawyer?"

"It's not always like that. Her lawyer has been very cooperative. They've answered all our questions. They gave us everything we've asked for. They brought us their phone records, credit card statements, everything. We have no reason to believe Jackson was killed and no reason to believe she's hiding something."

"Hiding something!" Hope yells. "She's been hiding something for two years! She married a married man. Of course, she's hiding something." When Stowe doesn't respond, she says, "She has an affair and marries a man who's already married. Isn't that a crime?"

"It's a crime to marry someone when you're already married. It was Jackson who was married. "

"I just don't believe her. If she'll lie about this, then what else is she lying about?"

"I really don't think she was aware he was married," Stowe says.

I shake my head and say, "I find that really hard to believe."

"No one knew. He started working more days at the Denver office and would fly back and forth. He was good…really good. Even his work had no idea anything was up."

"I want to see her!" I demand.

"Who?"

"Her…Sarah."

"Hannah?" Stowe asks.

"Yes, Hannah."

Hope jumps in and says, "She either killed him or she knows where he is. I guarantee it."

"Like I said, she asked for a lawyer. We can't question her. It's against the law."

"You can't," I say, pointing right at him, "but I can. Nothing stops me from talking to her, right?"

Stowe keeps staring at me like he's at a loss for words. He finally shakes his head and says, "No, but I urge you not to do this. You must be patient."

"I have been patient and where has it gotten me—nowhere."

"What do you think is going to happen? You think you're gonna knock on her door, and she's going to say, 'Nice to finally meet you, I've been waiting to confess. I killed your husband.'"

Hope looks at me and says, "I don't know if she killed him, but I know damn good and well she knows exactly where he is."

"Oh, I'm sorry," Stowe says being sarcastic. "Nice to finally meet you. I've been waiting to confess. Your husband is hiding across the border in Mexico."

Hope seems angrier about all this than I am. "Don't you see?" she continues. "He's in a lot of trouble, and she's covering for him. I don't want her to disappear someday with millions of dollars to live with him in Brazil, or Greece, or something."

"She can't. If she leaves the country, she'll be followed."

Hope starts to say something, but I raise my hand to stop her. "What if he's still in the country? What if he's hiding in the mountains, or New York City, or in some beach town somewhere?"

"Like I said, he'll be caught. It's just a matter of time."

"And those trails around our home?"

"We've been over this Mrs. Kennedy. Yes, we looked…and we asked. No one's seen him."

I sit back and say, "She's a woman. Now she's a mother. Everything changes when you become a mom. When she sees me, when she sees what Jackson's kids look like, it has to affect her. For all I know, we may be on the same side. I want to talk to her. I want to hear what she has to say. Yes, I want her to tell me where Jackson is."

Stowe raises his hand and squeezes his eyes shut. After taking a deep breath, he says, "I urge you not to do that. Right now, she's still cooperating. All you can do is mess things up."

"I don't care. I've waited eight months now and nothing is happening. I want to know the truth. I want to find him. If I have to do it myself, then I will."

Stowe stands from his chair and moves towards the door. When I also stand up, he says, "Mrs. Kennedy, don't do anything that will jeopardize the case. We want to find him as much as you do. You have to be patient."

"It feels like nothing's happening. I just want to know, is he dead…is he gone…what?"

"I don't like it," Stowe says. "I don't like it at all. I urge you to wait and let us do our job."

"I'm sorry," I say one last time, "but I'm through waiting."

– CHAPTER 16 –

I call Mr. Wood and explain why I need to go to Denver. He doesn't ask a lot of questions. He simply asks what day I want to leave and when I want to return.

"Don't you have a home in Aspen?" he asks.

"Yeah, but it's too far for me to drive all the way from Aspen to Denver. It's easier to stay at a hotel."

"Do you need tickets for the kids?"

"I don't think it's a good idea to take them. Hope is going to watch them for me."

"Let me see what I can do," he says. "I think this would fall under an emergency expense."

"Thank you so much," I say wanting to sound grateful.

Before hanging up, he asks, "Grace…what are you hoping to find?"

"I'm not sure. I just want answers and I'm getting nothing here."

The next day, I received an email with one first-class ticket, reservations at the Ritz-Carlton Hotel, and a rental car reservation for a luxury vehicle to drive.

For the first time, I'm starting to get a little concerned. I don't want these extravagant reservations to drain the trust of all the money. I go to Mr. Wood's office to let him know what I'm thinking.

"Mr. Wood, you booked a room for me at the Ritz-Carlton and you rented me a luxury vehicle."

"Yes ma'am," he says, sounding matter-of-fact.

"Well…I don't want this to sound ungrateful, but I checked with the Ritz-Carlton. My room is $950 a night."

"I think that's right," he says.

"Mr. Wood, I'm concerned. I do not know what the future holds for me or Hope. I don't want the money to run out."

"Mrs. Kennedy—"

"Feel free to call me Grace."

"Grace, before your father was killed, he changed his will to remove Kate as the trustee. He asked me to take over, but I didn't really want to do it. I have enough on my plate with my own family. He insisted. It was very important to him, so I eventually agreed to do it. Your father spent a great deal of time explaining everything to me and how he wanted the trust assets handled. When he died, he left specific instructions on how I'm supposed to distribute the money. I assure you; I'm following his instructions to the tee."

"Are you being paid to do this?" I ask.

"Grace, I loved your dad. He was a great friend, a great father, and one of the best men I've ever known."

My dad hasn't been gone long enough for me to talk about him without feeling the pain of his death. My eyes tear up and I can't talk.

"He was the best lawyer I've ever known, and he helped me every time I needed it. It was only because of him that I was able to open my own law office. Am I getting paid? Not a penny."

I wipe the tears from my eyes and say, "I'm sorry. I didn't mean to question or second guess you."

"You okay, Grace?" he asks gently, resting his hand on my arm.

As a tear rolls down my cheek. I shake my head and say, "I miss him."

"Grace, your dad loved you kids more than anything in the world. I know you look just like your mother, but when I see you, I see your father. When you were born, he adored you so much. You two were always so close—everywhere he went, you followed right behind him. You're smart, successful, and your personality…you both have many of the same qualities. He loved you so very much."

I look at him and ask, "Are you aware of what happened to my mom?"

He sits back in his chair and takes a deep breath. "Your father and I went to law school together. We've been friends ever since. I was his best man at his wedding. Yes, I know all about your mom and dad."

"So, you knew?"

"Not at the time, but he told me afterwards."

"And what did you say?"

"You know, Grace….I don't feel comfortable talking to you about this. All I can say, is your dad had a very difficult time after losing you kids. After the custody hearing, he had a breakdown. He stopped going into the office, stopped seeing clients, stopped living—he felt like he had lost everything. I was really worried about him. I tried to talk to him, but nothing mattered to him anymore. I don't think he was thinking straight."

"Mr. Wood, I want to ask you something. When I went to my mom's gravesite, I found a piece of paper stuffed in the bottom of the flower holder. I wasn't sure what it was, because it was all written in Thai. After I got home, I took it to someone and found out it's a receipt—the yearly payment to the cemetery for them to take care of my mom's gravesite."

Mr. Wood just sits there.

"Mr. Wood, I need to know the truth."

"I'll answer to the extent I'm able," he says.

"Please tell me….did you pay this?"

He stops for a minute, like he's not sure whether to answer. Then he says, "I did not. Maybe your dad paid it before the car accident."

"No," I say, shaking my head. "The receipt shows it was paid seven months after my dad died."

"Maybe he arranged for it to be paid."

"Maybe," I say, considering this for a second, "but this receipt was sitting in the vase in perfect condition. It sat there for five months and wasn't rained on, or faded, or anything. It looked practically new. I don't know why this was put there. Please tell me, is my—."

Wood interrupts and says, "Grace, I'm late and I have to go."

"Just tell me, please, please tell me…is my dad—"

Mr. Wood leans forward in his chair and says, "Grace, I've heard all the rumors and gossip surrounding your dad's death. Any time someone important dies under suspicious circumstances, people are going to talk, because they love controversy. Some people were saying Ryan drove over that cliff on purpose. Some think the car was empty. A rumor was going around that he was on his way to kill Kate. A couple of lawyers I know swore it was Kate who killed him. Hell, it was going around the courthouse that one of the big companies he was suing put a hit out on him."

I link my fingers together and press them against my forehead while he continues.

"I don't listen to all that crap and I don't think you should either. Everyone's looking for the next conspiracy. If you listen to these nuts, you'll be convinced we never landed on the moon...or...or the world is flat. All I know, is the wreck was investigated and nothing came of it."

I get up from my chair and extend my hand to him. "You're right. Thanks again for everything you've done for me."

He gets up and says, "Have a pleasant trip to Denver."

Tom Flint,
— Day 247

– CHAPTER 17 –

Flint drove into Waco, unsure if Ryan was alive or dead. He left convinced that sum bitch is now alive and well living it up somewhere while he's still stuck in Austin facing charges for murder. Not just any murder, but the murder of that stupid kid who wouldn't shut his big, fat mouth. Now to find out it was Ryan who tried to set him up! All he can think is: *If you're alive, you won't be for long!*

His next stop to track Ryan down is Houston. What's in Houston? It's the closest U.S. Passport Office to Austin where someone can get a passport. Flint was here ten years ago when he needed a fake passport for Zachary Bell and he's quite sure Ryan would head here if he needed another identity.

It's a three-hour drive from Waco to Houston. Flint drives right past the passport office to a company called Passport Service Center, Inc. two blocks away. The company was founded eighteen years ago to help individuals get their passports when they live far away from the passport office and don't want to drive to Houston.

It's a good idea to turn your passport documents in ten to twelve weeks before you plan on traveling, but there are lots of people who have to travel on short notice or simply forget about the whole passport thing until it's too late. Twelve years ago, Justin Hunter, the owner of Passport Service Center, Inc. developed a close friendship with a supervisor working inside the Passport Office. This friendship comes in real handy when you're in Justin's line of work. For a *friendly* $500 tip over dinner, Justin's friend agreed to push through a last-minute application for a client in needed of a passport in an emergency. Soon Passport Services, Inc. became known as the company who can get you a passport when no one else can.

Justin knew he was sitting on a gold mine. The only problem, even a gold mine wasn't enough for him, and he knew just how to get even more gold. For an even friendlier $5,000 tip over drinks, Justin's friend could produce a fake passport as genuine as the real deal. Justin charges each client $25,000 for a passport so you can change your identity and just disappear.

There was one little problem. Everyone disappearing with one of these passports soon learns there's a hole in the plan—passports only last ten years and then you're back at square one. Passport Services, Inc. eventually teamed up with a company in New York and for $30,000, Justin can get you a matching birth certificate and take care of all your problems—forever. It isn't cheap, but when you want to disappear, you better have a lot of money.

Ryan had a client who fled an abusive husband and got new passports and birth certificates for her and her children. It was Ryan who introduced

Flint to Passport Services, Inc. and the passports they provide. Flint knew damn good and well this is the first place Ryan would go if he's still alive.

Flint walks through the front door to a nicely decorated waiting room. There's a large gold sign in the waiting room that reads, "Passport Service Center." There's an expensive Persian rug on the floor, a comfy couch along one wall, and two matching chairs.

This place has really improved since I was here last.

Flint walks up to the receptionist who asks, "How can I help you?"

"I'm Tom Flint. I called earlier about seeing Justin Hunter. You said he'd be in at two o'clock."

"Oh, yes sir. Hold on just a minute."

A few minutes later, a man in his late forties comes from the back with an extended arm. "Hello Mr. Flint, I'm Justin Hunter. Why don't you come on back?"

They walk back to Justin's office. "How can I help you Mr. Flint?"

"I'm trying to locate someone."

"I'm not sure I'm following you," Justin says with a puzzled look.

"I have reason to believe you provided a passport and birth certificate to someone I'm trying to locate."

Justin raises both his hands in protest. "I don't know what you're talking about. We expedite passports....we have nothing to do with birth certificates. I'm happy to give you the local office if you need to get a copy of your birth certificate."

"Mr. Hunter, I'm well aware of the service you provide. I'm not interested in a passport or a birth certificate. I need to find someone who you provided a passport."

Justin looks Flint up and down and says, "Mr. Flint, our service is confidential. The information people provide us is private. I cannot disclose confidential information." He rises from his chair and says, "I'm sorry, but I'm unable to help you."

Flint leans over the desk, looks over his shoulder towards the door, and returns to Justin. "Quite frankly, I know exactly what you do here because I've used your services myself. Do you remember Zachary Bell?"

"No sir."

"It doesn't really matter," Flint continues. "I'm only interested in one individual. Now we can make this simple or go another route."

"Who exactly are you?" Justin asks.

Flint unclips his badge from his belt and shows it to Justin. "I'm Officer Flint. I'm with the Sheriff's office."

"Duval County….where is Duval County?"

Flint comes around the desk and shoves Justin against the back wall causing photos and a wall clock to crash to the floor. He holds Justin in place by his forearm against his neck and brings his face only inches away from Justin's nose. His cowboy hat is pressing against Justin's forehead.

"Listen to me, you little shit. I don't give one good goddamn about privacy or confidential information. Honestly, I don't give a shit what you do here. I'm interested in one man….a very, very bad man. All I have to do is make one call, and I'll have a search warrant here within an hour.

We'll take your fancy computer and every file in here. When I find what I know I'll find, the Feds will make sure you rot in a federal prison."

Flint grabs a family photo that just fell to the floor and says, "You got a pretty family. How old is your little girl….six?"

"Five," Justin says, all rattled.

"Sweet little girl," Flint says, shaking his head.

Justin brings his head down, now beginning to tear up.

"I'm sure my contact at the IRS would love to know about your little side business here."

Justin, still pinned against the wall, says, "Mr. Flint…please."

Flint gives him another shove for good measure. "No, sir…do this the easy way and we keep it all private. I'll head on back home and you can go on like nothing ever happened here."

Justin is so shaken he can barely talk. "I'm…I'm sorry, Mr. Flint. I just can't disclose—"

Flint releases Justin's neck with one last jerk. He opens his cell phone and speed dials his own home phone. His recorder comes on after the second ring. "You've reached the home of Tom Flint. I'm not—"

"Sheri," Tom yells, looking straight at Justin. "I'm gonna need that search warrant we talked about—pronto. Have the judge make it as broad as possible. Oh, and call Lance at the IRS."

Justin frantically waives both his hands in front of Flint to get his full attention. "Okay, okay," he says, just loud enough to be heard over the phone.

As the recorder beeps in his ear, Flint holds up his finger to Justin and says, "Sherri…Sheri, never mind. We're not going to need a search warrant after all."

Justin sits back down at his desk, takes a deep breath, and dries his sweaty palms on his slacks. With a shaky voice, he asks, "Who are you looking for?"

"I have reason to believe a man came in about seven months ago wanting a passport and a birth certificate."

"And who's that?"

"Ryan….Ryan Brunick."

Without even looking it up, Justin leans all the way back in his reclining chair and covers his eyes with each hand. "Oh God, Mr. Flint. I thought you were looking for a murderer or something. Anyone else…please."

"So, you got him a passport?"

Still leaning back, Justin closes his eyes, slowly nods his head, and says, "Yes, sir."

"Do you have a copy of his new passport and birth certificate?"

Justin leans forward, types something on his computer, and a moment later Flint hears his printer turn on and two pages slide out. He grabs the papers off the printer and hands them to Flint.

"Scott Edward Richards," Flint reads. "It's great. It looks exactly like the real deal."

"It is the real deal," Justin says.

"Did he tell you where he was going?"

"I have a strict, *don't ask, don't tell* policy."

"Did he tell you when he was leaving?"

"No, sir, but he wanted the passport right away. I got the feeling he was leaving the country pretty soon."

Flint rolls the papers tight in his hand before walking out.

"You know, I like Mr. Brunick." Justin says, "Is he in trouble?"

"Tom tips his cowboy hat with the roll of papers and says, "You bet your ass he's in trouble."

Flint starts to walk out, but his mind goes back to that dark place. He turns around and says, "I think this takes care of things for now, but it'd be a shame if I had to come back."

"What are you saying?" Justin asks.

"Well, as an officer of the law, I'd hate to make those phone calls again when I get back to my office. For a small cash contribution to the Duval County Sherriff's Association, I can forget this place forever."

"How small?"

"I don't know. I think for twenty-five thousand we can afford this new cruiser we've been needing."

Justin looks down, shakes his head and says, "You're really something."

"You're right," Flint laughs. "I should just do my job."

Justin walks out, leaving Flint in his office. He returns with a big fat envelope stuffed with cash. He holds the money out to Flint.

"Just drop it there on your desk," Flint says.

Justin places the money on his desk, and Flint picks it up, flips through the money with his thumb and says, "Thanks for your generous donation."

Grace Kennedy,

– CHAPTER 18 –

I'll never forget the first time I met Hannah. I wasn't sure how it would go, but I had to meet the woman who ruined my life. I had to meet the woman my husband married and had a baby with.

Driving my Mercedes Benz towards Hannah's house, I get this strange feeling. I feel like the dog that finally catches the car. I'm not even sure what I'm getting myself into. I'm not sure what I'll say.

For some reason, I thought, or maybe just hoped, they would be living in some small house—maybe like the one Jackson and I lived in when we first got married. When I arrive at the subdivision, I cannot believe the place. This neighborhood is as nice as our neighborhood in Dallas. Every house looks like it costs half a million dollars or more.

My GPS leads me right to her house. It's a large two-story home that looks just as expensive as ours. It has a large front yard that's well taken care of with a long driveway leading to the garage. Just looking at this house causes my blood to boil.

Before coming here, I gave a lot of thought to showing up unannounced, knocking on the door, and introducing myself, but I decided against it. I called ahead of time, told her who I was, and told her that I wanted to meet her. At first, she seemed quite surprised—really shocked—but she agreed to meet me whenever I wanted.

I slowly drive up the driveway and park in front of the garage. I get out and walk across the sidewalk to the front door and stand here, unsure what I should do next. I need to keep my cool, but I'm visibly shaken just walking here. I don't think I've ever been more nervous in my life.

Ring the doorbell, I keep telling myself unsure what will happen once I push this button. I actually don't know what I'll say when she answers the door. *Hello, I believe you're married to my husband. I'm his first wife and you ruined my family.*

I take a deep breath and muster the courage to ring the bell. I can hear the doorbell chime throughout the house. I stand there waiting for Hannah to come to the door. *Oh God, please help me.* I hear nothing—nothing at all.

I reach up and ring the doorbell a second time. I stand there waiting, but again, there's nothing. I look at my watch and see it's almost two-thirty. All my fears are for nothing—at least for now. I back my car down the driveway and out of the neighborhood.

I go back to my hotel and lay down for a few hours. I wake up at five o'clock and grab something to eat at the hotel restaurant. When I arrive back at her house, I'm hit with the same anger. *How in the hell is he paying for two new houses?*

This time when I approach the driveway, the garage is wide open with a new Lexus parked inside. My hands shake, as I creep slowly up the driveway and park behind her car. *Please help me,* I pray.

I walk back up the sidewalk until I'm standing at the front door again with my finger barely touching the doorbell. *Do it Grace....do it!* I push the button and hear the same chimes ring on the other side of the door. My heart is beating so fast, and I feel all the blood drain from my face as the front door opens.

"Hello," the girl says as soon as she opens the door.

She's really pretty. She has red hair, ivory skin, and her eyes are as blue as mine. She looks about ten years younger than me.

"I'm Grace….Grace Kennedy?"

"I know," she says, a little shaken. "I've been expecting you."

"I came by earlier, but you were gone."

"Sorry," she says, putting her hand on her forehead. "It took longer at the doctor's office than I expected."

"I didn't know. I thought maybe you changed your mind. I wasn't sure if you were going to slam the door in my face and demand I get off your property."

"No, no," she says, moving to the side. "Please come in. Come in and sit down."

I walk into a house every bit as nice as mine. I can see a pool in the backyard. I don't even have a pool!

"Beautiful house," I say, looking around.

"Thank you."

We sit down on the living room couch. I'm not sure what I was expecting, but she's very attractive and she actually seems like a sweet woman. "Can I get you something to drink?" she asks.

"I would love a cup of coffee or some water," I say.

She goes into the kitchen and leaves me looking around this home like the jealous wife I am. This place is beautiful. Hanging over the fireplace is a family portrait of her with my husband and a tiny baby girl. Scattered across the mantle are numerous crystal frames, with their family looking as happy and as legal as ever. Anyone visiting here would never know there's another home, eight hundred miles away, with very similar photos on my wall.

First, I pick up the five-by-seven photo of Jackson and Hannah on their wedding day. She's in her wedding gown, looking up at him in a tux. It makes me wonder what the hell I was thinking of coming here. I pick up another photo and stare at my husband holding his newborn daughter. She looks only a week or two old. I'm feeling an emotion, or emotions, I cannot describe. It's pain, and anger, and hurt. All these emotions are rising from my stomach and about to burst out of my body.

I feel a soft hand on my back and turn around to see Hannah standing behind me, trying to provide *me* comfort. "I'm sorry. I'm so sorry," she says.

I lower my head and, she lays her hands on my shoulders. I step forward and cry on the shoulder of the woman I was so sure I would hate. I stay there in her arms until I stop gasping long enough to say, "It hurts so much. I don't even know who I am anymore."

It surprises me, when I don't hear her crying too. We're in the same boat, but she shows no emotion at all. I eventually pull myself together, lift my head off her shoulder, and wipe my eyes. "I'm sorry to just show up like this. I must look so stupid."

She shakes her head and says, "You're not stupid at all. I'm glad you came. I have as many questions as you do."

I sit down on the living room chair where a cup of coffee is waiting on the end table. She sits down across from me with her own cup of coffee.

"So, you're Hannah," I say.

"Yes."

"…and your last name?"

"Kennedy," she says.

I look up and away to hide the tear that just fell from my eye. "Of course, you are," I say, wiping it away.

She hands me a tissue and says, "I'm really glad you're here. Thank you for calling me. I just want you to know that I knew nothing about you."

I'm not sure if I believe her or not. I look up at the family picture hanging over the fireplace and say, "When did you meet Jackson? How did you meet?"

"I was working at the downtown Grand Hyatt. Jackson would usually stay here for business. He was always friendly—even a little flirty. You know, I was at work so I tried to keep it professional, but he kept coming back to talk to me. He had this way about him."

Here we go. This is what I came for. As I hear this story unfold, I'm shocked. "How soon was it before he started coming on to you?" I ask.

"I don't know. I think it was the third time I saw him at the hotel. He kept coming to my counter, asking questions and making small talk. It became obvious he was flirting with me. Then he asked if I'd like to have dinner after I got off work. It was our first date. He took me to this beautiful restaurant for dinner, and then we had a few drinks at this little downtown piano bar. He was such a gentleman."

Any thought she wouldn't want to talk to me is long gone. It's obvious she's holding nothing back. I look down and ask, "What did he say about me—about his kids?"

"Nothing…absolutely nothing. He said he lived in Dallas and he was single. He said he worked for DMD, and I could see from his corporate account that he was the CFO. I had no suspicions whatsoever. He said he was primarily living in Dallas, but he was also working out of Denver. Well, he started coming to Denver more and more. Eventually he got an apartment here."

"An apartment? When was this?"

"I don't know, pretty early on. We were probably dating three months when he said he'd be coming to Denver more often. He actually talked about transferring to Denver."

"You know, I remember this," I say. "He told me the office in Denver was really picking up and they were transferring people here. He started talking about moving to Denver, but I had my job, and my mom and dad, and sister. I didn't want to move. He'd bring it up again and again. We were kinda' at a stalemate."

Hannah looks down and shakes her head.

"So, you were the reason he wanted to move? It was all about you?"

"Maybe it was about me…maybe he really did need to move here. I don't know. He kept saying how much he loved Denver. He bought a little place near Aspen, where we'd go to relax."

"You'd go? You'd go to relax? That's our vacation home."

"I thought it was *our* vacation house. He loved to go there when he finished with business. He loved to get away and hike, or fish, or just hang out. Sometimes we'd go, and he'd work from there."

"Son…of…a…bitch," I say, drawing out the words. "I knew it. I knew something wasn't right. About a year ago, I went to Aspen with the kids. I hadn't been there in months. When I arrived, the place was all fixed up. There were pretty curtains on the windows, a new bedspread on the bed, and decorations all over the place. He said he did it all, which really surprised me. He never cared one bit about decorating. There were candles and pot-pourri that looked like they'd been lit. I knew it wasn't right."

Hannah gives a quick laugh and says, "No, that was all me."

We sit there for a minute without talking. Finally, she gets this look on her face and asks, "Wait a minute, did you have a white, furry jacket with a light gray furry collar?"

"You know, I forgot all about that. I left it there and completely forgot about it."

"I found your jacket in the closet. I didn't understand why a woman's jacket was there. Jackson said the maid must have left it. The next time we came, it was gone. He said the maid came and took it."

"What a freakin' liar," I say.

"Yep."

This all infuriates me, but she's remaining pretty calm. I look at her and ask, "How are you able to talk about this so easily?"

"You didn't see me when I first found out. I've cried until I can't cry anymore. I think I'm all cried out. Let me know if it's too much for you and I'll stop."

"No…I have to hear what happened. Weren't you suspicious? Didn't you wonder why he was going back and forth from Dallas to Denver all the time?"

"Not really. When we met, he was living in Dallas. He would come here once every couple of months. I was happy he was coming here more often. I thought he was going to move here. We were spending more and more time together. He'd call and say, 'let's go on vacation.'"

"Wait…wait a minute," I say, stopping her. "You went on vacation? Where?"

"Well, mostly little getaways. We went to Vegas together a while back. His company was having some company convention. He asked me if I wanted to go."

"Was this at the end of July—maybe two years ago?"

"Yes….July."

I get up from the couch and start pacing back and forth. It's all coming together now. I cross my arms and practically scream, "You've got to be kidding me!"

"What?"

"Did you stay at the Bellagio?"

"Oh my God!" she whispers. "You're kidding."

"What a bastard. He said he wanted to go to Vegas before the kids returned to school. He wanted us to have a family vacation. We spent all our time in Vegas doing kids' things—you know, the rides and the knight show at the Excalibur. We went to the big pirate ship and watched the water shows. We took a day trip out to the Hoover Dam and stopped off at that little cowboy town."

"Wow!" Hannah says. "As far as I knew, he was working….busy at his company conference. We'd get together in the evenings or at night. We'd eat dinner at a fancy restaurant, gamble some, and maybe watch a show or something. Then we'd go back to our hotel room until he had to get back to his conference."

My blood is boiling, but I try to stay calm. "It all makes sense now. After running around all day, we'd come back to the hotel, and he'd say he wanted to gamble for a while. He'd crawl back in bed the next morning like he'd been up all night long. He showed me some chips…said he lost all track of time. I never even questioned it. I thought he was gambling all night."

I can't hide my anger any longer. I cover my face and squeeze my eyes shut so tight, trying to process it all. I shake my head in my hands and then stop myself. I lower my hands and stand there with my eyes shut and my mouth open as I think about the unthinkable.

"What?" Hannah asks.

"Did you…did you go to Cancun maybe nine months before he disappeared?"

"We sure did," she says.

"Where did you stay?" I ask.

"Temptation something."

"The Towers of Temptation?"

"That's it," she says, "the Towers of Temptation."

"I knew it. I knew something wasn't right," I say, now angrier than ever. "By this time, we were so distant, so I arranged a vacation. This was supposed to be *our* time together. He kept leaving…saying he had to take care of something at work. He'd be gone for hours and I was left all alone. It ruined the special time I had planned. He made me out to be some controlling….some controlling bitch. He said that *I* was the one ruining everything—that he took all this time off work for my vacation. He said he wanted to have a good time, but I didn't know how to have a good time anymore."

"Did you stay on the top floor, right by the elevator?" Hannah asks.

"Yep…right by the elevators."

She shakes her head with a little smile and says, "I think our rooms were side-by-side."

"Why do you say that?" I ask.

"Again, he told me there was some business conference there," Hannah explains. "He said he had to work, but he'd make time for fun. I didn't question it for a second. I'd lay out on the beach all day, go to the spa, and look through all the little shops. Well, one time I lost my room key, so I went to the front desk and asked for another one. She handed me a room key, but it wasn't mine. It was the key to the room next to ours. I told her it was a mistake and repeated my room number. She looked at her computer with the strangest look. Next thing, she called her boss over and they said something in Spanish. Then, with a giant big smile, the manager handed me another room key—the one to *our* room. I thought it was strange, but I shrugged it off."

"Oh my god!" I scream. When I'm calm enough to talk again, I look down and say, "I have to ask you something. Did you make love? Did you have sex during the stay?"

She looks down at her lap without answering, but the look on her face says it all.

I stand up and pace back and forth with my hands on my hips. I raise my hand and say, "Okay, okay, okay....I don't want to hear the answer. How stupid can I be?"

Hannah looks at me like she wants to say something, but she's holding it inside.

"There's a reason why I'm asking. We made love the first night we were there. Then...then he wasn't interested—wasn't interested in me or us. I knew something wasn't right. I wanted to know why...why he was so distant. I wanted to know why he kept leaving to "take care of business," I say, making quotation marks with my fingers.

"I was so angry, so he blamed everything on me. He said I was ruining another trip. Why would he want to have sex with someone who....who....who nags him all the time?" I'm barely able to get the last words out.

Hannah stands in front of me and takes me in her arms. Gasping for air, I cry, "He said he wanted a...a....he wanted a divorce. I promised my father before he died that I'd do everything in my power to make my marriage work. I felt like I had failed, and I promised him I wouldn't fail. Then something clicked in my mind—like a light just turned on. I looked straight at Jackson and asked if he was seeing someone else. This just infuriated him. He yelled, 'Here I am killing myself for you and the kids, and all you do is accuse me of God knows what. I'm done!'" He turned around and walked out the door.

"I laid in bed crying all night, waiting for him to come back so we could talk. Well, he didn't come back—he was probably with you. When he came back the next morning, he sat on the edge of the bed and said we needed to talk. Before he could say more, I knelt down on the floor in front of him. I opened his legs and moved forward to hold him."

"'No Grace,' he said like he didn't want me touching him. 'I just can't do this anymore.'"

"I'm sitting there holding him in my arms and I started crying. I told him I'm sorry—I love you—I'll make everything right. I swore I'd make this right again if he'd just hold me."

"He said, 'I can't,' and tried to break away."

"I begged him—I begged him to forgive me, but he kept saying he was done."

"We hardly made love anymore, so I figured this was the problem. I'm not as sexual as I was before our baby was born, and I wanted to make it right. I pushed him back on the bed and kissed him with tears pouring down my cheeks. I opened his shirt—I practically tore it off him like you'd see on television or something. The more he said no, the harder I pressed. I tried to undo his belt, but he grabbed my wrists and held me back. I told him I wanted him, but he kept saying no."

"I don't know if I've ever wanted him more than I did at that moment. I pulled away and undid his pants. I held him and kissed him. I made love to him, doing my best to wash away everything I'd done to ruin the love he once had for me."

Hannah hands me a tissue, and I stop for a moment to wipe my eyes.

"When we were done, I laid on top of him in the dark, holding his face in my hands. You know….I felt like I had my husband back and everything was going to be all right. All I had to do was start having sex more often. I kissed his face and told him I loved him, but he didn't say anything back. I thought he must have fallen asleep, so I kissed him again and rubbed the side of his face with my hand until he opened his eyes. While he laid there looking at me, I told him how much I loved him. Barely speaking above a whisper and with no emotion whatsoever, he looked away and said, 'Can we please not talk?'"

Hannah gives me this sad look—like this is the saddest story she's ever heard.

"I actually thought we could start all over again. I told him we should have another baby. For some stupid reason, I thought a baby would draw us closer together. He gave me this look….this look like I must be crazy. He closed his eyes and turned his face away from me like he couldn't stand to look at me. Then he moved me off of him without saying anything more. He never once said I'm sorry…I love you…nothing."

Hannah shakes her head, and with puffy, red eyes, she grabs a tissue.

"Now I know why he looked like that. Yeah, he was having a baby alright…except it was with you."

Now, Hannah looks down and wipes a tear from her own eyes. Catching me completely by surprise, in a quiet, sad way, she says, "I'm so, so sorry…can you please forgive me?"

This touches me so deeply. I hold her close and say, "You know, when I came here, I didn't know what to expect. I blamed you for everything almost as much as I blamed him. Now I see…now I see you were as much in the dark as I was."

"Or just as stupid," she says, still looking down.

After a moment, I bring up the hardest part for me. "So….now you have a baby?"

"Yes, we…well *I* have a baby girl."

"Can I see her?" I ask.

She gets up from the couch, and I follow her into a nursery that's decorated with a crib, dresser, changing table, and a rocker that all match. The room is full of stuffed animals, a giant bear in the corner, and rainbows and unicorns painted on the walls. "Our Little Girl" is painted on the back wall.

I walk over to the crib and see this little baby girl sound asleep on her stomach. She's so tiny and so beautiful, wearing this little pink jumper and white socks with pink bows. Her hair is curly and red, just like her mother's hair, but the rest of her looks like Jackson. She's so peaceful lying here, sound asleep. When I get close, she stirs a little, lifts her head, then goes back to sleep. Something draws me to her.

Standing over her looking down, I can imagine their life together with their new baby. He probably starts his day eating the breakfast Hannah made, and his daughter about to wake up in this beautiful nursery. I'm sure their life is full of all the sweet things we shared the first years of our marriage—romantic dinners, walking arm in arm through the park, weekend date nights, and late mornings lying together in bed. They probably never argue. I close my eyes and wonder: *Why? Why wasn't I enough? What did I do that was so bad that he would go to another woman?*

I want to reach down and pick her up, but I don't dare ask. Instead, I stand here until my need to cry goes away. Then I turn around and walk out of the room, doing my best to hide the pain of seeing their beautiful girl. As we walk out, it's pretty obvious this isn't easy for me. Once back in the living room sitting on the couch, Hannah talks to me like we're two friends without a care in the world. "I understand you have two kids," she asks with a smile.

"How'd you know?"

"I did a little investigating myself. They're darling."

"What's her name?" I ask, motioning back to the nursery.

"Savannah….when Jackson and I went to Savannah, Georgia while I was pregnant we both thought it was so cute we agreed—"

This is just another revelation I can't believe I'm hearing. I think she sees the shock and sadness on my face and backs off the story she's probably told everyone. She reaches forward and puts her hand on my knee. "I'm sorry. Tell me about your kids."

I compose myself and say, "My daughter just turned five. Her name is Bonnie. My youngest just turned one. His name is Wesley."

Learning about it all, I'm surprised Hannah is taking everything as good as she is. I guess some people are stronger than others. Still, I don't really understand it. The more we talk, the more I warm up to her.

"Hannah, I like you—I can't believe I'm saying this, but you're very beautiful and very sweet."

"So are you," she says. "Who would cheat on a woman like you? It proves that men are…just men. It doesn't matter how good, or how beautiful, their wife is, they'll still cheat. I guess it's all about the thrill of the chase."

"You know, I'm sure we would have been friends under different circumstances."

"I know," she says. "Maybe we can still be friends. Our kids are now siblings."

I sit down on the couch and say, "You know, I would have never thought—never in a million years—that I'd be sitting in the home of my husband's new wife and baby."

"Truthfully, I feel like I should have known," she says. "Months ago, he started acting so strange…like something was wrong. He talked about moving away, moving out of the country. He asked me where I'd like to live if I could go anywhere in the world. I thought it was all just playing, or dreaming, or something. I told him I'd like to go to Paris or Australia. Now, looking back, I think he was dead serious. I think everything with you and me was just too much. It was all closing in on him. I'm sure he wanted to leave. He wanted us to start over on the other side of the world.'

This is not what I was expecting at all. Here I was trying to save my marriage, while he's planning to move away with another woman. This whole thing blows my mind.

We spend the next day getting to know each other. I know it's crazy, but we have this bond, and our kids are related whether we like it or not.

Instead of going back to my hotel, we stay up so late that I spend the night at her house. Unfortunately, it only adds insult to injury. She shows me all the cards he gave her that are full of love and a bunch of crap I haven't heard in years. It's a slap in my face. I can't take it anymore. We agree we won't talk about Jackson for the rest of the weekend.

On Sunday evening, she drives me to the airport and walks with me to the counter.

After I have my tickets, she smiles at me and says, "I'm so glad you came to see me."

"I am too," I say and give her a hug. "Do you mind?" I ask reaching for Savannah.

She places her in my arms, and I look into her bright blue eyes. I see Jackson all over her. She gives me this sweet smile as I hold her against me and rock her from side to side a few times. When I pull away, I kiss her right on the mouth before I realize what I just did. Hannah gives me another smile, like she knows exactly what I'm feeling.

So embarrassed at what I just did, I look at Hannah and tell her, "I'm sorry."

"Don't be sorry," she says, still smiling. "I understand completely."

"Goodbye, sweet girl," I whisper and hand Savannah back to her mommy.

– CHAPTER 19 –

Flint sits in his pickup truck with the air conditioner blowing on "MAX/AC" until his truck finally cools down a little. Once the heat is halfway bearable, Flint turns down the fan to make a phone call.

Armed with proof—the smoking gun evidence—that Ryan is alive, Flint calls J.D., his contact at the Austin Police Department. J.D. is an old friend who, for not-so-small a fee, has always been there whenever Flint needs some inside information on a case. Now Flint wants to return the favor and have the whole Austin Police Department join him in his search for Ryan.

"What the hell are you calling me for?" J.D. begins.

This takes Flint by surprise. "Why the hell are you talking to me like that, J.D.?"

"Tom, you're fire around here. You can't be calling me."

"What the hell are you talking about?"

"You're charged with murder, for God's sake. I can't be caught talking with you anymore."

"That's a bullshit, trumped-up charge," Flint promises. "They got nothing. It ain't gonna stick."

"That's not the word around here."

Flint is surprised by this response but knows better than to confront him. "J.D., I called to give you some information—to do you a favor." When J.D. says nothing in return, Flint continues. "You remember that whole mess with Ryan Brunick? How we had suspicions about the whole thing? Well, we were right."

"Oh my God, Tom….enough already. You're like a broken record. How many times are we gonna go over this? It's over, let it go! I don't want to hear any more about Ryan Brunick."

"Shut the fuck up and listen," Tom yells. "He's alive and I can prove it. He got a fake passport and birth certificate two weeks before his bullshit car wreck."

Flint is ready to strut around like a peacock and say, "I told you so," but J.D. doesn't react at all like he's expecting. He bursts right in, spoiling Flint's parade. "What's that prove…nothing! Maybe he thought about leaving. Maybe he even planned on leaving, but he got drunk and crashed his car off that cliff…end of story. APD closed this investigation long ago."

"What investigation?" Flint asks. "You jackasses didn't investigate a damn thing."

Talking to Flint like a child who you have to keep repeating the same thing over and over again, J.D. says slowly and clearly, "Because there's nothing to investigate. Ryan did nothing wrong. He wasn't charged with any crime. There's no reason for him to fake his own death, and even if he did, it's not a crime."

Flint knows Ryan has plenty of reasons to fake his own death, but he isn't about to bring up the whole thing about the death of either Faith or

Zach. Both those trails lead right back to him. Instead, he goes a different route.

"What about getting a fake passport? That's damn sure a crime."

"Big shit, Tom. Even if he did, Ryan's gone. We're not gonna go around the world chasing ghosts for no reason—especially when we pulled his body out of that car."

"Oh, come on. How stupid are you? For a couple thousand dollars I can get a cadaver from a morgue, funeral home, or any medical school hard up for money. It's not that difficult."

"Actually, it's not that easy, and it's against the law. You're telling me a university is going to break the law to help Ryan Brunick? I don't think so."

"Someone might do it," Flint says, "if you pay them enough."

"Yeah, and an elephant can fly over a barn if it were a bird...so what?"

"So what? Why would he be cremated? Why would he demand to be cremated immediately?"

"God Tom, I don't know what your deal is with this case, but you've got to let it go."

Flint calms down, lights a cigarette, and now talking like J.D. is a close friend, he says, "J.D. I need a favor....just one little favor."

"I'm through doing you favors, Tom. I can't even be seen talking to you."

Now the *old friend* routine is gone. Flint throws his cigarette to the ground, and yells, "You listen to me, asshole. These bullshit charges are going to be dropped. It's all a bunch of horseshit and everyone knows it.

When they are dropped, and all these shenanigans are behind me, I'll remember this."

"Tom, I've got to go," J.D. says, shutting him down. "You need to take my advice and let this thing go. If I were you, I'd be more concerned about your own charges."

J.D. hangs up the phone, leaving Flint fuming. Over and over in his mind, he hears, *Let this thing go. Let this thing go.*

"LET THIS THING GO?" Tom finally screams. "I'LL LET THIS THING GO WHEN RYAN'S ON HIS WAY TO HELL!"

– CHAPTER 20 –

The following Friday, Hope and I go back down to the police station for my weekly meeting with Detective Stowe. I'm sure he's exhausted with me, but I want answers—I deserve answers. After sitting in the waiting area for far too long, Stowe walks up and extends his hand.

"Mrs. Kennedy, how nice to see you again. Come on back."

We walk back to his office. He pulls out my file—or Jackson's file—from his side drawer and lays it on his desk.

"Any news?" I ask.

"Nothing…..there's been no charges on his cards, no activity on his phone. We still haven't found a trace of anything."

"Are you trying? Are you still searching?"

"Of course, I'm searching. Your file is my top priority. I keep it on my desk. I take it home at night."

"Why can't you find him?" I ask.

"We're doing everything we can."

"You keep saying that, but you aren't finding him."

My hard words take Stowe by surprise. He draws back and fumbles through his file before saying anything. "Mrs. Brunick, eventually he's going to slip up—they always do. Over time, they drop their guard. Eventually they start thinking we've forgotten…or that we're not looking for them anymore. They start walking the streets again and eating out. They even get a driver's license, or start driving without a license. You wouldn't believe how many people get caught running a stop sign or driving over the speed limit. People miss their family, and they'll call or come home for a visit."

"Are you tapping their phones?" Hope asks. "Are you following his brother, or this Hannah woman?

"I can't tell you everything we're doing to find him, but trust me, we're going to find him. It's just a matter of time."

"What if he left the country?" I ask.

"He probably did," Stowe admits.

"Well, I have some news," I crow. "I think I know where he's at."

"And where is that?" he asks.

"He went to Paris…or Australia."

"Paris or Australia? And why do you say that?"

I sit there without answering.

"You've been talking to Mrs. Kennedy…to Hannah, haven't you?"

"Why?"

"Because she told us the same thing."

"So, you've known this the whole time? Have you checked there?"

"We're checking every lead. The authorities in both countries have been notified."

"And that's it?" I ask. "That's all we can do?"

"Mrs. Kennedy, it's like I keep saying. It's not easy to live in a foreign country—especially if you're a fugitive. The FBI is searching for him in every country. You can't fly on a fake passport like you once could. With all the face and eye recognition, if you show up on one passport and later travel using a different passport, you're going to be stopped."

Making sure they're still looking here in America, I ask, "Detective Stowe, it's been nine months now. How can you be so sure he's still alive?"

"I didn't say I was sure. I'm not eliminating anything, but at this point, everything points in the opposite direction. When people die—or are killed—they don't just disappear. A body pops up by now."

"What about our house in Aspen? That was his getaway. He loved going hiking in the mountains."

"We checked. There was nothing out of the ordinary. We scanned for fingerprints but, no big surprise, his prints are everywhere. We asked everyone around there and no one ever saw him. It was a dead end."

"What about Hannah's prints?" Hope asks.

"Her prints were there too, but that's no surprise either."

"So that's it?" I ask. "You're not checking there anymore?"

"Again, everyone knows to contact me if they see him."

I haven't really talked to Hope much about my visit with Hannah. I didn't want to let her know how much I like her. Hope jumps in and says, "Well, I don't trust this…this Hannah. I think she's the one you need to be looking at. You want to know where Jackson is…where the money is…she knows."

"I understand the way you feel—both of you. Please know we're on it. Everyone's on it, and we're not going to stop until we find him."

"Then find him," I say and walk out of his office.

– CHAPTER 21 –

Flint has a hearing every six to eight weeks. All defendants must show up to make sure they haven't skipped town or been doing something they shouldn't be doing. Each time he comes, Flint mostly sits there for an hour or two while the lawyers try to work out a plea.

The prosecutor first assured Mr. Fanning that an indictment would be coming for capital murder, but he'd agree to life in prison without parole if Flint accepted the deal immediately. "Your client better take the deal," he said, like he's talking to one of these court-appointed lawyers who just graduated from law school.

But each meeting, the deal got better. The prosecutor went down to life with the possibility of parole and at the last hearing he offered Flint forty years—a "gift" as he liked to call it. Fanning relayed the offer to his client, but Flint has no intention of spending forty years, or forty days, or forty minutes in prison. He wants a dismissal so he can go about his life.

Flint calls Fanning for an update. "How you doing, Tom?" Fanning asks.

"Oh, 'bout as good as a pit bull in a butcher shop."

Fanning laughs and says, "Well, that's just great, Tom."

"Where we at?" Flint asks.

"Still forty years."

"Listen, where are we at on filing our motion to dismiss?" Flint asks.

"I'm working on it."

"Good deal, well let's get that filed. I'm sick of these charges hanging over my head."

"Tom, these motions are never granted. You think judges just go around throwing out murder charges? You have a better shot than most, but it's still an uphill battle. Let me see what I can work out with the prosecutor. If I have to, I'll talk to the District Attorney."

"Is this the same prosecutor who was at our hearing four months ago?" Flint asks.

"Sure."

"Wasn't he listening?"

Starting to get irritated, Fanning asks, "What are you getting at, Mr. Flint?"

"That chicken shit's got nothing!" Tom laughs. "They got a big handful of shit, and they know it. So, some jackass sends a letter saying I got it in for him. Big deal; he can't testify. Their only other witness killed himself."

"Like I said, you have a better shot than most. I also think you should consider a plea agreement. Right now, I might be able to get them down to fifteen or twenty years."

"Fifteen years!" Tom shouts.

"Tom, you're charged with First Degree murder. Fifteen years would be a gift."

"A gift? Are you out of your mind?"

"You'll probably be out in ten."

"I don't have ten years left, and I'm damn sure not gonna spend my last years in some prison. I'm a cop. You know damn well a cop won't last a week with those animals."

"I'll file your motion, but the prosecutor is more likely to cut you a deal now. If the judge denies your motion, any offer I can work out will be withdrawn."

"File the motion," Flint demands.

"Fine, I'll get it filed."

"Good," Flint says. "Did you….did you give the judge the ten thousand dollars?"

"Tom!" Fanning shouts before he says more. "I have no idea what you're talking about. We can meet when you're back in Austin and discuss your case more in person."

Flint knows exactly what's going on. He was stupid to bring this up over the phone. "Just file the motion and do everything you have to do," he says. "I'll do everything I have to do. I want to get this case dismissed right away."

"Goodbye, Tom," Fanning says, shutting this conversation down.

"Goodbye, see you next week."

– CHAPTER 22 –

Growing up in Austin, I spent half my life in a normal family with my mom and dad. Then I lived in a broken family living mostly with my mom but going back and forth between my mom's apartment and my dad's house.

I grew up in the kind of family most kids can only dream of. I went to school in one of the best school districts in the state. Every afternoon, I'd come home from school knowing my mom would be waiting at home cooking dinner, cleaning house, washing clothes, and doing all the other things a stay-at-home mom does. I'd usually eat a quick snack and get started on my homework.

My dad would come home a few hours later, and we'd all eat dinner together at the kitchen table. We'd usually watch television together or pick up a movie from Blockbuster. Now and then, my dad would gather us all together to play some silly family board game before we went to bed. When the weekends finally rolled around, we'd spend the day swimming in the pool, going to the park, heading to Fiesta Texas with our season passes, bowling, or spending the day on our boat. As far as I knew, we were one big, happy family.

Then everything changed. It seemed like it all happened overnight. I never saw it coming. Yeah, I heard my parents argue sometimes, but don't all parents argue? I argued with my brother and sister all the time, but I didn't get to call it quits and move out. I thought it was just a part of life. Parents argue and then they make up.

One day, we all sat down in the family room to have a talk. I thought someone was in trouble or something. I knew it must be serious, because we didn't have these "family talks" very often. I wasn't sure what happened, but I felt pretty sure it wasn't about me. My room stayed pretty clean, my grades were up, and boys were the last thing on my mind. Whoever was in trouble needed to be honest. Don't make matters worse. Fess up and take your punishment.

Instead, my dad sat there looking at us, and then at my mom, like he didn't know what to say (which wasn't like him at all.) He finally turned to my mom and said, "You want it? Why don't you tell them?"

My mom glared at my dad in a way we were starting to get used to. She turned to us and said, "Kids…..kids sometimes mommies and daddies can't get along." This is about all she got out before her eyes started tearing up. My little sister got off the couch, went right up to my mom, and asked, "Why are you crying, mommy?"

My mom grabbed a tissue, dabbed her tears away, and said, "It's okay, sweetie. Mommy's okay."

My brother, who was a few years younger than me at the time, asked, "Are you guys getting a divorce?"

Hope turned to Dad and asked, "What's a 'vorce'?"

"No," my dad said, shaking his head and looking back at Mom. "You know how sometimes Dad has a big case, so he stays in a hotel until it's over? Well, think of it like that. Dad is gonna get a hotel and stay there for a while."

"And then come back home?" Colt interrupted in the saddest voice, with his eyes tearing up.

Dad looked over at mom and said, "Sure I'll come back home. Mom and dad just need to work through some things."

Dad always taught us not to lie, but I knew this was either a lie or not the whole truth. Now that I'm older, I know sometimes you have to lie to your kids.

"Tell Santa Claus what you want for Christmas."

"How much did the Tooth Fairy bring you?"

"Mommy and Daddy are taking a nap."

"Sure, Daddy's coming home."

Now it all made sense. They weren't talking as much anymore. Mom no longer met Dad at the door when he came home from work, and we've been doing more and more things with only one parent.

About a month before we had "the talk" I saw my mom go into the guest bedroom, so I walked in a few minutes later to ask her a question. I saw clothes hanging in the closet and jewelry sitting on the dresser. I asked her why she had all her stuff in there. She said something about cleaning out her closet. I just left it at that and never really thought much about it.

Now here we were having a family talk. It would be the last family talk we'd ever have. I wasn't buying it, and I don't think Colt was buying it either. I think I was in shock. I couldn't believe this was actually happening. I sat there and said nothing.

Colt, however, looked right at my dad and said, "I want to go with *you*, Dad."

"Come here, buddy," my dad said, pulling him close. "There's nothing to worry about. Mom and Dad still love each other, they just need some time."

My mom gives him another one of her looks.

My dad ruffles Colt's hair. "What's important is that you kids stay together."

It was looking to me like "us kids" would be divided up. Colt made his intentions clear, and Hope was holding my mom's hand and leaning against her. She was only two, maybe three, so I'm pretty sure she had no idea what the heck was going on.

I, however, wasn't two or three. I was fifteen, and I knew exactly what was going on. My best friend's parents divorced two years ago. They had the same talk about how dad was moving out for "just a little while" until they figured things out. He never came back. In fact, a year later, he moved to Tennessee with his girlfriend. He now had a new family. Then my friend only saw her dad for half the summer and on Christmas breaks. Her mom mostly cried a lot. She told her the whole story about how her dad "ran off with that slut from his office." It made me wonder if my dad was running off with some slu— well, I wasn't allowed to use those kind of words at that age.

Something told me that wasn't the case. My mom and dad loved each other. They were always kissing, holding hands, giving presents, and writing cards that were full of *I love you's*. There were a few cards we weren't even allowed to see. We went to church every Sunday and on Wednesdays. My mom and dad taught Sunday School for God's sake. No, neither of my parents were one of those parents who have affairs.

So, I sat there saying nothing. Actually, I was trying to think of something to say to make this all go away, but nothing came to mind. When my brother said, "Don't go, Daddy," my eyes filled up, but I wiped them away with both hands before anyone could see.

My dad must have seen me wiping my eyes, because he reached out to comfort me and said, "Come here, sweetie." He held me on one side and held Colt on the other. I leaned my head against his shoulder and asked, "So, when are you leaving?"

"I'm leaving tonight, baby," he answered with a squeeze.

Obviously, it was too late for me to say or do anything. My mom called me to her. I walked over, stood beside her, and she said, "You know, you did nothing wrong. Mommy and daddy love you."

I nod my head several times without answering such a silly question. All I could think was: *Why would I think I did something wrong?*

I turned to my mom and asked, "Can I go to my room?"

With that, I walked upstairs to my room, closed the door, and cried.

You'd think this whole scene would cause my parents to go back into their bedroom and work things out. They'd come out a few hours later and tell us how mom and dad love us too much to tear our family apart. Instead, we all watched as dad put his suitcase in his trunk and drove away.

Once my dad got settled into his new apartment, we spent one week at home and one week at his apartment. If this wasn't bad enough, about a year later there was some trial and we were "ordered" by some judge (who never even talked to me) that I would live with my mom and visit my dad every other weekend. That's when things got really crazy.

For some reason, adults today think kids are so strong. They say things like:

"It's no big deal. Lots of kids today have divorced parents."

"Kids are resilient."

"They get over to it."

Some people even joke that kids actually like having their family torn apart because now they get two birthdays and two Christmases.

Of course, they eventually get over it. They don't really have a choice, do they? All these smart people never mention how kids have to bounce back and forth between two homes like some kind of Ping-pong ball—leaving their bedroom, their friends, their pets, and the home they know. They leave out the part where dad (or mom) moves away and now you go and visit them only once or twice a year. Soon Dad meets his new "friend" or Mom's new boyfriend pops up unexpectedly for dinner, and we're supposed to act like we're a brand-new, happy family. A few arguments later, and everything starts all over again with a different new friend or a different happy family.

My mom went from staying at home every day to being gone all the time. I'd come home from school to an empty house and a list of chores to do. I was expected to take care of two kids who wouldn't listen to a thing I said. My brother was too old for me to watch, and my little sister was too young.

I had to hunt for a ride home from volleyball practice or theater like I was poor or something. It was so embarrassing. I was left at the school with no ride home more than once or twice.

First, there was that Paul guy; and then some guy named Don….or Dan…and then other guys I never cared to know. By that time, I had a car and made sure I was gone as much as possible.

No one asks the kids what they want. Well, I wanted none of it. I wanted my mom and my dad back together again. I wanted to hear them laugh again, argue again, and make up again. I wanted one Christmas and one birthday. I wanted to climb into my parent's bed when I couldn't sleep, and see that look on their face like I just interrupted something.

When my parents were together, I never asked myself who I loved more or who treated me better. No one asked who I wanted to live with. They were my parents, and I wanted to live with them both. Suddenly, I was stuck in the middle of it all. It felt like some stupid contest to see who was the best parent, and I was the prize.

I must not have been one of those strong kids everyone talks about. I was strong on the outside when everyone was around, but so many nights I'd go to my room and cry. Eventually, I stopped crying. In fact, I never cried again until that day when a police officer came to the door and said my dad was killed in a car accident, and I'd never see him again.

I was so determined that this wouldn't happen to me….or to my kids. To me, love was bigger than just me. Love is a husband, a wife, kids, a home, and the memories you make together. No matter what I had to do, I would make my marriage work. Now here I am raising my two kids all by myself.

Grace Kennedy,
— Day 440

– CHAPTER 23 –

I can look back on what coulda', woulda', or shoulda' been, but what I need the most right now is a good bankruptcy attorney. I have so many bills, threatening demand letters, and civil lawsuits, that I don't know what to do. Jackson took off and left me to deal with all his mess.

I go to the Trustee with a folder full of all the letters, bills, and lawsuits I've received over the last weeks. While he glances over the documents, I shake my head and say, "I think I need to file for bankruptcy."

"Bankruptcy?" he says, still looking down and looking over everything. "I don't think that will be necessary. Why don't you leave all this with me. I'll take care of it."

He finds me the best contract attorney in Austin. By the time I meet with this attorney, he has more documents than I came in with.

To me, my situation is hopeless. On our first visit I ask, "Is there anything you can do to help me?"

"Oh yeah," he says. "These folks have way overreached and they know it."

I don't really understand how all the legal stuff works. I grew up with a lawyer for a father, but now it all sounds like Latin to me. My new lawyer fights my legal cases every step of the way. I never so much as see a bill. I just show up in court when I'm told, looking like the poor wife and mommy I am. I shut my mouth and let my attorney do all the talking.

He files my response to DMD's request for an injunction. To my surprise, he tells the court they are entitled to nothing. The embezzled money is long gone and if anyone is to blame, it's DMD! Jackson stole the money over a two-year period. The company should have had better oversight and control measures in place. Now the money is gone and not "one red penny" was spent on my household. None of the money in my account was stolen, and it's all my community property. They have no right to any of it. If they want their money back, they need to track down Jackson and ask him for it.

– CHAPTER 24 –

J.D. may be a dead end, but Flint's not done—not by a long shot. It's a lot easier being a private detective when you were born and raised in the same area. Old high school buddies are a great source of information—especially if they now work for Homeland Security. Well, Flint has just such a friend. His name is Kevin Davis. They went to high school together. Kevin joined the Marines right after graduation and came back a war hero. While Flint was busy arresting bad guys, Davis went to some important college and now works for Homeland Security. He comes in real handy whenever Flint has a problem that's bigger than just the State of Texas.

"How you been, Kevin," Flint begins.

"Tom Flint….how you been, old buddy?"

"Ah, I can't complain," Tom answers.

"Well good, something I can help you with?"

"Now that you ask, I need a teeny favor. I've been hired to track down a bail jumper. I'm pretty sure he left the country. Can you check the flights to see if he got on one?"

"Oh, hell Tom, you know the last time I did this for you, it was like finding a needle in a—"

"No, no, no, no," Tom interrupts. "Not this time. I can narrow it down to a pretty small window. I only need you to check over a three-week period. September twenty-second to October fourteenth of last year. I think that's when he left."

"What do you have on the guy?"

"I have his passport and his birth certificate."

"And you only need me to check from the twenty-second to the fourteenth?"

"That's it," Flint agrees.

"No problem at all. If he left the country on any commercial flight, we'll find him."

Flint knows Ryan's smart enough to avoid a commercial flight if he can. "What if he got on a private plane?"

"That's a whole different matter. As a pilot, we can possibly find him, but it's damn near impossible to locate all passengers. All I can check is commercial flights."

"I'll fax over the passport and birth certificate as soon as I get back to Austin."

"Sounds good."

"Listen Kevin, how long do you think this will take?"

"I'm working on something right now and then I'll get on it. I'll try to get something back to you within a couple weeks."

"Thank you, Kev."

"No problem," Kevin says. "And make sure you look me up the next time you're in the Houston area. We'll grab some lunch and catch up."

"Hell yes," Flint says and hangs up.

Sitting in his truck, all Tom can think about is Ryan tipping off Zach. Flint did so much work for Ryan's clients. All their skeletons are now hidden safely away in a closet somewhere because of Flint's expertise. Now to find out Ryan called to warn Zach about everything. He might as well have called the police. Now Ryan is far away, living it up somewhere while he's stuck here in Austin with a murder rap hanging over his head.

I've got you…now it's just a matter of time.

Grace Kennedy,
— Day 477

– CHAPTER 25 –

It's been a year and a half since Jackson left. I'm used to being alone for holidays and birthdays, but this is too much. I'm sitting here doing my best to cope with the fact that my husband (at least I thought he was my husband) married another woman and stole millions of dollars from his company.

Every minute I'm alone with my thoughts—like when I lie down to sleep, read a book, take a shower, watch television, or drive down the road in my car—my mind always goes back to Jackson. When I first found out about this giant lie, I felt a hurt beyond anything I've ever felt before. He betrayed me. I gave him my love, my life, and he threw it all away for some....some woman he met at a hotel. *Why?* I've asked myself that question a thousand times. I can't understand for the life of me how he could do this to me.

For weeks, I wondered how I'll ever be able to go on. The pain is just too deep, but step-by-step, day-by-day, I slowly start picking myself up and getting back on my feet. I really don't have a choice. I have a precious little girl and a beautiful baby boy to take care of.

Over the next few weeks, the pain and the hurt I've been living with turns to anger and then the anger turns to hate. I hate what Jackson did to me. I hate what he did to our children. I hate Jackson.

So many nights, I have this dream—the same horrible, horrible dream over and over again. It always starts with me sitting in the park on a blanket. It's a bright, beautiful, sunny day. While lying on the soft grass enjoying the beautiful day, I look up at the sky, and see the darkest storm clouds I've ever seen roll across the sky far, far away like the unfolding of a black scroll that divides the heavens as it gets closer and closer. The black sky rolls towards me, bringing an icy chill behind it.

I'm terrified by the darkness coming closer and closer, so I run...and run...but the dark sky rolls over me, and everything turns so dark I can't see a thing in front of me. I stumble over dirt, and rocks, and the hilly ground, but I continue to run as fast as I can. Suddenly, my body disappears when I fall into a well hidden in the ground in front of me. It seems like forever as I plummet down, down, down to the bottom of the well and land with a *thud* on my back.

I lay on my back, looking up at the top of the well, hoping someone will save me. The well is so dark and scary, with dirt and roots creeping out above me. The top of the well is so high above me that the opening looks small. "Hello!" I scream. "Is anyone there?"

Looking up, all I see are the dark clouds soaring across the sky. Then the hole above me slowly opens bigger and bigger. Without warning, a large stone falls down the well right at my head. I jerk to my left and it hits right beside me, barely missing my face. I can feel myself almost jerk awake in my bed as I see another stone falling down the well—and then another and another. Stones hit my legs, my arms, my stomach, my chest——each one hitting harder and harder.

I'm trapped in this hole as the stones keep coming. As one, and then another, and another stone crashes down on me, my body is about to disappear. I'm going to be buried alive. Unable to move, I look up and catch a glimpse of the devil leaning over the well, looking so evil it terrifies me.

Like a fog slowly lifting, the face at the top of the well comes clearer and clearer. Right as he's about to throw another stone at me, I can see it's Jackson above me throwing all those stones!

No matter how many times I have this dream, it never gets any better. If anything, it keeps getting worse. Every night I have this dream, I wake up soaked in sweat, screaming or crying, and shaking with fear. It's horrifying when you realize the person you love and trust the most is the one who's hurting you the most.

The thought of everything Jackson did is overwhelming. I feel like I never knew him. While I was taking care of his kids, he was raising another family and in love with another woman. Now I'm left dealing with the tornado he's left behind.

I never thought I could hate someone so much. I know it's not healthy, but I can't let go of that hate as hard as I try. There's a raging fire burning inside me, ready to explode. I want Jackson found. I want to find him myself.

– CHAPTER 26 –

When Flint gets back to Austin, he goes straight to his office. There's no reason to hurry back to his dark, empty apartment. This is the first time he's been back since he got out of jail and took off to Waco and then Houston.

Because of his arrest, his investigation business has closed down. The lawyers who were once waiting in line for his services now won't even return his calls. Everyone knows Flint pushes the envelope—hell, he tore the envelope up long ago and threw it in the trash. He's been all the talk around the courthouse nowadays. There are rumors going around town that Flint's indictment for the murder of Zachary Bell is just the beginning. The hammer is about to drop and there are several lawyers terrified they're going to drop with it. One local lawyer was just about to hire someone to burn Flint's entire office down to the ground.

When Flint pulls into the parking lot, he's a little surprised that his secretary's car isn't parked out front. Actually, he's been looking for an excuse to let her go, and this is as good an excuse as any.

He takes two steps up the front stairs and freezes in place. *This is where those bastards threw me against the wall and slapped the handcuffs on me. That little punk even shoved my head against the car door while helping me into his cop car.* This was a trick Flint knew very well from all his years of throwing people in cop cars. It's just one of the many tricks up his sleeves when someone wants to get mouthy, or pushy, or starts talking about who pays whose salary. There's always some kid whose daddy or uncle somewhere will "sue the shit out of me, and I'll be fired by morning."

Flint opens the front door to his office to find a gigantic mess inside. The place never looked the office of some upscale big-shot, but this is a disaster. You'd think some bad guys came in and ransacked the place, but Flint knows better. This is the work of the good guys—the same good guy club he was once a legitimate, badge carrying, member—except back then the only way you could tell the good guys from the bad guys was by their cowboy hat, the uniforms they wore, and the badge on their hip.

Standing in the reception area, Flint turns around and sees a pink copy of the search warrant attached to the inside of his front door. He rips it off and throws it on the floor.

His receptionist's area was obviously the first victim of the search. The cabinet and desk drawers are hanging open. This doesn't concern Flint a bit. He can't imagine anything in those drawers other than a bunch of pens, pencils, paper clips, and other ordinary office supplies.

The only thing missing from her area appears to be the computer that always sits on her desk. *Nothing to find there except her Facebook and Instasomething posts, searches on Amazon for a new skirt or something, and about a million hands of solitaire.* The shelves behind her desk are usually nicely arranged, but now things have been moved all around. The only thing anyone would find on those shelves is a bunch of cheap decorations and knick-knacks that you could buy at Wal-Mart or some garage sale for less than twenty dollars.

As Flint walks from room to room, the place looks like someone just moved out and left all their junk behind. It's not until he enters his own office that things really get crazy. Just like the reception desk, they went through his personal desk looking for evidence. *Good luck finding anything there!*

His desk is seldom used. It's mostly just a place to meet clients, because he prefers to work out of his pickup truck. The stack of bills Flint left on his desk are still sitting at the same place waiting to be paid. *Didn't want the bills, huh?*

Looking at the mess in front of him, Flint laughs out loud and says, "I hope you assholes enjoyed yourselves."

You can't miss the empty space where his computer once sat. The only thing left now is his printer, his Internet and power cords, his mouse, and a bunch of dust. Flint can't imagine his computer could provide anything worth looking at. He is computer illiterate. He rarely writes letters, or sends emails, and he's never so much as signed up for one of those silly social media sites. If he wants to be social, he goes hunting, or fishing, or plays Texas Holdem' with his old buddies. A five-year-old knows more about computers than he does.

Flint does use the Internet to investigate people, but he knows better than to leave anything incriminating on his computer. He was in law enforcement long enough to know that nothing on your computer is ever really erased. It's hidden in the far corners of your hard drive, just waiting for some computer geek to run a sophisticated program and bring all your deleted files back to life. Flint never so much as made a call that could be traced—he damn sure didn't use his computer when working on his "top secret files."

Flint spins his chair around to face his credenza. It also has very little value—unless you're looking for a stack of *Playboys, Field and Stream* magazines, a half empty bottle of Jim Beam, or a drawer full of potato chips, candy bars, beef jerky, and microwave popcorn. You won't find any photos of a wife or kids siting on his desk or credenza. His wife is long gone and turned all his kids against him on the way out. He hasn't talked to them in years. He heard he had a couple grandbabies a few years back, but after all these years he "wasn't welcome" at the hospital. The whole damn family acts like he's a murderer or something.

Suddenly, he remembers his little safe that stays locked inside the left door of his credenza. He reaches in his pocket, pulls out his key chain, and inserts the smallest brown key. As soon as he tries to turn the key, he realizes the lock to the credenza drawer is now broken. *"You sum bitches!"*

He opens the broken door to find the cash box missing. The only thing they'll find is the cash he keeps in case of emergencies. When he last checked, there was $16,000 inside. *Take the damn money if you want it!*

The money doesn't really matter. There's so much more buried in a Yeti cooler underneath an old mesquite tree fifty feet from his favorite fishing spot. Flint doesn't trust banks—even if those banks are located on the other side of the planet. No, they'll never find the rest of his money unless they start digging holes three feet deep out in the middle of Duval County.

Looking around his office, he can tell some things are missing, but it's hard to know just what. They even took his cheap art off the wall like he's Bill Gates or something who has some big safe hidden behind his picture of a bunch of cows grazing in a Bluebonnet field out in the hot Texas sun. He picks up the picture, blows the dust off the front, and returns it to the nail hanging on the wall. He's pretty sure they got nothing that could be incriminating. No, they came all the way here just to go home with empty pockets! All they did was cause one hell of a mess that he'll have to clean up.

Suddenly his eyes light up and his head, his hands, and his whole body shake with terror. His heart beats so hard he feels like he's about to have a damn heart attack. He leans beside his desk and coughs up some of the crud from fifty years of cigarettes, beer, and cheap whiskey.

"SUM BITCHES!" he screams through his cough. It's not the mess that shakes him. It's not his office, his desk, his missing computer, or his missing safe. He jumps to his feet and runs to the back of his office. His boots bang against the old wood floors as he enters the storage room.

The door is already wide open, and the place looks like some kind of bomb exploded in there. There are files sitting lopsided in file cabinets, other files are sitting in stacks on the floor, and boxes are on the floor with lids hanging to the side.

There's only one file that he cares about. It should be hidden up in the attic in the "secret file cabinet" along with all the other *special files*. The file cabinet is hidden so no one can find it. His secretary pulled the file when Hope arrived, poking her nose around things that were none of her business. Flint closed the box for good after that Zach boy died and he told his secretary to return it to the attic. He reminded her for the third time a week later when she was walking out the door to go home for the day, but never followed up on it again.

Flint gazes up to the heavens and presses his palms together like Jesus praying in the Garden of Gethsemane. *Oh Lord, please let it be here.*

He opens his eyes and looks to his right. There it is, still sitting on the floor right where he left it. "BRUNICK V. BRUNICK" is written in large letters and "PERSONAL AND PRIVATE" is written underneath. It's like God answered his prayer.

He closes his eyes before slowly opening the lid. The second he opens his eyes, he yells, "SUM BITCH!" The box is completely empty. All the files, the photos, the receipts, the credit card charges, and his personal notes are now in the hands of the prosecutors!

Flint backs up and slams his head against the wall behind him again and again until it creates a large hole in the sheetrock. He covers his eyes with his hands and shakes his head back and forth screaming, "SHIT, SHIT, SHIT."

He goes over to the attic and pulls down on the spring door. He climbs up the creaking ladder until he reaches the top. *It's hot as hell up here.* He flips on the light and can see from the mess that they even searched up here. He walks back to the false wall, gives it a push, and it feels secure. He circles around to the back, releases the latch, and the wall opens right up. Every file is sitting there untouched.

Flint hired his receptionist a year ago after his old secretary "got sick and tired of all the sexual harassment" and threatened to sue. His new secretary came in right out of high school wearing a miniskirt and a tight blouse that showed all the right curves. He was more concerned with her nipples showing through her blouse than her resume. She was gorgeous, but you could tell the second she opened her mouth that she was no brilliant intellect. But how much of an intellect do you have to be to answer a phone call here and there, fix a cup of coffee, or pick up some office supplies now and then?

She hadn't been working for two months before the troubles began. She usually came in late, took long lunches, and called in sick every time you turned around. Like most eighteen-year-olds, she got so mouthy you might have thought she was the boss.

He threatened to fire her once, but she threatened him right back with a sexual harassment claim after one little slap on the butt. *What the hell has the world come to?* Flint thought at the time. *There was once a day when women knew their place. If you want to work in a man's world, or at least in a man's office, you better learn to toughen up.*

In the end, she already knew way too much and Flint had no doubt, given half a chance, she'd run her big mouth to anyone and everyone. Before it was all over, Flint gave her a huge raise and told her to only come in on Monday through Thursday.

"DAMMIT YOU LITTLE BITCH!" Flint screams as loud as possible. *If, for once, you just did what you were told! If you just put that damn file back where it belongs, I'd have nothing to worry about.*

Now....now....holy shit.

Flint walks back down the rickety ladder to his office down below. The air conditioning provides immediate relief from the heat, but the hot Texas summer is the least of Flint's problems. Now he knows exactly what the prosecutors have—a treasure trove of information. They're probably popping corks and high fiving each other at this very moment.

All the optimism Flint's had about these "bullshit charges" is now long gone. He has every reason to be terrified of the long prison sentence he's facing. He sits in the chair behind his desk trying to consider his next move—nothing comes to mind. Burning down a courthouse in the age of computers and digital backups is a silly thought. Flint knows no judge, or prosecutor, or "Duke of Duval" who has his back.

He reaches back and pulls out the bottle of Jim Beam. He tilts the bottle to his lips, starts chugging, and doesn't let up until the last drop is gone. The burn that only cheap whisky can deliver hits him particularly hard going down.

Grace Kennedy,
— Day 489

– CHAPTER 27 –

Flint wakes up the next morning passed out on the floor with an empty bottle of Jim Beam still in his hand. He picks himself up, and stumbles over to his desk. His head is killing him. He looks at his watch and sees it's 8:15 a.m. He calls his lawyer's office, but an answering machine picks up.

"You've reached the Law Office of Whitney Fanning. The office is closed right now. Please leave a message and we'll return your call as soon as possible."

Flint hangs up the phone, waits until 8:40, and calls again. He's relieved when the receptionist answers, "Law Office of Whitney Fanning. How can I help you?"

"Get Fanning on the line!" Flint demands.

"Okay," the receptionist draws out, shocked at how rude Flint can be. She knows exactly who's on the phone ordering her around, because he's done the same thing several times in the past. "Is this Mr. Flint?" she asks sarcastically.

"Yes, it's Flint and I need to talk to Fanning…NOW!"

"Yes sir," she says like a soldier taking an order.

A moment later, Fanning comes on the line and says, "This is Whitney Fanning."

"Fanning, did you file the motion to dismiss?"

"Yes, I filed it. We have court next week. Make sure you're there."

Flint takes a deep breath, lets it out, and says, "We got a problem. We got a big goddamn problem."

"What are you talking about, Tom?"

"They searched my office. They went in and tore the whole damn place apart."

"O..k..a..y," Fanning says cautiously.

"They got my file. They got the damn Zachary Bell file."

"Wait…wait….wait. I thought you knew nothing about Zachary Bell?"

Flint chuckles a little and says, "Oh, come on, Fanning."

"So, what's in the file?" Fanning asks.

"Look, just get this case dismissed – NOW!"

"Flint, what do they have?"

"Everything!"

"Flint, there's no way the judge is going to just dismiss your case if they have hard evidence."

"Did you give the judge the money?"

"Mr. Flint, I can't just—"

"Did you give the judge the fucking money or not?"

"Did I give the judge a campaign contribution? Yes."

"Then get it dismissed!"

"He won't dismiss it, Tom! Even if he does, he'll dismiss without prejudice to the state bringing charges later."

"Then make a deal," Flint says, talking so fast he's almost impossible to follow. "They want twenty? Tell them I'll take ten."

"Slow down, Tom."

"I'll take ten years!" he repeats.

"Tom, first, they don't *want twenty*. They were at *forty*. I told you I could *probably* get them down to twenty. That was before. If you were stupid enough to leave them a box full of evidence, they're going to withdraw their current offer. Everything is off."

"What if I show up at court? Will they arrest me?"

"Well, the judge set your bail so low because the State had no case—he made that clear. It's very possible the judge will raise your bail substantially. Depending what they have, he might even deny bail. In that event, you'll be taken into custody right then."

"And what if I don't come to court? What happens then?"

"If you don't come to court, there will be a warrant for your arrest."

"What do I do?" Flint asks.

"Tom, let me call the prosecutor. Let me find out what he has. I'll see if we can plead the case out. Are you willing to take the forty years if it's still on the table?"

"What about the twenty?" Flint asks.

"Tom—" Fanning says, exacerbated.

"Try to get the twenty. I'll be out in ten, right?"

Irritated, Fanning says, "I'll call the prosecutor and call you back."

– CHAPTER 28 –

A few hours later, Flint's back in his apartment checking his phone again and again for some news—any news from Fanning. Three hours later, he gets the call.

"What the hell took you so long?" Tom growls.

"I just got off the phone with the prosecutor. Well, actually it was thirty minutes ago. I was waiting for his fax. He sent over the motion he's filing."

"Well?" Flint asks.

"I don't know what exactly they got, but he kept calling it a *game changer*." What do they have, Flint?"

"I told you. They got the whole damn world."

"Evidently so. They've filed a motion asking the court to deny you bond based on the new evidence. They're asking you to be taken into custody immediately. The District Attorney is coming up to argue the motion. They wanted to schedule an emergency hearing, but I told him I wasn't available. I'll put it off as long as possible, but I'm sure we'll hear it on your next scheduled court date. By that time, I'll know exactly what they got from your office."

"Shit, Shit, Shit…okay Fanning, just settle the case."

"It's not so simple anymore, Flint."

"I don't give a damn, just do it. I'll take thirty years."

I talked to the prosecutor about a plea. "They won't offer thirty years. You can forget it."

"Shit! If I get forty years, how soon will I be out?"

"Tom, they're withdrawing the forty years, too. They say they're going to indict you for capital murder. Maybe, just maybe, I can get them to back off and drop the death penalty if you'll accept life without the possibility of parole."

"They're bluffing. Tell them I'll take twenty-five. I'll be out in what….maybe fifteen years. Just tell them twenty-five. They'll—"

"Flint, I have to level with you. Usually I can pull a few strings, but this is bigger than the prosecutor, or even his boss. The Feds are looking over his shoulder."

"The Feds?"

"It seems the FBI had an active investigation on you after you were acquitted of murder. What, twenty years ago?"

"What in Sam Hill does that have to do with this case?"

"That kid you killed, well now his dad is some big-wig oil man in Houston. He's making waves."

"That little punk had it coming to him."

"He was shot in the back of the head for a taillight?" Fanning asks.

"I was acquitted—not guilty."

"Yeah, that's what it says."

"Then tell his daddy to shove it up his ass, and get this case settled."

"Well, it's not just that case. It seems a lot of people had it coming when they crossed your path. The FBI was putting it all together when you disappeared. It was probably the smartest thing you've ever done. After a while, they figured you were dead, and closed the file. They also have reason to believe you made off with a lot of money from Duval County. When you paid your bail in cash, they put two and two together."

Flint doesn't want to hear all this crap. All he wants is a plea deal.

"Did you threaten to kill a Texas Ranger?" Fanning asks.

"Hell, I don't know. That was thirty years ago. Him and me got all sideways. He's actually lucky. He had a good country ass whooping coming to him."

"Well, that Ranger is now a Special Agent Supervisor for the FBI. This has become personal for him."

"I'm seventy-two years old, for god's sake. I'm an old man. I just want to go off fishing somewhere."

"Yeah, that's what everyone was thinking—let bygones be bygones. Then the old fisherman struck again. They don't want to let it go this time. I think they want an eye for an eye, as the Good Book says."

"Whose side you on?" Flint yells.

"Look, I'll know soon exactly what they have when we go to court. Let's keep calm until then."

"Keep calm? How the hell am I supposed to keep calm?"

"I'll see you next week, Mr. Flint. We'll know more then."

Without responding, Flint simply hangs up the phone.

Fanning looks at the receiver and whispers, "You asshole."

Grace Kennedy,
— Day 500

– CHAPTER 29 –

It's been a while since I first met Hannah. She sent me a friend request on Facebook, and then she sent the same request on Instagram. I accept them both. Now we've been talking and texting pretty regularly.

I think this might sound crazy, but my whole life has been pretty crazy. Hope doesn't understand it—maybe no one can understand it unless you've been here. Hannah and I have this connection. Like it or not, our children will be related forever. We both agree we don't want to hide this from our kids. We don't want them to grow up one day and find out they have a brother and sister out there who they've never known. Whatever Jackson did, it's not their fault.

With so much uncertainty in my life, I just want to get away for a few days to clear my head. I take the kids to our vacation home in Aspen, and I invite Hannah to meet us there with her little baby.

Walking into my home—yes, *my home*—I see it so different now. There's this cute little rug right inside the entry. Frilly pillows are laying on our sofa. A pot-pourri pot is sitting on the counter. Matching dish towels and washcloths are hanging in the kitchen.

Nope….nope….nope….nope, I didn't buy any of them. How stupid I had to be to think Jackson, who could barely match his suit and tie, could or would decorate an entire house.

Once Hannah arrives a couple hours later, I can't help but ask, "Did you buy the pillows on the couch?"

"Yep," she answers. " I got them at the mall."

"And the dish towels and washcloths?"

"Target."

"The bedspread in the master bedroom?"

"Dillard's."

"How long have they been here?"

"A long time," she says.

This goes on and on until I finally stop before I make myself crazy. The bottom line, my house was slowly decorated, not by my husband like I thought, but by my husband's wife! At one point, I'm so furious I want to just sell the place, but I agreed not to sell anything while the lawsuit is pending.

Later that evening, I hear her little girl crying from the guest bedroom. "Can I pick her up?" I ask.

"Sure."

I walk into the nursery and see her little girl laying in her playpen crying. She's grown so much since I last saw her. "Come here Savannah," I say, picking her up and laying her head on my shoulder. "Shhhhhhhh," I whisper, bouncing her so lightly. She eventually stops crying.

I lift her off my shoulder and look at her face. Now she looks even more like Jackson. She has the same eyes, the same mouth, and the same straight, pointy nose. "You're a beautiful girl," I say, pulling her close and holding my face against hers. I turn my head and kiss her little cheek. She gives me this smile that looks just like Jackson's smile. I'm filled with this feeling of love—the kind of love you only feel for your own children. I pull her closer and kiss her on her forehead.

When I turn to walk out of the room, Hannah is standing at the door watching everything. My eyes are full of tears and one falls down my cheek. "I'm sorry," I say, handing her Savannah.

She takes her little girl and says, "It's okay, I understand."

"It's so hard," I say, wiping my eyes. "I see Jackson every time I look at Savannah. They look so much alike. I hate him, but I also miss him. I can't help it."

"You gonna be okay?" she asks.

I can't really talk, so I simply shake my head. I'm nodding yes, but it's obvious I'm not okay at all.

"Don't you miss him?" I ask.

"I don't know," she says. "It's not like it was with you guys. We were only together for two years. I was so angry for so long, I think it sucked all the love out of me. There's nothing left now but hate. You know what they say, hell hath no fury like a woman scorned."

"I hate him too….most the time," I say, shaking my head. "Other times I miss him so much. I don't know what to do. I feel like I'm losing my mind."

"You're not losing your mind. You were together a long time. He was the father of your children."

"Do you know how hard it is to find out your husband is married and has kids with someone else?"

Hannah gives me this look like maybe I am losing my mind.

"Sorry," I say, looking away.

The more time we spend together, the closer we get. We spend the weekend walking through the park, looking at the shops and galleries, and eating dinner at this pleasant little restaurant. We seem to have so much in common. I really enjoy spending time with her.

On Sunday morning, we're enjoying breakfast at another cute restaurant, before I have to catch my flight back to Dallas.

"So, how you holding out?" I ask.

"Good, I'm doing really good."

"How? How can you go on like nothing ever happened?"

"Maybe I'm lucky," she answers. "I didn't have time to get jaded. I'm not going to let Jackson ruin me for all men. I know it's silly, but I still believe in love. As far as Jackson is concerned…good riddance."

Her attitude surprises me.

"Plus, I met someone else. He's nice and simple. No more lies. He loves me and Savannah. Who knows, sometimes I think I might love him too."

"So, when did you start dating him?"

"I guess about six months ago."

"Where'd you meet?"

"At work. I meet so many guys at work."

"And you love him?"

"It's still early but yeah….I think I do."

"And that's it? You're done? You can just move on?"

"I'm tired of crying. I'm tired of being depressed. I'm done."

"That's great," I say. "I just don't know how you do it. I'll never love again. It hurts too much."

"Don't focus on love. Go out and meet someone. It will help you get over all this mess."

"That's what my sister says. She wants me to join this dating site, but I'm not ready."

"You know what they say," she jokes. "Want to get over one man, just get under another."

I've never heard this, and I can't help but laugh a little. Once I stop laughing, I say, "The last thing I need is a man. Honestly, I'm so broken right now. If I found a good guy, I'd just ruin him."

"You never know," she winks.

"It's not so easy for me. Bonnie lost her grandpa, and she just learned her father is gone. Right now, I need to focus on her."

"Yeah, Savannah's so small she won't remember any of this."

When we're finished eating, we refill our coffee and sit for a while talking. "How did your interrogation with the police go?" I ask.

"It started great. They started by asking normal questions they'd ask anyone. After a half hour of this, it became clear I was their prime suspect.

They kept pushing…repeating the same questions, but wanting different answers. Eventually, I freaked out. I told them I wanted an attorney."

"You were smart," I say. "I don't know why I didn't leave. They questioned me for five hours. I was treated like a criminal."

"Five hours," she says, surprised. "Why didn't you just leave?"

"That's a good question," I answer. "I'm sure I said too much. I just want them to find Jackson. Maybe that will bring closure and I can start all over again."

There's one thing I've been wanting to ask for months now. It's been on my mind, and I have to ask her before I go home. "So….what about all the money he stole?"

She looks at me and smiles for just a second before it fades away. Looking serious now, she says, "I know nothing about the money."

"Come on," I say. "You can tell me."

She laughs before taking a sip of coffee. "I wish I did know where it is. I keep looking around the house, hoping to find a box full of thousand-dollar bills. Do they even make thousand-dollar bills?"

"I don't think so," I laugh.

"Well anyway, I didn't steal anything, and I didn't get a penny. If I find a box full of money, you'll be the first to know. I'll split it with you."

"So, you know nothing?" I ask.

"I know nothing," she says, holding up two fingers as if to say, scout's honor. "All I got is a box full of bills. I'm sure they're going to repossess this house in a couple months. Then…."

"Then what?"

"I don't know. I guess I'll have to figure it out."

When I left Dallas, I forgot my phone charger so my phone lost all power this morning. When we get back home, I borrow Hannah's charger and get my phone up and running again. There are ten missed calls. Two are from Detective Stowe and the rest are from Hope. I push play on one message after another until I've heard them all:

****

"Mrs. Kennedy, this is Detective Stowe. It's very important I meet with you right away. It's very urgent. I'll be over in a few minutes if that's okay."

****

"Grace, it's Hope. That Stowe guy is here. He's at the front door and I don't know what to do. Call me right away."

****

"Grace, call me! Two more police cars just showed up. Stowe is waiting in his car. He probably knows I'm here. Call me."

****

"Mrs. Kennedy…um….its Detective Stowe again. I need to speak to you. I'm waiting outside your house. Please call me."

****

"Grace, where are you? Call me now!"

****

"Grace, now there's news trucks outside. I don't know what to do. I'm afraid to answer the door. Please, please call."

****

My heart starts pounding. *Oh my God.* I call Hope and she picks up immediately. "Grace!" she practically yells.

"Hope, I'm sorry. I was having lunch with Hannah. What the hell is going on?"

"I don't know. There are three police cars outside, and the street is full of news trucks and reporters. Something has happened."

"Hope, I'm on my way back. I'll call Stowe and let him know. I'll catch the next flight back."

"Something's not right," Hope says. "I'm afraid."

"Me too. Call me if anything else happens."

I hang up the phone and call Detective Stowe. "Detective Stowe, what's happening? Why are you at my house?"

"I've been trying to reach you all morning. When are you coming back home?"

"What is it? What's going on?"

"I'd prefer not to talk about it over the phone," he says. "How soon can you be home?"

"I'm out of town. My flight doesn't get in until seven-thirty this evening. It's only a two-hour flight back. I'll head to the airport right now and catch the next flight back."

– CHAPTER 30 –

When I explain everything to the lady at the ticket counter, she prints out our paper tickets for the next flight to Dallas that's just about to board. She walks us to the front of security. Once through, I run through the terminal to my gate, pushing Wesley's stroller as fast as I can with Bonnie running by my side. When I finally get to the gate, everyone has already boarded.

"Come on, come on, come on," the woman at the counter says, waving me to her. She scans my ticket and helps me inside before they close the gate.

I barely sit down before the plane takes off. Luckily, it's a quick flight. If it was any longer, I'm not sure I would have survived it. The whole time, my mind is racing through every possibility.

They found Jackson.....

Jackson is dead....

They're at my house to arrest me....

One part of me is afraid to go home. Another part of me can't get home fast enough.

– CHAPTER 31 –

Flint was so afraid he might miss Fanning's call that he declined all other calls he received that day. A week later, while checking his messages, he notices he missed a call from Kevin Davis, his buddy at Homeland Security. It's hard to believe. For almost a year, finding Ryan Brunick has been Flint's primary purpose in life, but now he forgot all about it. He plays Kevin's message:

"Tom…hey, it's Kevin. Listen, I finished the search for all flights leaving the country during the weeks you're concerned about. Give me a call so I can tell you what I found."

"Hey Kevin," Flint says when Kevin picks up his call. "How's it going, buddy? I just saw your message. I've been so busy lately."

"Yeah, Tom…hold on a second." Kevin puts the call on hold and comes back on the line a minute later. "Ah, here we are. Scott Edward Richards. You wanted me to check to see if he was on a flight leaving the U.S.?"

"Yes, sir."

"Last year, from September twenty-second to October fourteenth?"

"So, what'd you find, Kev?"

"We got a hit on September twenty-fifth. Your bail jumper was on a flight from Austin to Dallas, and then from Dallas to Zurich."

"Anything after Zurich?"

"Nothing, it's like he up and disappeared. Listen, was this Richards on an ankle bracelet or anything? I can work with that."

"Nah," Flint says.

"Then send me over an arrest warrant. I can show my boss. With that, he'll be fine for me to press a little further. I'll check with the authorities in Zurich—I'm sure we'll find him."

Flint knows he's skirting the law, but what else is new? He's spent his whole life with one foot on one side of the law and another foot on the other— taking from both sides. He's tore up so many tickets with a "friendly contribution to the Duval County Sheriff's Association"—like such an association even existed. Of course, Flint has no arrest warrant, but there're ways around that as well. For now, he'll keep that card in his back pocket.

"Thank you, Kevin," he says.

"No problem. Let me know if you need anything else."

– CHAPTER 32 –

My car rolls forward, but I can't drive down my own street. The sun is just about to go down, and there are news trucks, satellites, and three police cars in front of my house. Many of my neighbors are gathered outside.

As I drive a little closer, a police officer approaches my car window and says, "Ma'am, this street is temporarily closed off."

"I'm Kennedy….Grace Kennedy," I say.

"Mrs. Kennedy," he says, "follow me." He walks through the crowd, barking at everyone to move out of the way.

The reporters are slow to move. They crowd against my car with cameras pointing into my front and side windows, saying:

"Mrs. Kennedy…Mrs. Kennedy…give us a statement?"

"What do you have to say, Mrs. Kennedy?"

"Any comments?"

I open the garage door when I get closer, and shut it behind me closing out all the chaos.

When I enter the kitchen, Hope comes right up and takes Wesley from my arms. "They're in the living room," she whispers.

Bonnie holds my leg like she's as scared as I am. "Mommy, there's policemen in our house," she says.

"I know, baby."

"Why are they here, Mommy?" she asks, looking afraid.

I kneel down, hold her in my arms, and say, "Everything's going to be okay, baby."

When I walk into the living room, there's one officer standing by the entrance to the door and another officer sitting in my recliner, who rises to his feet as soon as I walk in. Both Detective Stowe and Detective Fleming are sitting on the couch. They both get up and walk towards me as soon as I enter. For a second, I fear Stowe is here to put handcuffs on me.

"What's going on?" I ask.

"Mrs. Kennedy, I think it's best you sit down."

– CHAPTER 33 –

Why in the world would they need so many cops in my house? Once we're all seated, I wait to find out why my house looks like an episode of *Cops.*

"So, did you find Jackson?" I ask.

They had to know I was going to ask that question, but both Stowe and Fleming look at each other like I caught them by surprise. Stowe turns back and says, "Yes, we have."

"Thank God," I say.

"Well, it was actually someone else who found him."

"Someone else? Where is he? I want to talk to him."

He was actually found near your vacation home in Aspen in the Rocky Mountains. You know the area they call the Maroon Bells?"

"I'm very familiar with it. We'd go hiking there all the time. So, how long has he been hiding out there?"

"No ma'am," Stowe says, looking down. "A hiker was down there and found his body pretty hidden down in the brush. It looks like he took a long fall."

"So, he's," I say, covering my mouth with my hand. "He's dead?"

"I'm afraid so."

As soon as I hear these words, everything goes blank for a second. "No," I say, barely above a whisper. "I know where he is. He's….he's in Paris… or maybe Australia."

"Yes ma'am," he says again, looking over at Fleming. "We're quite sure it's him."

"No," I repeat, looking forward like I'm in a trance. "You said he wasn't dead. You said he'd show up somewhere…get a ticket or something."

"Mrs. Kennedy, I'm—"

"You've got it wrong. Jackson isn't dead. He's in Paris."

"He's not in Paris, Mrs. Kennedy."

"How?" I cry. "How can you be so sure?"

"It's been a long time, so an identification won't be easy, but—"

"But what?" I interrupt.

"Well, Mrs. Kennedy, his wallet was found in his jacket, along with his keys."

I take a big sigh, and say, "Oh my God, that doesn't mean it's him. Someone could have stolen those things. Sure, someone probably just stole them."

"Ultimately, we'll get dental records, but it looks like him. I know this isn't easy, but I have to ask. Did Jackson have a scar on his back?"

I'm not sure if I heard him right. "A scar?" I ask.

"Yes, a scar on his back, to the left of his armpit?"

I put my head down and cry into my hands. "Yes, a scar by his armpit. He fell when he was a boy. He was in a tree, and he fell back on a branch. It caused the scar that looks kind of like a check mark."

"We're going to need you to identify him. I don't think you want to see his face, but the scar on his back and the clothes he has on should be fine for now."

"Now?" I ask.

"No, not now," he says. "He's still in Colorado. We need your permission to bring him back to Dallas."

"Of course," I say.

"We should have him here by tomorrow. I'll send someone to pick you up if you like."

Hope hands me a glass of water and says, "I can drive her down to the station."

"Mrs. Stowe, I had an agreement with the news to hold off on the story until you got home. I'm sure they've run the story by now."

"I want to see it," I say. "I want to see the news about my husband. Where's the remote?"

Hope picks up the remote and turns on the news. There's "BREAKING NEWS" flashing across the bottom of the screen. When I turn up the sound, they're already reporting.

"Again, the police are reporting that a body has been found at the base of the Rocky Mountains near Aspen, Colorado. They have reason to believe it's the body of Jackson Kennedy, the Dallas executive who disappeared almost two years ago from his home in Dallas, Texas. I believe we're going to take you to Aspen, Colorado, where we have a reporter on the scene."

The reporter in Aspen is standing beside a man who looks like he's in his late thirties. He has on a red flannel shirt, hiking pants, and boots. You can see dirty blonde hair poking out from under his cap.

"We're here at the scene with Sean Campbell. He's the hiker who discovered the body of Jackson Kennedy. Mr. Campbell, I understand you were hiking in the area?"

"Yes ma'am, I was hiking back down the Maroon Peak when I saw something shiny down in the thick trees below. I wasn't sure what it was. I thought it might be gold or something. I lowered myself down, and I could see it was a man's body."

He points to the trees behind him and says, "It was pretty well hidden by the shade of these thick trees over there."

"Do you hike here often?" she asks.

"No," he answers, removing his cap and brushing his hair back. "First time. I'm just visiting…you know…on vacation. I just came to spend a few days hiking and maybe fishing."

After the reporter finishes talking with this hiker, the story goes back to the CNN newsroom, where some hiking expert is on TV describing the area:

"Yes, the Maroon Bells, near Aspen, is made up of Maroon Peak, which is about fourteen thousand one-hundred feet, and North Maroon Peak that's fourteen thousand feet. It's very beautiful—one of the most photographed spots in Colorado. Unfortunately, it's also very

dangerous. Most hikers refer to it as 'The Deadly Bells.' It's an eleven-hour hike that's long and very challenging, both mentally and physically. It's one of the most deadly hikes in America."

"Aren't there signs warning hikers?" the reporter asks.

"Sure. There's a U.S. Forest Service sign on the access trail that says, 'The beautiful Maroon Bells have claimed many lives in the past few years. They are not extreme technical climbs, but they are unbelievably deceptive. The rock is down-sloping, rotten, loose, and unstable. It kills without warning. The snowfields are treacherous, poorly consolidated, and no place for a novice climber.'"

"It appears Mr. Kennedy went hiking without adequate hiking boots and protection from the harsh early winter. He fell—"

Turn it off!" I say, turning away.

Hope grabs the remote from the coffee table and turns the television off, sparing me the horrible details.

"Please, please, please," I beg Stowe. "Isn't it possible there's been a mistake?"

Stowe takes a plastic baggie out of his jacket pocket and holds it in front of him. Hiding in the corner is the gold and silver wedding band Jackson always wore. My chin and my lower lip start to quiver as I slowly reach out and take the baggie. I bring the ring to my chest and hold it there so tight. I know this ring well.

My eyes glass over and tears start building in the corners. I bend over on the edge of the couch and moan with pain. You'd think I was just punched in the gut. "Oh Jackson," I sob into my lap. "Oh, my baby…oh my baby."

I get up from the couch and start into the kitchen. "I…I….I…I need…I need some water," I mumble before I walk out, Stowe takes the baggie out of my hands.

Hope follows me into the kitchen. I pour a glass of water, take a drink, and lean over the sink. Hope lays her head on my back and stays here holding me while I cry.

I knew this day would come, but I didn't know it would hurt so bad. I gasp for air, but can't catch my breath. Still in a fog, I spin around and throw my arms around her. "He's gone," I cry. "He's really gone."

Hope, still holding me tight, is the only thing stopping me from collapsing. She eases me down to the kitchen floor as I cry in her arms. I'm sobbing so hard I'm sure the police sitting in my living room can hear me. They stay away, giving me time to grieve.

Hope and I walk back into the living room arm in arm. I sit back on the couch and ask Stowe, "Can I see the ring again?"

Detective Fleming reaches out and takes the baggie with the ring from Stowe. She puts my hand in hers and hands me the baggie. Showing her concern, she says, "I'm so sorry, Mrs. Kennedy."

I sit on the edge of the couch holding his wedding ring in the baggie. When I open the baggie to take it out, Stowe puts his hand over the baggie to stop me. "Mrs. Kennedy….please don't. This is evidence. We don't want to contaminate it."

I crumple the baggie in my hand and say, "I don't understand."

Stowe gently takes the baggie from me and says, "This wasn't the ring he was wearing at the time. It was in his pocket."

"So, he didn't have a ring on?" I ask.

Stowe looks down, shakes his head just a little, and says, "I'm sorry…."

"What?"

"He had his other ring on."

– CHAPTER 34 –

Just like he promised, Detective Stowe calls a couple days later to let me know the body—Jackson's body—is back in Dallas. Hope and I drive down to the Dallas County Medical Examiner's Office. I think I was expecting something old and scary, but it's a professional white building accented with red brick.

Stowe is already there when we arrive, and someone who identifies herself as the Chief Medical Examiner meets us at the front. The whole thing is so upsetting, that I'm really not thinking straight. "Mrs. Kennedy," she begins, "I know this isn't easy for you. I want you to know there's no rush. Take your time and proceed only when you're sure you're ready."

"Thank you," I say, sounding pretty shaky.

Working at the hospital, I've seen dead bodies before. Still, I feel so lost and alone as Hope and I walk out of the elevator to the end of the hall.

"Mrs. Kennedy, I want to prepare you. Your husband took a long fall. It crushed his skull and his face. His body has been outside for almost two years. The long winters preserved his body to some extent, especially since it was high in the mountains where it was frozen for most of the year. At the same time, it's still been subject to the elements and wild animals."

Without fully grasping what she's trying to say, I nod my head and say, "I understand." Hope doesn't say anything.

"All I'm really asking is for you to identify his scar as well as the watch on his wrist."

When we walk in, Jackson is covered with a white sheet. "Are you ready to proceed?" he asks.

I nod my head and say, "I think so." Hope walks up beside me.

They carefully turn Jackson over, including the sheet, to prevent me from seeing his face. I can tell from the scar to the left of his armpit that it has to be Jackson. It looks like the same check mark I've seen so many times.

This all seems so strange. I reach out and gently lay my hand on the sheet covering his body. "Oh, sweetie….oh sweetie," I say with my eyes full of tears.

The medical examiner then moves the blanket just enough to expose his wristwatch, which is dirty and worn. I'm not sure where he got it, but it's the watch he wore the most. For a brief second, I wonder if Hannah gave him the watch.

"Yes, that's his watch," I confirm.

"Are we good here?" Detective Stowe asks.

"I think that's all we can do," she says.

Seeing his lifeless body covered by a sheet, I wonder if this is the last chance I'll ever have to see him—to say goodbye. I turn to Stowe and say, "I want to see him."

The medical examiner steps forward and says, "I don't think that's a good—"

Before he can stop me, I pull the sheet back from his head and look down in horror. It's impossible to tell who, or what, is lying here under this sheet. It doesn't even look like a person.

"God no," I scream when I see what looks like a skull that's completely crushed in with no eyes and most of his face gone. I almost throw up. Hope must have caught a glimpse, because she looks as shocked as I am.

I immediately turn away, I hold on to Hope for support. We walk arm in arm back down the hall. Stowe stops Hope and me and asks if we need help with grief counseling or any other services. Still shocked by the nightmare I just witnessed, I walk out the front door in Hope's arms and collapse in her car.

– CHAPTER 35 –

I'm not the first woman to marry a man who treats her wedding vows more like a guideline than a rule. What is a woman supposed to do after finding out her husband, the man she loves, has been sleeping with another woman for two years? I really believe I could have handled a cheating husband. I could forgive, maybe even forget one day. Maybe I would have filed for divorce and started all over again. But to discover he has another wife, another house, another baby, and a whole other life? To find out he's been stealing millions of dollars from his company? And now to learn he's been dead the whole time? There's no instruction manual to tell you what to do.

How do I tell my little girl her daddy is gone—and he's never coming back? I sit down on the floor and pull Bonnie to me. As I rock her back and forth in my arms and stroke her hair with my hand, I try to explain how daddy is gone, and he's not coming back home. Her eyes turn red and her chin quivers. I hold her tight while she cries…and then I cry. I tell her everything's going to be alright, but the truth is things won't be alright…ever again. All the anger, all the hurt, all the pain I felt for Jackson disappears in that moment. All I feel is the pain my little girl is feeling.

Jackson's funeral is a pretty low-key affair. There are three rows of chairs and most are empty. Jackson's brother is his only family member present. I sit on the front row holding our baby boy with Bonnie sitting between Hope and me. Bonnie cries when she sees the beautiful casket I chose sitting there covered in flowers.

A picture of Jackson in a blue suit sits beside the casket. This is the Jackson I want to remember. This is the dad I want my kids to remember.

In the middle of the service, a black limousine pulls up to the gravesite and stops on the side of the road. I wait for someone to get out, but the door never opens. The dark, tinted window rolls down just enough to hear the preacher talk about God's love and forgiveness.

I know who's inside. I have a son, and she has a daughter who will never know her daddy. I'm sure her pain is just as real as mine. I turn around and motion for her to take a seat next to me, but she never gets out of the car.

When the service is over, I turn to Hope and say, "It's Hannah."

"What?"

"It's Hannah in the limousine."

I figure Hannah wants to spend a moment with the man she believed was her husband. I get up from my chair and walk to the limousine to let her know she can come to the casket. As I get closer, she rolls up the limousine window and drives away. For some reason, she doesn't even want to talk to me.

– CHAPTER 36 –

Flint wakes up when his phone rings for the second time. Right when it's about to go to voicemail again, he realizes it's his lawyer calling.

"Hello," Flint answers, sounding tired and grumpy.

"Mr. Flint, this is Tracy, with your attorney's office. I was just calling to remind you that you have to be in court on Thursday at nine o'clock in the morning."

"Thursday," Flint mumbles, rubbing the sleep from his eyes. "Okay."

"Have a good day."

Tracy knows all too well how difficult Flint can be. Just when she thinks she made a clean getaway, in the same rude voice, he says, "Hold your horses there. I need to talk to my lawyer."

Instead of just hanging up like she never heard him, Tracy says, "Hold on a minute. Let me see if he's available."

Flint lies in bed with the phone to his ear for almost fifteen minutes listening to light elevator music, before Fanning comes on saying, "This is Whitney Fanning."

"Shit Fanning, I was on hold for thirty minutes."

"Sorry about that. I was with a client. How—"

"I'm a client, for God's sake," Flint grunts.

"Of course, you're a client. That's why we called. We don't randomly call people off the street to be in court. How can I help you?"

"Did you talk to the prosecutor?"

"Not really. I was in court yesterday on another case and said, "C'mon, he's an old man—give him a break.""

"And…"

"She just looked at me like I was crazy."

"Are they going to revoke my bond?" Flint asks.

"That's what they're requesting. We'll see."

"What do you think?"

"I can't tell you for sure. I'll argue that you've made all your court appearances, you have ties to this community, and you're seventy-two years old, so you're not a flight risk. But the prosecutor will say you showed up because the case wasn't too strong. Now, with the evidence they seized, you're sure to flee."

"Cut the crap, Fanning. Is the judge going to revoke my bond?"

"There's a good chance."

"Then I want a continuance."

"I can't. They wanted this heard weeks ago, and I kept putting them off. There's no way they'll agree to a continuance. Plus, I have to be there on another case."

"Tell the court we need more time to prepare, or there's a missing witness, or some shit."

Fanning, exhausted with this entire conversation, says, "Fine, I'll file the motion, but I wouldn't count on it."

Once Flint hangs up the phone, he sits on the side of his bed, contemplating everything. *What the hell's the matter with people these days?* He looks at the receiver and says, "Piece of shit lawyer."

Flint has no doubt Ryan Brunick would have found some way out of this mess—some witness, or piece of evidence, or some statute, to make this all go away. This jackass lawyer doesn't have any idea what the hell he's doing.

– CHAPTER 37 –

Flint wants to make sure whatever happens to him, Ryan Brunick gets what he's due. No matter how long it takes, or how much it costs, Ryan will pay for what he did.

Flint calls Jesse Garcia—the only person he can rely on for things like this. Jesse proved long ago he's as loyal as they come. He'd rather go to prison than be a rat—even that time when it meant going to prison for ten years.

"Jesse, Tom Flint here."

"Yes sir, Mr. Flint. How can I help you?"

"You in town?"

"Sure," Jesse answers.

"How would you like to meet for a cup of coffee?"

"Meet for a cup of coffee" has always been their code word for them to meet at a little Mexican restaurant in Alice, Texas, to discuss business.

"No problem, Mr. Flint. See you there in two hours."

Two hours later, Flint walks into the restaurant he's known all his life. He's personal friends with the owners. The place looks like the kind of Mexican food restaurant you'd find in Mexico. The walls are painted red, orange and yellow; there're sombreros hanging on the walls; red and green lights are strung along the back wall; and each table has salt and pepper shakers inside Jose Cuero beer bottles.

Flint nods at the cashier and walks right through all the regular tables to a room in the back where they usually hold parties, banquets, and other large get-togethers. Jesse is sitting at a little table in the back near a window. The curtain next to the table is pulled shut.

"Jesse," Flint says with a firm handshake.

"Mr. Flint," Jesse responds, pointing to the chair across from him.

Right about then, the waitress walks up with a basket of tortilla chips and a red bowl of homemade salsa. They both order a margarita—none of this Tex/Mex crap, but the kind of 'rita you get in Mexico. It's mostly Agave tequila with a splash of lime juice and salt on the rim of the glass. It's not smart for anyone to drink more than two.

Once the waitress disappears out the door, Jesse says, "How's it going, Flint?"

"It's all shit," Flint says.

Jesse leans closer and asks, "What's all this news with that Zach boy?"

"That's what I want to talk to you about."

"That was clean as a whistle. What the hell happened?"

"We have a problem. His name is Ryan Brunick….you ever heard of him?"

Jesse shakes his head.

"Well, he was the reason I had you take care of Zach. It was all because of him. Well, the sum bitch got cold feet and called Zach—gave him the heads up you were coming. What'd Zach do? That idiot sent a letter to the cops letting them know if anything happened to him, it was me who did it."

"Shit," Jesse says.

Both Flint and Jesse take a sip of their rita. Jesse leans forward and says, "So what? You know me, it was clean…..not a trace. They won't find a fingerprint or a drop of DNA anywhere. You're good, Mr. Flint. They can't do nothing."

"Well, now they have some evidence tying me to it. It's something I have to deal with."

"So, you need my help?"

"Not with that. I need you to take care of Ryan Brunick."

"Another suicide?" Jesse asks.

"I don't give two shits how it's done. I just want it to be painful. Burn him, cut off some fingers, stick a cattle prod up his ass. Just make sure you send a message to all future rats what happens when you run your mouth."

"No problem, Mr. Flint."

"Just one thing….he's in Zurich."

"Zurich, Texas," Jesse asks.

"Where the hell is Zurich, Texas?" Flint asks. "No, we tracked him down in Zurich, Switzerland."

"Switzerland?" Jesse asks. "I don't know about this."

"I'll make it worth your while," Flint says. "I'll pay you twelve thousand."

"Twelve thousand?" Jesse says, "I've never been to Switzerland. I want fifty thousand.".

Flint came with fifteen thousand dollars. That's five thousand more than he paid last time. He was prepared to pay all the money before anything happened to him, but he never expected this.

"Fifty thousand!" Flint says louder than he wanted to. He leans in and almost whispers, "Good God, Jesse."

"You want me to go all the way to Ireland, Mr. Flint?"

"Switzerland," Flint says.

"You know me. You want it clean? You want to make sure no one will rat you out? I need a lot more than twelve thousand….and I'll need a fake passport."

"Sure, but fifty thousand?"

Then get someone else," Jesse says, getting up.

Flint reaches out to keep Jesse from leaving. Once he sits back down in his chair, Flint breaks a chip in half and dips it in the salsa while he contemplates the cost. He still has plenty of money in his cooler, but he's never been one to throw money all over the place.

"Fine, fifty thousand," Flint says, "but like I said, I want to make sure I get every penny's worth, you understand?"

"No problem. I'll bring you ten fingers and toes—my gift to you."

"Thanks, Jesse," Flint says, peeking through the curtains to make sure no strange cars are waiting outside.

"Did you bring the money?" Jesse asks.

Flint reaches in his pocket and pulls out an envelope with fifteen thousand dollars inside. He slides it to Jesse under the table and says, "Not that much. Here's a down payment. Meet me tomorrow at two o'clock at my fishing spot by that old mesquite tree. I'll have the rest of your money."

Jesse puts the envelope in his pocket in such a subtle manner you'd never know anything happened. He takes a drink of his margarita and says, "Damn, that's strong."

Flint hasn't touched his drink yet. He drinks half of it down without so much as a flinch.

"Listen Jesse, I might be going away for a while. No matter what happens to me, I want you to take care of Ryan. You understand?"

"You know me, Mr. Flint. Have I ever let you down?"

"That's why you're here," Flint says.

"You get me the fifty thousand and I'll take care of this Ryan idiot."

"One thing," Flint says. "He's going by Richards…Scott Richards. Tomorrow, I'll give you his passport and birth certificate."

"Richards….Ryan…he can go by Santa Claus for all I care. I'll take care of them all."

Flint stands up and slaps Jesse on the shoulder. "That's my man," he says with a grin.

He stands up and walks out of the restaurant without finishing his drink. When he opens the front door, he looks all around to make sure the coast is clear. He does this a lot nowadays. He gets in his pickup and drives away satisfied Jesse will handle the job.

– CHAPTER 38 –

For the most part, today's just another day at the courthouse. It's mostly a bunch of routine hearings except for one custody trial down the hall, and a DWI trial a couple of floors down.

Fanning meets briefly with the prosecutor and asks one last time if he'll agree to twenty-five years. When the prosecutor practically laughs at the idea, Fanning asks about thirty years.

The prosecutor hands Fanning the updated motion to revoke Flint's bond and says, "You might want to review our motion. We got everything on your guy. It's as good as a confession."

Fanning sits in the jury box and reads the motion that outlines the evidence. Recovered during the search of Flint's office. "I'll be damned," he says, as he flips from one page to the next. After scanning the last page, he closes his eyes and whispers, "What an idiot!"

The court calls, "The State of Texas vs. Thomas Wayne Flint."

Fanning looks up and walks to the bench. *It's gonna take everything I've got to pull this one off.* "Good morning, Judge," he begins.

"Ah…Mr. Fanning. Good to see you today," the judge says with a smile.

"Nice to see you too, Your Honor."

"So, what is the hearing about today?" the judge asks.

"The prosecutor walks forward, lays the Motion to Revoke on the judge's bench, and says, "Your Honor, the state is asking the court to revoke the Defendant's Bond."

"Didn't the court already rule on this matter?" the judge asks.

Fanning jumps to his feet and says, "Exactly, Your Honor. As the court will recall, we had an extensive hearing on this matter. The prosecutor wants two bites of the same apple."

"Has Mr. Flint violated the terms of his bond?" the judge asks.

The prosecutor steps forward and says, "We have new—"

"Has he violated the terms of his probation?" the judge repeats.

"Before the prosecutor can respond, Fanning says, "Absolutely not. He's complied with all the conditions you set out."

"Has he missed any of his court dates?"

"No sir," Fanning continues. "He's shown up at every appearance date."

The judge, appearing irritated, looks at the prosecutor and says, "I've already ruled on this matter. I've got a full docket. If the defendant is complying, then I don't know why we're even here today."

The prosecutor holds his motion up in the air and says, "Your Honor, there was a search of Mr. Flint's home, recovered in the search is—"

Fanning raises his own stack of papers and says, "Just to make the court aware, we plan on challenging that search and everything recovered from the search. There was no probable cause for the search warrant…none. The state relied on an anonymous, unreliable informant who they can't even name. I've set the hearing on my motion for August fifth, and I'm asking the court to sign an order barring any further examination of any documents or records until the court can rule on my motion, including any appeal….if necessary."

"Very well," the judge says. "Bring me your motion."

The judge spends the next ten minutes flipping through each page, including the attached cases and affidavits. Halfway through, the prosecutor says, "Your Honor, the state"

The judge raises his hand to cut him off while he's reading. Fanning shakes his head, like he can't believe anyone could be so stupid. When the judge finally looks up, he asks, "Mr. Fanning, do you have an order for me to sign?"

After Fanning hands him the order, the judge asks the prosecutor, "Have you reviewed this motion and the order?"

"Yes, Judge, we got it yesterday evening."

"Do you have any problem with the order?"

"The order looks fine, but we don't agree with the motion."

"Counselor, I'm not ruling on the veracity of the search. I don't know who this informant is. I'm sure you'll have plenty to say about it on the fifth. That's what….six, seven weeks away? All this does is maintain the status quo until I can hear this matter in a few weeks. I would have this informant in court if I were you. If the order looks fine, then I'm prepared to sign it."

Fanning picks up his briefcase, sets it on the table, and locks his file inside. He can barely hide the smile on his face as he waits for the judge to return the order. Then the judge stops, sets down his pen, and asks, "Mr. Fanning, where's your client?"

Fanning already knows Flint is not in the courtroom. He tried to call him before the hearing, but both of his calls went to Flint's voicemail. Then he called his office and told his secretary to call Flint.

He looks around the courtroom like it's the first time he's even thought about it. "I....I don't see him, Your Honor."

"Have you talked to him, Mr. Fanning?"

"I spoke to him on Tuesday," Fanning answers.

"Did you let him know he had court today?"

"I did, Your Honor."

The judge turns to the bailiff and says, "Go out in the hall and call the Defendant's name three times. Mr. Fanning, you might want to try to reach your client as well."

As the bailiff walks out of the courtroom, Fanning pulls out his cell phone and calls Flint one last time. Again, the call goes to his voicemail. Everyone in the courtroom can hear the bailiff yell, "Mr. Thomas Wayne Flint." There is a brief pause before he again yells, "Thomas Wayne Flint.....is Thomas Wayne Flint here?"

The bailiff returns to the courtroom and the judge asks, "Did you announce for the Defendant three times?"

"Yes, Sir," the bailiff answers.

"And did anyone answer?"

"No, Sir."

The judge turns his attention back to the file on his desk. "Well, this changes things," he says, writing on the docket sheet. He then looks across the courtroom and announces, "The court hereby grants the State's Motion to Revoke Bond. The Defendant, Thomas Wayne Flint's bond is hereby revoked. A warrant is issued for the arrest of Mr. Flint."

At a time like this, Fanning usually has a lot of sympathy for his client. He might even argue for the court to give him more time to locate his client and come in by agreement. Mr. Flint, however, has been nothing but a rude pain in the ass. Fanning wasn't at all surprised when he failed to show up today after reading all about the documents seized from Flint's office. Deep down inside, he knows Flint will soon be right where he belongs.

The prosecutor wastes no time getting the arrest warrant to the Sheriff's Office downstairs. He practically runs through the halls. He walks in the door out of breath with the judge's order in his hand. "I need you to execute this warrant immediately," he says leaning over the counter. "Bring plenty of backup."

Grace Kennedy,
— Day 558

– CHAPTER 39 –

Every time I go into my closet, I'm reminded of Jackson and the life I thought we had together. Two months after his funeral, I decide it's time to take his clothes out of the closet and put some of his belongings in storage.

Holding a pile of shirts in my arms, I can smell Jackson all over them. Sorting through his shirts, and pants, and socks, and underwear, something happens I never expected. It hits me how long we've been together, and how alone I am now. I lived with his fragrance for years. Now I have no one to talk to, no one to come home to, no one to hold, and no one to make love to me. I actually start missing him.

Sitting in my closet, my rage turns into a deep, deep depression. I put the kids to bed, go back into our closet, and open the shoebox full of all the cards and letters Jackson and I gave each other over the years. I sit on the floor and read every card going all the way back to the first year we were together. Good thing I didn't read these cards a month ago. I would have thrown them all in the trash. Now that Jackson's gone, they're all I have left of him.

When I finish the last card, I lie down on the floor and cry. Hope walks into the bedroom and asks, "Grace…are you okay?"

With my face covered in tears, I'm still holding the first card I ever got from Jackson.

I sit up and say, "You know, dad and mom got divorced. I didn't want that. I didn't want it for my kids and I didn't want it for myself. Jackson and I promised each other that we'd be different. We'd beat the odds. We swore we'd make this marriage work and love each other forever."

Hope sits down beside me and says, "I'm really sorry."

"You know, the whole time growing up, Mom and Dad were so romantic. They were always giving each other cards and flowers; always holding hands everywhere we went. They'd kiss in front of us and leave on Friday or Saturday night for their date nights alone. Dad couldn't keep his hands off her. Colt and I would always say, 'Get a room.'"

I wipe away my latest tear and say, "They really loved each other."

Hope pulls her knees close and says, "I never saw any of that."

"Christmas and birthdays were always so special. They made sure *all* holidays were special. This is what I wanted for my family."

Hope takes the card from my hand and asks, "Are these the cards you and Jackson gave each other?"

A smile fills my tear-stained face as I reach down and pick up the first card I gave Jackson so many years ago.

"I never told you about this," I say. "Right after Jackson and I got married, we went to dinner on Valentine's Day. I looked on the Internet to find the most romantic restaurant in Austin and made reservations. I wanted everything to be special. It was silly, really. I went and got my nails done and pulled my hair back to look really beautiful. I bought this red dress—you know, my dress that zips up in the back?"

When Hope shakes her head, I say, "Anyway, I went to Victoria's Secret and got this tiny, sexy, see-through teddy and matching panties for later."

Hope sits here, listening as I continue.

"Well, we ate dinner, drank wine, and ordered this little Valentine's cake. It was white with pink roses on the side. After the waiter set the cake down between us, I handed Jackson this big red envelope with the card I spent over an hour at the store picking out. I wrote this long note inside the card about how much I loved him and how happy I was to be his wife. It filled up the whole card. Then I gave him a gift in a little bag covered in red and white tissue paper with a pretty red bow. Inside was this stupid needlepoint I spent three weeks making. It was all about how much I love him. I told him he could put it on his wall at his office."

I see the hint of a smile on Hope's face as she starts to tear up listening to my story.

"Do you know what he got me for Valentine's?" I ask.

Hope looks in my eyes, waiting for my answer.

"Nothing…not a card, not a gift, not a single flower. After he read my card and opened my present, he sat at the table with this look on his face…a look that told me he brought nothing."

"Figures," Hope says.

"He was so embarrassed that he showed up empty-handed. He looked across the table and said, 'I'm so sorry baby…I…I just didn't know.'"

Hope reaches over and gives me a hug.

"I kept telling him it was no big deal—that it's not about the present. As hard as I tried to convince him, I think he could see the disappointment on my face."

"We went home, and from the bathroom I said, 'I have something else for you.'"

"'More?' he said like this is his worst nightmare."

"I walked out in my little nightgown and we made love. Still lying there on top of me, he brushed my hair out of my eyes and said, 'Grace, I'm so sorry about the present thing.'"

"It looked like he was going to cry. I kissed his eye and said, 'I love you, sweetie. I don't need gifts. I love you no matter what you do. I'll always love you no matter what.'"

Hope sits there beside me, wondering why I'm saying these things. I wipe my eyes clear and pick up two cards off the floor before continuing the story. I hand both cards to Hope and say, "My birthday came around two months later and these are the two cards he gave me. He showed up with a birthday card and a giant Valentine's Day card. The Valentine's Day card was covered with 'I love you' written over and over again across the whole card. He gave me more presents, so beautifully wrapped, than I've ever received in my life."

With a little laugh, Hope says, "That's saying a lot given the gifts dad would always give us for our birthdays."

My lips start trembling, as I do my best not to start crying all over again.

"From that day on, whether it was Valentine's Day, Easter, Christmas, my birthday, or our anniversary, it didn't matter. He never showed up empty-handed again. It was so funny," I laugh. "He showed up on Thanksgiving with a handmade card, and this time I was the one with nothing. We agreed—no more cards on Thanksgiving."

Both Hope and I laugh together.

"You know, we built a life together. There were so many good times. Jackson was there when I graduated from college, and when I got my job at the hospital. I was so proud when he was named the CFO at his company. We went to the French Room to celebrate. We ordered the most expensive bottle of wine they had."

Hope doesn't know what to say. I stay on the floor, slumped over, gazing down at my feet. There's a mist covering my eyes, and my voice is mild, showing my loneliness.

"Remember when we moved to Dallas? I was so afraid—afraid to move away from my family. I told Jackson I didn't want to move, but he was right—it wasn't that far, and we were starting our own family now. We built this beautiful house and together we made it our home."

"It was the happiest day of our life when Bonnie was born. You know, he was the only one in the delivery room when Bonnie and Wesley were born."

Hope stares at me in silence.

"She was the first grandchild…for both families. I thought our parents would get into a fistfight over who got to keep her first."

"I remember," Hope laughs. "I was first in line."

"You don't know what it's like to see your own child take her first step, or say mamma and daddy, or go to her first day of kindergarten."

We sit here in silence. I take a deep breath and exhale.

"Good times and bad…right?" I ask, wiping my eyes. "When his mom had breast cancer, I sat at the hospital for weeks before she died."

I pause for a few seconds to collect myself.

"God, how I loved her. She was the mom I never had. I loved his dad, too. When he died of a heart attack a year later, it was almost like my own father died." Still looking down, I say, "He wouldn't have done this. His parents loved me too much. He wouldn't have done this if his parents were still alive. "

Hope lays her hand on my leg and says, "Don't do this to yourself."

"You know, he was a witness to my past. He knew me before I was a doctor—when I was a silly little college girl. He knew my dad. We were just kids and became adults. Together we learned about life…and love. I can never say that about anyone else I'm with."

Hope rubs my leg and says, "I know what you're saying, but he ruined all that. He had everything but he, he….he threw it away. He was the one who—"

"Not really," I say, stopping her. I turn slightly towards her and say, "You know, I've blamed him for everything, but the truth is, it's not that simple. It wasn't all his fault."

Hope gives me this puzzled look.

"The last three years were so hard. When you almost died from that overdose, it hurt me so bad. I stayed at the hospital the whole time; afraid I was going to lose my best friend. The whole time you were in rehab, you were all I could think about…all I could talk about."

Now a tear rolls down Hope's face.

"Then Bonnie fell into the swimming pool and almost died. I spent the next months taking off work at the hospital and going back and forth to doctors, and therapists, and doing all this testing. On top of this, I still had Wesley to take care of. I had no time for Jackson. He was busy at work, and I was busy working and running around all over the place. We were lucky if we even ate dinner together."

Hope looks at me, trying to understand where I'm going with this.

"He complained….he complained that we never had sex, which of course, I denied. He said, 'Oh yeah, then tell me the last time we've had sex.' You know, I couldn't even remember. He closed his eyes, and said, 'Grace, we didn't even have sex on my birthday.'"

"I don't know what the hell happened to me. I used to love sex—I couldn't get enough. Between work, and Bonnie, and Wesley, I was just so exhausted all the time. I didn't have time to think about sex. Eventually, Jackson just stopped asking and stopped complaining."

"When you came back from Thailand and told me how mom died in that prison, it hit me—but not the way it hit you. After watching mom after the divorce, I was determined not to do the same thing to my kids. I'd be supermom. I became so obsessed with Bonnie and Wesley. I spent all my free time with them."

"You're a great mom," Hope says.

"Then you found that fucking watch. I couldn't believe he'd do it. I don't know if I was more angry at what he did to mom or what he did to me. I loved him so much, and now things would never be the same between us again. I wanted to talk to Jackson about it, but I couldn't. He looked at my family like we were all crazy or something—like there was this curse over our family that he didn't want on his. I think it was just too much for him. Then, just when I thought it couldn't get any worse, dad was killed in that car wreck."

"But, isn't that why you get married?" Hope asks. "I carry you when you're down, and you carry me when I'm down?"

"Maybe that's how it's supposed to be, but I don't think it usually works out that way. I was devastated…and I pushed him away. Jackson kept saying dad got what he deserved. Every time he said it, it would infuriate me. We fought about it…we fought about everything. We fought all the time. It seemed like the only thing we could agree on was yelling and screaming at each other."

"A couple years ago, we had this big fight about the amount of time he spends at work. He just missed Bonnie's class party after missing her school play two weeks earlier. I told him he loved his job more than he loved his own children. I told him how my dad went to everything—it didn't matter what it was. Well, this was the wrong thing to say. Jackson went on and on, yelling how sorry Dad was. It was just too much. He knew…he knew how much I loved Dad and how bad his words hurt. It was like 'open the wound and pour in the salt.' I broke…I just broke. I…."

"You what?" Hope asks.

"I screamed…I lunged for his face."

Hope gasps with her eyes open wide.

"He held me back while I went off on him. Words I should have choked on came pouring out of my mouth. I told him I hated him. I said dad begged me to make this marriage work, and the only reason I stayed with him these past few years is because of my dad. Now that dad's gone, I told him I didn't want to be married to him anymore. I told him I wanted a divorce."

Hope gives that face—you know, that face that says, "Ouch!"

I cover my face with my hands, look down, and say, "I don't know how everything got so crazy. I loved him. God, I loved that man. I would have loved him forever."

We sit there in silence. Finally, I look down at all the cards on the floor and say, "It's easy for me to sit here and blame him for everything, but it's not all his fault. I did my part too. I think we just took each other for granted—we took our love for granted. Now…now that love is gone. I have this hole in my heart, and I don't know what to do. Sometimes I hate him so much. Other times I miss him…or I miss what we had."

For the first time, I decide to tell Hope everything. I take a deep breath and hold it for a second. Looking away, I say, "Hope, there's something I have to tell you that no one knows." Hope sits there waiting for me to continue. Finally, I look at her and say, "God, I don't know how to say this."

Hope lays over me and whispers, "Don't blame yourself, Grace. You were a good wife. It's not your fault."

"Does it really matter now?" I ask, tearing up again. "Does it matter whose fault it is? I'm alone. He's gone and I'm all alone. My kids will grow up without their daddy. His fault….my fault…I don't give a damn. I'm tired of hating. I'm tired of being alone. I'd give anything to have him back one more time and tell him how sorry I am for what I did."

Hope leans over and holds me in her arms. "You've got me," she says with a squeeze. "You'll always have me."

– CHAPTER 40 –

Flint's been to court enough to know even the best lawyer can't get him out of this fix. The box of evidence the police took from his office lays everything out. It was all in there. Flint knows once he's taken into custody, he'll never see the light of day again.

Right now, what Flint wants more than anything is a little peace and quiet. He needs a little time to get right with the Lord—like one of those sinners-on-the-cross kind of stories.

He drives his pickup truck to this fishing creek in Duval County, just a few miles outside of town. He parks off the side of the road and walks down to his favorite spot underneath the mesquite tree. After living in the county most of his life, Flint knows the fish tend to gather under the shade of this tree. He always feels closer to the Lord here.

Exactly twenty feet from the tree is a large rock that marks the spot where Flint buried all that money. He grabs his shovel and digs, until he hears the thump of the Yeti cooler. Once he has everything he needs, he covers the cooler with dirt again and replaces the large rock over it. Not a soul on this earth knows about this spot and the small fortune hidden there. It isn't even mentioned in his will. The way Flint sees it, some lucky fisherman will stumble upon it one day. Yeah, that's probably best.

Someone who loves to fish in a creek under his favorite mesquite tree deserves the money as much as anyone.

The fish aren't biting at all, so Flint sits beside the creek, drinking cold Lone Star Beer and shots of Jim Beam. For Flint, it's not so much about catching fish, anyway. It's about enjoying this cool October day.

Flint has never been one of those kind of men who are troubled by the things they do. By his count, he's killed six men and one boy. This total doesn't include the three fellas he killed after they shot at him first. Those killings were completely legal. The seven not-so-legal killings aren't as bad as it might sound at first, because three of those men who he killed were shot together on the same night. He prides himself on the fact he's never killed a woman—although several needed a good killing.

There's one killing, just one, that won't just fade away like all the others. It was October 20, 1969. Flint suddenly realizes today is the anniversary of that terrible night. Flint remembers this guy's first name was Brian, but he can't remember his last name to save his life. The whole name thing might be hazy, but Flint remembers the rest of the night like it happened yesterday.

Brian was this teenage boy who came back from college and was trying to get everyone all fired up and change the world—or at least the way things had been run in Duval County for the past seventy years. As far as they were concerned, change was coming and it might as well start in Duval County.

Flint warned them—several times—but these kids today are just too hard-headed. Well, the Sheriff's office got a tip these troublemakers were holding another one of their political get-togethers in a little trailer home just outside the city limits. Flint hid his patrol car along the side of the highway and waited for the orange and yellow Volkswagen van covered with "PEACE" and "LOVE" stickers to come by. As soon as the van drove past at a little after midnight, Flint turned on his lights and siren and pulled the kid over on the dark and quiet county highway.

As the Lone Star Beer and Jim Beam take hold of Flint's faculties, and his better judgment, he drifts off to sleep along that little creek. With a cool breeze keeping him sound asleep, Brian is, once again, alive and well in his memory.

Flint walks up from behind Brian's van and looks through the curtains hanging in the back window. He has to make sure he has the right hippie, and that he's all alone. Flint goes around to the driver's side door and hears that hippie music these kids are listening to nowadays blaring from the van. Flint waits there for Brian to roll down his window. Instead, Brian fumbles around in his wallet for his driver's license. Brian finally cracks the window just enough to slide his license out to Flint.

"Hello, Officer Flint," Brian says, like the little smart-ass he is.

"Please turn down the music," Flint commands.

Brian turns down the music and gives a big smile. "Would you prefer a little Hank Williams, Mr. Flint?"

Not amused, Flint asks, "Do you know why I pulled you over?"

"To remind me about the upcoming election?" Brian laughs.

Brian always acts like he's smarter, or more clever, than everyone else in the room. This always gets under Flint's craw.

"Watch your mouth, son," Flint warns.

"Sir, I have no idea why you pulled me over. I believe I was driving under the speed limit."

"I pulled you over for your broken taillight."

"My broken taillight?" Brian says, confused by the accusation. He looks in his rearview mirror like he can actually see the taillight. He rolls his window halfway down and looks back, before saying, "Well, I didn't even know I had a broken taillight. I'll have that looked at."

"Why don't you step out of the vehicle and take a look back here," Flint suggests.

"Well, it's late, and I'd prefer to take care of this tomorrow if you don't mind."

"Well...the problem is...your vehicle is illegal, and I think you've been driving with this illegal vehicle for quite a spell. I can't have you running around our beautiful county in this illegal hippie van—even if it is all marked up with your love and peace stickers."

"Be the change.....right, Mr. Flint?"

"I reckon," Flint answers. "Right now, I'm concerned about your taillight."

"As I said," Brian says like he gets to call all the shots, "I'll have that looked at first thing in the morning. I believe you can issue a citation for a faulty taillight."

"So now you're a goddam lawyer or something?"

"No sir. I'm no lawyer, but I just finished my Constitutional Law class. You probably took the same class to become a police officer."

"My what class?" Flint asks.

"It's just that it's late, and I want to go home and go to bed."

"Please step out of your vehicle," Flint commands.

Brian tries to stand his ground. "I'd prefer to stay right here, if you don't mind. Please issue me your ticket and I'll have the light checked out first thing in the morning."

This was back in 1969, when cell phones and body cameras were a faraway dream. Out here, Flint is God and right now God wants Brian the hell out of the van.

"I don't give a good goddam what you prefer, you little shit. Step out of the van or you and me are gonna get sideways. You understand?"

"No, sir...I'm not getting out of this—"

Right then, Flint unholsters his pistol and shoves it right in Brian's face. Brian, who's always able to remain calm and in control, starts shaking like a leaf on a tree in a Texas tornado.

"Okay," Brian says, raising his hands for Flint to see. "I'll get out."

Brian reaches down and opens his car door. The latch releases, but like most days, the door doesn't open. Brian throws his shoulder hard against the inside of the door, causing it to fly open and hit Flint square against his leg. Brian can't help but grin when Flint loses his balance and falls backwards.

Brian's whole life turns on that one little grin. Flint grabs Brian by the back of his shirt with his nostrils flaring, and throws him out of the van so hard Brian falls to the ground. Still holding his revolver in his right hand, he gives Brian a good kick in the ass, which causes Brian to fall forward towards the back of the van.

This meeting between Brian and Flint has been a long time coming. Now Brian finds himself all alone on a dark Texas highway with the man who's threatened his life on more than one occasion. Brian knows better than to say anything else.

Brian tries to get up from his hands and knees, but Flint grabs a thick head of hair, leans down until his thick, dirty, mustache is touching Brian's ear, and says, "You try to get up one more time, and I'll scatter your brains every which-away."

It's clear to Brian that Flint is speaking like a man who has no doubts. Brian is about five-foot-eight and weighs maybe 145 pounds. Flint is twice as big. He grabs Brian by the back collar, like you might grab a young pup, and drags him between the van and his patrol car.

Right then, another motorist comes driving down the highway towards them with his headlights on high. Just as he passes by, Flint is standing over Brian with his revolver against Brian's head. The driver hits his brakes, causing his pickup truck to come to an abrupt stop about a hundred feet down the road. Flint stands still, waiting on the driver to mind his own damn business and move on down the road.

"Please come back," Brian prays from his knees, as Flint keeps a firm grip on his shirt collar.

Everything seems to freeze in place. Flint keeps Brian's head to the ground, making sure he doesn't do anything stupid. Flint sees the glow of the truck's white brake lights as the driver puts his truck in reverse, The man in the pickup drives back about fifteen feet, and stops again. Flint stands tall, giving a long stare at the driver stopped down the road. The loud sounds of crickets and katydids echo from the barbed wire fields on each side of the highway like they're yelling at the truck driver to keep coming back. It's like a weird modern-day cowboy standoff. Eventually, the brake lights on the pickup dim and the car continues driving down the highway.

"Help me!" Brian screams as loud as he's ever screamed in his life.

Flint brings the butt of his gun down hard on Brian's head with a loud crack. Brian blacks out for a couple of seconds before returning to the side of the road, still in the hands of a maniac.

Brian cries, "Mr. Flint....Mr. Flint I swear I'll never—"

"You talk when you're asked to talk," Flint yells, giving him another ass kick that causes his face to crash against the rocky shoulder.

Flint, more than a hundred pounds heavier than Brian, pulls him further off the road to give them a little more privacy to settle their dispute.

"Can you see the danger your little hippie van here creates to the good people of our county?" Flint asks, taunting Brian.

Brian looks up with blood dripping from the side of his face. The brake light doesn't show so much as a scratch. "I don't see a broken taillight, sir," Brian cries, showing his fear.

"Hey partner, you calling me a liar?" Flint asks. With another kick, he says, "I think you're calling me a liar, you little shit."

"No sir," Brian continues to cry.

Flint takes a step towards the passenger side, lifts up his boot, and crashes his heel against the van's taillight; causing the broken red pieces to fly everywhere.

"You're not such a big shot now, are you, partner?" Flint asks. "Where's all those liberal fliers you been handing out all over town? I bet they're stuffed in the back of your hippie van, aren't they?"

Barely able to talk from his face beginning to swell, Brian mumbles, "Yes sir," hoping this is what Flint's after.

"Well, all your college hippie friends can't help you now. No, it's just you and me all alone here. There's no Constitution class to save you."

Brian knows he's in trouble—big trouble. Holding himself up by his hands and knees, he pleads for his life. "Mr. Flint....I'll leave. I swear to God I'll leave and I'll never come back. Please just—"

The time for talking is over. Flint points his revolver at the back of Brian's head and cocks the trigger.

Hearing the click, Brian yells, "Please Mr. Flint," as blood drips into his mouth. "Don't kill me. I'll do whatev—"

Flint takes his boot and slams it down hard on Brian's back, causing him to collapse on the ground. "Did I tell you to talk?" he yells.

As Flint looks down at Brian doing his best to protect himself from another blow, all the hippies who've been running down his country flash through his mind. He didn't go across the world to fight in Vietnam for these punks to burn flags down at the courthouse. For God's sake, he fought for that flag. His friends died for that flag. Flint puts his finger on the trigger of his thirty-eight special and gives it a squeeze. The boom echoes through the night. A group of cows that had wondered up to find out what was going on take-off across the field.

When Brian heard Flint pull that trigger on his gun, he jerked his head to the left. Instead of shooting Brian in the back of his head, Flint's shot blows off the side of Brian's face. He collapses on the ground and starts gurgling and choking with blood bubbling out of the hole in the side of his mouth where his cheek used to be.

The sight of this boy lying on the side of the road, moaning and crying for his mother, is too much even for Flint. This is what he can't get out of his mind. It's as vivid in Flint's dream forty years later as it was on that very night.

"Oh, good God," Flint says shaking his head in disgust and still feeling no sympathy. Wanting to put an end to this pathetic sight, he bends down, looks right in Brian's face, and says. "Just shut up already."

These are the last words Brian would ever hear.

Flint cocks his gun again and shoots Brian a second time square in the back of his head. Brian's lifeless body lies there on the side of the highway while his blood flows out of his body and into the grass. All the katydids and crickets that were once making so much racket you could barely hear yourself think, go completely silent as if they're shocked at what they just witnessed.

Flint looks down at his smoking gun and sees some of Brian's brain splattered on his hand. He gets back in his car, wipes off the mess with a McDonald's napkin laying underneath his empty hamburger wrapper, and calls dispatch.

"Sharon Jean, I'm gonna need backup out here. One of these punks just tried to jump me."

The shortest verse in the Bible is: "Jesus wept." There's little doubt, Jesus shed a tear or two for Brian that night.

– CHAPTER 41 –

Flint is jarred out of his nap by the sound of sirens coming down the little country road. It sounds like three—maybe four—police vehicles. Then he hears the sound of the police chopper's blades slapping overhead.

There's no way Flint is going back to prison. No, if they want to take him, they're going to have to come and get him. As the sirens get closer and louder, Flint can tell it's more like seven or eight patrol cars. Flint peeks around the tree and sees them all parking along the road about five hundred feet away.

Once everyone's in place, he hears the sound of the caliche crunching under their boots as they walk closer. When they're about half-way to him, they all stop and someone says, "Tom Flint….Tom Flint is that you?"

The man talking sounds so friendly you might think he's a friend who just stopped by so they can fish together; but Flint knows better. He grabs the shotgun leaning against the tree and sets it on his lap. With twelve empty, crushed beer cans floating in his cooler, Flint grabs the bottle of Jim Beam soaking in the cold ice and takes a big drink.

"Mr. Flint, this is Officer Hadaway with the Texas DPS. We have a warrant. Can we come forward?"

Flint takes another big drink and shouts, "No sir, I reckon you should stay right where you are."

"Are you armed, Mr. Flint?" Hadaway asks.

"Yes, sir." Flint answers.

"Take cover," Hadaway shouts to the men behind him. Flint can hear the sound of men running back so fast you might have thought he just announced he has a bomb. "Mr. Flint, we don't want anyone to get hurt now do we? Why don't you come out here so we can talk?"

"Nah," Flint says. "I reckon I'm just fine right where I am."

Hadaway can tell Flint's been drinking—a lot. "Mr. Flint…do you mind if I come a little closer?" he asks.

"I don't reckon that'd be too smart on your part," Flint answers with a little chuckle.

"Okay, okay…I'll just sit right here." Hadaway finds an old tree stump and sits down. Once he's in place, he asks Flint, "You catching any fish?"

How did it all come to this? Flint once ruled this county and now, at seventy-two years old, he doesn't have a wife, a child, a relative, or a single good friend to grieve his passing. He's coming to the end of the line all alone.

"Not a single bite," Flint says.

"What you fishing with?" Hadaway asks.

"You know, mostly worms."

"I'll be damn," Hadaway says.

As Officer Hadaway settles in for a long talk, Flint raises his shotgun to his chin and cocks the trigger. Hadaway raises his hands to get Flint's attention.

"Mr. Flint….Mr. Flint….no need for that. Nothing can be all that bad. We just need to bring you in so you can take care of this little legal matter. I'm sure you can work things out."

"I knew when I fetched up here, you'd be coming," Flint says. "I just wanted to do a little fishin' first."

"When do you think you might be done?"

"I don't know," Flint says. "I reckon it might be a spell."

"I'll wait," Hadaway says, "if you promise not to lollygag."

Flint sits there holding his shotgun in his lap. Surrounded by police officers and a helicopter hovering overhead, he sees no way out. *How did my life go so wrong?* He lays his head back against the tree to stop his head from swirling from the fifth of Jim Beam he just guzzled. Slurring his speech, he says, "I sherved my country."

"What's that?" Hadaway asks.

Flint shouts, "I shays I sherves my country, Gos dammit!"

"What branch?" Hadaway asks.

"Army."

"I'll be damn," Hadaway continues. "I was in the Marines."

Flint is a man of few regrets, but in this moment it'd sure be nice to see his kids one last time—maybe hold his grandbabies. He starts to cry, but stops himself. He hasn't cried in fifty years, and he's damn sure not about to start crying in front of a bunch of fellow officers. Instead, he puts the barrel of his shotgun under his chin and reaches down for the trigger."

"Mr. Flint," Hadaway yells.

Flint closes his eyes tight and pulls the trigger. The shotgun blast is so loud it causes Hadaway to jump.

"Mr. Flint!" Hadaway yells. When there's no answer, he asks, "Mr. Flint, you still with me?"

Unable to see what's going on, Hadaway gets up and walks cautiously towards the tree with the other officers not far behind him. When he gets closer, he calls out one last time, "Mr. Flint, you here?

A couple steps closer, and Hadaway can see Flint's lifeless body hunched over.

"Mr. Flint….you okay?"

Standing next to the tree, it's obvious Flint is dead. There's a large, black hole under his chin and the top of his head is completely blown off.

"Yeah," Hadaway says to his partner. "I told you this old fart wasn't going to prison."

Flint isn't the villain in Duval County that he is around the rest of the state. The only guy from the local Sheriff's Department who knows the area well turns to Hadaway and says, "How fitting."

"What do you mean?" Hadaway asks.

"This reminds me of old George."

"George?"

"You know, old George Parr."

Hadaway shakes his head.

"He and his father ran this place for almost a hundred years. You know….the Duke of Duval?"

Hadaway shakes his head again.

"Anyway, he was convicted of tax evasion, and they sent half the State of Texas out here to get him. He went out to his ranch and shot himself right there in the front seat of his car."

Hadaway kicks a stick out of the way and says, "You know, I think I've heard something 'bout that."

"Him and his father are legends around here. Flint used to work for old George."

Hadaway looks down at his shirt and sees the splatter of blood that hit him. "What a mess," he says, shaking his head.

As the officers investigate the scene, they find Flint's beer cooler full of empty beer cans and an empty fifth of Jim Beam spilled over on its side. Hadaway picks up a blood-spattered envelope sitting next to the cooler and says, "Holy shit!"

"What is it?"

Hadaway thumbs through the stack of hundred-dollar bills stuffed inside and says, "There's a shitload of money here."

"What for?" his partner asks.

"I have no idea. There's nothing written on the envelope."

"Why the hell would he bring so much money to go fishing?"

Hadaway sees a few folded papers in Flint's back pocket. He pulls them out, opens it up, and sees the photocopy of the passport belonging to Scott Edward Richards.

"Any of you fellas know a Scott Edwards Richards?"

All the officers at the scene either shake their heads or shrug their shoulders.

Hadaway shakes his head and says, "Well, it looks like Flint owed Mr. Richards a stack of money. Knowing Flint, it was probably a bribe or something."

To everyone's surprise, underneath the page with the photocopy of the passport is the old tally sheet from the 1948 Senate race between Lyndon Baines Johnson and Coke Stevenson. It's been missing for seventy years.

The last 202 names are all in alphabetical order;

Each entry is written in the same color ink;

All the voters signed in the same handwriting.

The police close off the road to the park and stop all traffic from coming in or out. Twenty minutes later, Jesse Garcia drives up the road and stops at the police roadblock. Once he's beside the officer, he rolls down his window to find out what's going on.

"The road is closed," the officer says. "You gotta turn around."

"I was going to fish for a little bit," Jesse says, pointing to his fishing poles. "Is there another road in?"

"There's no other way in. The park is closed."

Jesse was really counting on the rest of that money. He turns around and heads back to the little Mexican food restaurant where he always meets Flint. He waits for further orders.

After sitting at the restaurant for an hour eating chips and salsa, Jesse calls Flint a couple of times. None of his calls are answered. The next day, Jesse learns from the local newspaper, and all the scuttlebutt around town, that he's never getting his thirty-five thousand dollars.

Whether or not Flint ever got right with God is only known by Flint and the good Lord upstairs.

– CHAPTER 42 –

After two months of legal briefs, depositions, and letters back and forth, we finally go to court for the injunction. The hearing lasts three days and I'm on the stand for most of the third day.

DMD hired some expensive forensic accountants to lay out in a lot of detail how Jackson, through a number of complicated schemes, set up a system to funnel off millions of dollars from the company's accounts receivable. He took a little at a time, without anyone knowing. Their expert goes on and on for hours. I can't really understand what happened; even when he's explaining it to everyone. At one point, I almost fall asleep. My lawyer sits there, barely writing a thing on his legal tablet. I just figured he knows we can't win.

I'm no lawyer, but everything sounds pretty bad. They use the word, "Kennedy" so many times and I'm the only Kennedy in the courtroom. It looks like someone needs to pay for this, and I'm the only someone at the table.

Once this guy is done with all his poster boards, charts and graphs, and pointing at things with his laser pointer, my lawyer gets a chance to ask his questions.

First, we break for lunch. My lawyer sits beside me, eating his tuna fish sandwich, like he doesn't have a care in the world. He never so much as asks for my thoughts or anything. Finally, towards the end of lunch, I say, "That guy seemed really smart."

"Really?" he answers. "I thought he was pretty boring."

That's about all we ever talked about. I didn't know if he had it all under control or, like me, thought the case was hopeless.

Back in the courtroom, he asks their witness the same thing he'll ask every witness, and they all pretty much give the same answers.

"This all sounds like a big mess?"

"Yes, sir, I'd say so."

"Now let me ask you, do you have any reason *whatsoever* to believe Mrs. Kennedy was involved in the theft of DMD's money?"

"No, sir," each witness answers.

"Do you have any reason *whatsoever* to believe Mrs. Kennedy had any knowledge of the theft?"

"No, sir."

"Come on. Before you came all the way in here from….where did you come from again?"

"My office is in New York City."

"Good Lord!" he says, like there's something wrong with this. At this point, I'm still pretty lost. If there's something I need to be doing to help, I'm not sure what it might be.

"Before you came in here today all the way from New York City asking this judge to take every penny this woman (pointing right at me) needs to support her little girl and her newborn baby, surely you found an email proving she knew what was going on here….right?"

"No, sir."

"A phone record?"

"No, sir."

"A text message?"

"No, sir."

"A Post-It?"

This causes the witness to smile before saying, "No sir." Several people behind us laugh at it all.

"Anything?"

"No, sir."

"Do you have a *shred of evidence* that any of the stolen money went into Mrs. Kennedy's account?"

"No, sir."

"Or that she or her family benefited from the money in any way?"

"No, sir."

When the other lawyer was talking, the trial was so boring that the judge and several other people watching the trial actually dozed off. I may have dozed off myself. Now the judge is wide-awake watching every move my lawyer makes. I've gone from thinking I'm going to owe a lot of money to agreeing with my lawyer—what the heck did they sue *me* for?

My lawyer gets this puzzled look on his face and says, "So I've got to ask you, where did all the money go?"

"Well, we haven't figured it all out yet."

"Now when you were sitting in your office there in New York City doing all your calculating, you eventually figured out how the money was taken, right?"

"Oh, yes, sir."

"And how long did it take you to figure out exactly who did what here?"

"I was hired eight months ago."

My lawyer whistles and then shouts, "Eight months!" like it's the biggest number he's ever heard in his life. "And you had a big office, a fancy desk, and all the company books, records, and accounts available to you, right?"

"Yes, sir."

"And everyone at DMD was happy to cooperate with you, right?"

"Yes, sir."

"They gave you whatever you wanted….you know all these poster boards up here and that fancy pointy laser you keep using?"

"Well, we already had the pointy…I mean, the laser pointer," the witness says.

"Anyway, it sounds like a daunting task. I bet you earned every penny you were paid."

"I would say so. It was a very complicated scheme."

"By the way, how much were you paid?"

"I'm not really sure. I'm not involved in accounts receivable."

"Well, how much has your office billed so far?"

"Approximately one hundred and eighty thousand."

"Two hundred thousand, and you still can't find the money?"

"No, sir."

"And what school did you go to?"

The guy looks at the judge with a smile and says, "I graduated from Harvard with a Master's Degree in—"

"Harvard! Way up there in Massachusetts?"

"Yes, sir, Boston."

"Master's Degree, huh?"

"Yes, sir."

"And, if it took a smart guy like you eight months to figure it all out, do you *really* think this little woman (pointing right at me again), who spends her days at the hospital right down the street from here in Dallas, Texas, helping sick folks get better, would have any idea what the heck is going on?"

"I can't say what she knew."

"Exactly!" my lawyer shouts.

Now I look around and can tell my lawyer has the whole courtroom captivated. I've been sitting here with my pad in front of me doing nothing, so I write, "LAWYER SAID EXACTLY!" on my pad.

"Have you given recommendations on how to end this complicated scheme so it never happens again?"

"Oh, yes sir."

"And did they do it?"

"Absolutely."

"And all those company executives down at DMD could have put those same policies and procedures—your recommendations—in place *before* the theft and prevented this whole thing from happening, right?"

The guy looks over at DMD's lawyers like he doesn't know what to say. He looks like he wishes he never came today. Finally, he sits back, shrugs, and says, "Uh.....probably so,"

"So, I have to ask you....how much of the stolen money is DMD asking those company executives and their wives and families to pay back?"

The witness looks back at the other lawyer again, hoping for some guidance. All three lawyers are looking down. When he doesn't answer, my lawyer says, "Well, I've looked over hundreds, if not thousands, of documents. They filed everything imaginable against this little lady, but and I don't see a single document asking this judge to freeze all *their* accounts."

"I don't know what the lawyers filed," he says.

My lawyer looks around the room and says, "Where are *their* wives? I don't see them sitting here like some kind of criminal."

After some objections that I don't understand, my lawyer says, "Let me ask you one last thing. You'd agree with me that if these DMD executives over here screwed up—dropped the ball—that's between them and DMD. It has nothing to do with their wives who are at home taking care of the little ones....right?"

He looks over at the other table, back at the judge, and says, "I guess not."

"Nothing further," my lawyer says with a smile like he's the nicest, friendliest man you'd ever want to meet. "Thank you for coming here today,"

In the end, the judge denies the injunction and issues an order preventing DMD from touching any of my money or Jackson's retirement.

The IRS is another matter altogether. Mr. Wood hired the best tax attorney in town. The IRS agent handling my case, who was once so hard and absolute, now seems to soften just a bit. At the beginning of our first meeting, I got the feeling my lawyer was a personal friend of his.

Every time we meet, my lawyer throws around the words "innocent spouse" again and again. It's not until our third meeting that I learn what it all means. I'm the innocent spouse. It was Jackson who stole the money without my knowledge, and Jackson prepared and filed the family tax returns. I signed them without even reading what the accountant prepared. As an innocent spouse, so I'm not responsible for him failing to report the stolen money that I knew nothing about. As an innocent spouse, and my money can't be seized because I'm innocent. The IRS finally released their lien and I never hear from them again.

The bill collectors, who keep calling my house at all times of the day, are met with the same thing. My attorney sends them each a 'CEASE AND DESIST" letter, threatening to sue if they dare call me again.

When the whole thing started, the calls, and letters, and lawsuits were more than I could handle. First, I lost my husband and now I have to deal with this? I was sure I'd be filing for bankruptcy. Now, one step at a time, I can breathe again.

– CHAPTER 43 –

. Love and hate are very similar emotions, and I'm living proof of that. I spend half my time hating Jackson, and everything he did to me, and the other half missing the man I dedicated my life to. Sometimes I wish I never met him, and other times I wish we could go back and start all over again.

I'm standing over the stove, making mashed potatoes to go with the chicken in the oven, when I hear Hope yell from the living room with an urgency you'd use if the house was on fire, "Grace, get in here."

"What's wrong?" I answer, hurrying to the living room as fast as I can and drying my hands on a dishtowel.

Sitting in front of the television with the news on, she repeats, "Get in here quick. You've gotta' see this."

"BREAKING NEWS" scrolls across the bottom of the television. Hope turns up the volume just in time for us to hear the news reporter say,

"We have breaking news in a story we first brought you over a year ago. As you recall, we brought you the story of the Dallas Executive, Jackson Kennedy, who went missing from his home in Highland Park, a suburb north of Dallas. Jackson's body was discovered deep in the Rocky Mountains after an apparent hiking accident. Well, in a stunning turn of

events, today the police have arrested Hannah Kennedy, the twenty-eight-year-old wife, or mistress, of Mr. Kennedy."

The reporter next shows Hannah in handcuffs, being escorted from her house—the house I've been to twice now. She's holding her head down, trying to hide her face from the cameras.

"Holy shit," Hope screams. "She killed him."

"Oh my God," I whisper, seeing my friend in handcuffs.

We stay in front of the television, waiting to hear more. When we flip to another station, all the news channels are showing the same coverage of Hannah getting arrested. After about an hour, the news goes to Dallas where Stowe is giving a press conference.

"After a thorough investigation, the Dallas Homicide Unit has reason to believe Mr. Kennedy's death was not an accident. The evidence leads us to believe that his death was a homicide. Tonight we've executed an arrest warrant for Hannah Kennedy."

"What was Mrs. Kennedy's relationship to Jackson Kennedy?" the reporter asks.

"Hannah Kennedy and Jackson Kenney were married a year before his death."

"Has she confessed?" someone asks.

"The evidence leads to only one conclusion. Mr. Jackson was killed and Hannah Kennedy was involved in the murder. Mrs. Kennedy has requested a lawyer, and we have honored her request."

"It can't be true," I say, shaking my head and covering my mouth with my hand. "I know her. I know she couldn't do this."

"I knew it all along," Hope practically yells.

"No…she didn't do it," I insist. "I know she didn't do it."

When I call the Sheriff's Office in Aspen, I find out Hannah is being held at the local jail. Inmates can make calls but can't receive them, so I catch a flight to Aspen to visit her. After passing through security and leaving my belongings in a little locker, I wait on a stool in front of a window with a phone hanging to my right.

Hannah walks into the visitation room wearing orange pants, an orange top, and flip-flops. It's hard to see her looking like a criminal. I know it must be hard for her to come to the window.

The second she sees me; she looks down in embarrassment. She sits down on the stool and hangs her head before finally picking up the phone hanging on the other side wall.

"You, okay?" I ask into the receiver.

She nods her head, doing her best not to cry.

"I came as soon as I saw it on the news."

"My arrest was all over the news?" she asks.

"It's all over everywhere—every channel."

"I've been charged with murder…murder!" she says.

"I know. That stupid detective got on television and told everyone you're guilty."

"I don't even know why I'm here, Grace. On the day Jackson disappeared, I was going—"

"Stop….Stop," I say, holding up my hand. "Don't ever talk about your case in here. All your calls in jail are being monitored—all of them. Have you talked to anyone else?"

"Just my mom."

"Oh God, did you talk to her about the case…about everything you were doing?"

"I just told her I'm innocent; but she already knows that. We mostly talked about Savannah."

"Good, never talk to anyone about your case while you're in jail except your lawyer. Nothing you say to him is being recorded."

"I won't."

"Have you seen a judge?"

"No, I just got here yesterday. I'm supposed to see a judge sometime today. I can't wait to get out of here."

"Hannah, I'm not a lawyer, but I'm pretty sure they don't give bond when you're charged with murder."

"What?" she says with her lip and chin shaking. "I have to get out of here."

She removes the phone from her mouth and holds it in front of her. She puts her head down and cries. When she looks back up again, her face is stained with tears. "What about Savannah? She needs me."

"I don't know. I don't know how all this works. My dad would know. He's represented people accused of murder."

"I didn't do it. I swear I didn't do it," she says so convincingly anyone listening to the conversation would believe her. "I could never do something like this."

This is the first time I've ever been inside a jail. I can't imagine being accused of something so terrible. "You don't even have to say it," I say. "I believe you."

She tells me all about the conditions inside the jail. I wish there was something I could say to make things better, but all I can do is be her friend.

"Where's Savannah?" I ask. "If you need someone to take care of her, I'll take her for you."

"She's fine," she answers. "She's with my mom."

"Hannah, do you have a lawyer?"

"I don't have money to pay a lawyer."

"You have to," I say. "You have to hire a good lawyer."

"They said the court will appoint me a lawyer."

"No," I insist, "you can't do that. If you get a court-appointed lawyer, you'll be convicted for sure."

"I have no choice," she says.

"What about your parents, or your grandparents?"

"I don't know. I'm sure they can help a little, but they don't have that kind of money. They spent most of their savings putting me and my brother through college. They barely came up with the seven hundred fifty dollars I paid a lawyer to come to the police station with me."

"What do the police have?" I ask. "You didn't confess, did you?"

"I don't know. When we last spoke, they told me they knew I was at the vacation home when he disappeared. They said my cell phone registered on the nearby cell phone tower."

"Oh my God," I say.

"I was there, but that's it. I was supposed to meet Jackson there when he flew in. I called him, but he never answered. After a few hours, I went home. I went home and went to bed."

Suddenly it occurs to me how I can help. If nothing else, I can pay for a lawyer for her.

"Hannah, don't do anything yet. Give me a little time. My dad left me some money. I'll find you a lawyer. I'll find you the best lawyer there is."

"Why are you doing this for me?" she asks.

"Because you're my friend and I care about you. You're not going to go through this alone."

"I don't get it," she says. "This is America. What about innocent until proven guilty?"

"No," I say. "In America, it's guilty until you hire a damn good lawyer. Don't worry, I'll be back with one."

– CHAPTER 44 –

Instead of returning to Dallas, I fly straight to Austin to talk to the Trustee, Mr. Wood. When I called his office from Denver, he told me to come right in.

"Quite frankly," he said, "there's something I need to see you about."

Over the past two years, he's never once refused my request for money; but this is big…bigger than anything I've ever asked for before. I'm not even sure how to ask him.

"How you been, Grace?" he says, once I'm sitting in front of him.

"Well, it's been tough. These last years have been hard. If it's not one thing, it's another."

"I'm sorry to hear about Jackson," he says. "You, okay?"

"I'm okay. More than anything else, I'm really sad for my kids. My son will never know his dad."

"I know. I wish there was more I could do."

"More you could do?" I smile. "You've done so much for me. If not for you, I'd be in big trouble."

"So, how's everything going with your case against DMD?"

"Didn't he tell you?" I ask.

"No, what happened?"

"This lawyer you hired was great. Before you hired him, they had all my accounts frozen—they wanted everything. We went to court, and he really turned things around. In the end, it was DMD who had to pay my attorney fees."

"Wow, that's great," he says with a smile. "He's the best at what he does."

Then Wood pulls out an envelope from his desk. "I actually asked you here because I have some news for you."

"More news?" I ask, closing my eyes, expecting the worst. "I don't know if I can take any more news. What's happened now?"

"I hope you don't mind," he says, holding the envelope. "I took it upon myself to send the insurance company a copy of Jackson's death certificate." He slides the envelope towards me. The top isn't sealed, so I easily pull out the paper inside. I'm shocked to find a check made out to "Grace Kennedy" in the amount of two million dollars. With a big smile, he says, "I believe this money belongs to you."

"Oh my God!" I say, about to cry. I get up from my chair, walk around his desk, and give him a giant hug. When I pull away from him, my eyes are full of tears. "Thank you. Thank you so much."

"You're very welcome," he says.

"I can't believe this. Don't I owe you a third or something?"

Wood closes his eyes and shakes his head. "Grace, I did all this because of your dad. He was there when I really needed someone. I owe everything

I am to him. The least I can do is help his little girl. You know you were always his little girl."

I put my head in my hands and cry; thinking about everything my dad has done for me and for so many other people. I look up and say, "I miss him so much. It's so hard going on without him."

He takes a deep breath and says, "Grace, there's something I need to talk to you and Hope about."

"What is it?"

"Your dad was concerned about what would happen after he was gone. He knew you and Hope would be left without a mother or a father. He wanted to make sure you and Hope stay close and be there for each other. He also wanted you to look out for each other."

"Of course," I say. "She's all I have left."

"Well, he had one last wish. It was to be fulfilled once the money is released to you, and I'm hoping you will honor his wish."

This is really confusing. I don't know what I'm supposed to do. "What is it?" I ask.

"I understand Hope is getting married soon, right?"

"The wedding is this May."

"That's wonderful," he says with another smile. "I'm sure he's a wonderful guy. Do you like him?"

"He's a great guy."

"Well, I think enough of the money has been distributed. I believe this is as good a time as any."

"What? What did my dad want?"

"He set some money aside for you two. He wanted you and Hope to take the money and go on a vacation together—to enjoy yourselves before you're so busy with life you can't go anymore."

"This is such an odd request. He wanted this?" I ask.

"It was his specific instruction before releasing all the money." He pauses for a second and says, "You know, I thought it was a strange request too at first, but now I agree with him. I think you both can use a little break right now…right?

"Definitely," I agree.

"Any idea where you might go?"

"I don't know, maybe California….or down to Florida."

"I think the media around your husband's death will be pretty intense now that they arrested the woman who killed Jackson. It might be a good idea for you and your kids to leave the country for a few weeks."

It's hard for me to think about a vacation with Hannah in jail and needing my support. Not wanting to let him know I'm going to give some of my money to hire her a lawyer, I nod my head and say, "That's a thought."

"I tell you what. I know someone who works in this area. She's planned several vacations for my wife and me. She can give us a few suggestions. Something easy and relaxing, right?"

"Right," I say with a smile.

He reaches out and says, "Well, let me get back to you with a few ideas."

A couple of days later, Hope and I return to Mr. Wood. He hands me a large envelope full of pictures and brochures to Montenegro—a place I've never heard of before."

"This is a country?" I ask.

"Oh yeah, Montenegro is an incredibly beautiful country. The woman I told you about just loves it. She booked a trip for my wife, and we had one of the best times of our lives. It's in Europe on the Mediterranean. It has all the beauty and glamour of the French Riviera, but costs much less. The country is home to some of the world's most beautiful beaches."

"Montenegro?" Hope says, reaching for the envelope.

"I told her you have a young girl and a baby. I let her know about the media surrounding your husband's death. This is why she thought of Montenegro. It's not real crowded… you'll be left alone."

Hope looks like she's already sold.

"It has some great sand beaches on the Adriatic coast, and the Bay of Kotor is a genuine miracle of nature. You can take a day trip to Italy, Croatia, or Greece. You can go wherever you like, but I think this is a great starting point."

"Montenegro?" I say, looking at Hope. "What do you think?"

"Montenegro!" she says, like she's thrilled with the idea. "Let's do it."

"All right then," he says, "I'll let her know. How's next week?"

We look at each other and Hope says, "Sure."

Wood gets up from his desk and, with a smile, says, "We'll take care of it. She'll book your flight, and hotel, and a couple getaways. The rest will be up to you. Do whatever you like."

Back home, Hope and I get on the computer and learn more about Montenegro. We call Wood to let him know we'll spend a few days there and finish our trip going down Italy's Amalfi coast. It all seems like an amazing getaway.

Grace Kennedy,
— Day 599

– CHAPTER 45 –

The following week our plane lands in Podgorica, the capital of Montenegro. We take a taxi to Budva, where we will be staying for the next four days.

As we've come to expect by now, Wood booked us at The Hotel Splendid, which is all about luxury. It has the fancy casino where James Bond gambled in the movie *Casino Royale*. The hotel has its own beautiful beach, indoor pools, sauna, hot tubs, and steam baths with Swarovski crystals.

We came into the city near the marina, so we find a restaurant on the water where we can eat dinner and relax after our long flight. There are so many incredible yachts and sailboats sparkling in the setting sun. Driving in from the airport, I saw more big houses and expensive cars than I've ever seen in my life. It looks like pictures I've seen of the French Riviera.

The next day, we walk around Budva. The city is protected by this old medieval fortress wall and beautiful mountains. We get a city map from the concierge and head along the city wall through all these really charming alleys until we reach the old town that's twenty-five hundred years old.

We walk down these cobblestone streets, through different narrow alleyways, and go in and out of the local shops and galleries until we finally stop for an early dinner at this cute restaurant with outdoor tables. After dinner, Hope and I drop the kids off at the hotel's kid's center and go to the spa for a one-hour massage.

After our massage, Hope leaves to check out some of the local bars and clubs in town that our waiter told us about. He said there's great music and the drinks are cheap. There's also some giant music hall she wanted to check out.

On our third day, we stay at the resort almost all day. First, we grab a quick breakfast before walking down to the hotel's private beach. The sand is white, and the water is so crystal clear—it looks turquoise. We all walk along the beach until we find an umbrella to get out of the sun.

Sometimes I complain that I'm left raising my kids all by myself, but the truth is Hope has been an incredible help—especially with Bonnie. Since Bonnie was the first and only grandchild for so long, everyone just attached to her. Sometimes I feel last in line. Ever since she came back, they spend more time together than we do. Bonnie often falls asleep in Hope's bed back home, and now in our hotel room she wants to sleep with Hope.

After a couple of hours sitting on the beach, I decide to take Wesley back to the hotel so he can get out of the sun and play in the indoor pool where it's not so hot. I don't think Bonnie will ever want to leave the beach, so Hope stays down there and they play in the water.

The hotel has a gigantic indoor/outdoor pool with palm trees, fountains, and a cool bridge to walk across. Wesley falls asleep on the hotel lounge chair, so I take this time to relax by the pool. Sitting next to him, my mind goes back to Hannah. The sight of her in a filthy prison, wearing a prison jumpsuit breaks my heart. While we're enjoying this vacation, she can't even see Savannah. I made sure I hired her a good lawyer before I left.

When she says she had nothing to do with Jackson's death, I know she's telling the truth. I'm not sure why they would arrest her. They have to have more than a ping off some cell phone tower.

The truth is, after everything Jackson did to us, I wouldn't blame her if she did kill him. I don't think anyone would blame her. Maybe she can plead temporary insanity, or self-defense, or…or that battered wife thing. If I was on her jury, I'd send her home with a big apology.

Almost ready to doze off in my lounge chair, I'm stirred out of my thoughts when another pool waiter with long hair walks up wearing white shorts and a colorful Hawaiian shirt. As he comes towards me, I'm blinded by the sun directly behind him, so I use my hand to shade my eyes. The service at this hotel is great, but sometimes it's overkill. Right now, I want to be left alone, and my drink is almost full.

He has long, dark hair and tan skin. All I see is the silhouette of his face until he gets close enough that his body blocks the sun. I'm just about to tell him I don't need anything, when I lower my sunglasses and almost have to do a double take. He's not a waiter wanting to bring me a drink. It's my dad standing in front of me!

Grace Kennedy,
— Day 599

– CHAPTER 46 –

The day I learned my father was dead was the day I lost a part of myself forever. Even before he died, I was already beginning to see how much of him was in me. His kindness, his sense of humor, and the love he had for his children were already a big part of the adult, and the parent, I've become. I'd catch myself saying many of the same sayings he would say; using some of the same facial expressions; or making the same gestures.

It took a while for it all to sink in. It was just too sudden. Jackson was gone for work that morning when the state trooper came to my door. I think I said something like, "What? My dad what?"

He stayed at the door, doing his best to keep everything really professional. "Your father was in an automobile collision," he repeated.

Unable to process what I just heard, I asked, "What hospital is he at?"

"I'm sorry, ma'am, but the collision was fatal."

Those words echoed through my head. I leaned against the wall to brace myself, and everything went blank. I think I invited him in for breakfast or a cup of coffee. When he politely declined, I asked him if he wanted to stay for dinner.

"Do you want me to call someone for you?" he asked.

I think he almost cried when, half out of my mind, I said, "Can you please call my dad?"

This is not the way it was supposed to be. I never had time to tell my dad goodbye. I was supposed to be there when he died and hold his hand; kiss his face; tell him I love him; and thank him for always being there for me. I wanted him to hold me in his arms one last time and whisper how much he loves me.

All I could think is: *What do I do now? How can I live without you? Where will I go when I need advice? Who will be there when I just need to talk? What does a person do when their life is broken like a giant jigsaw puzzle and the biggest piece to the puzzle is missing?*

So, what did I do? The first thing I did was call Hope, and we cried together. Then I went to bed in the pitch dark and cried myself to sleep. With the blinds down and the curtains closed, I lost all track of time. I thought, or hoped, or prayed, that if I just stayed asleep long enough, the pain would go away. But as one day, and then another, and another passed, the pain only got worse. Every dream I had crushed me.

Not all the dreams were bad. Some were beautiful, and those dreams hurt the most. In my dream, my dad is back as happy as ever. I'm confused and ask him what happened. Night after night, he'd explain how it was all some big misunderstanding and everything was going to be fine. In that moment, I feel love and peace, and my soul is healed. Then I'd wake up again and again to the reality that it was just a dream—not some big misunderstanding, and my dad is still dead.

For the first few days, Jackson (and everyone else) kept telling me how sorry they were…just let them know if I need anything. Then they went about their lives like my father never died at all. But not me. I just laid there in and out of sleep. For four days, I stayed in bed—unable to get up because getting up meant, in some sad way, that I was accepting his death. This was something I wasn't ready to do. It meant I would have to talk to other people, eat at the dinner table, smile, laugh, or God forbid, face a world without him in it.

Then, on the fourth day, Jackson came into our bedroom and threw open the curtains, blinding me with the morning sun. He walked over to the bed, and without lying down or even sitting beside me, he said something I'll remember for the rest of my days, "Grace, I know it may be hard, but life goes on. Get up. The kids need you."

By this time, I was already used to being alone; but never had I felt so lonely. When I needed love and comfort, Jackson offered neither. I looked at him, and for the first time, I felt nothing but contempt.

I threw off the covers and sat up on the side of the bed. He tried to kiss me, but I turned my face away. By this time, my heart was hard as steel. I felt a hate I never knew was possible. Things would never be the same between us again.

I couldn't help but wonder why I ever married this man. It's a terrible place to be, when you think you know someone and find out you don't know them at all. Still, I must have loved him at one time. I must have seen something in him that made me want to spend the rest of my life with him. Maybe so, but for the life of me, I can no longer remember what that something was.

The first thing I did when I stepped out of my bedroom was take my children in my arms and show them all the love my father always showed me. Bonnie, never at a loss for words, looked right at me and said, "Mommy, did Grandpa die?"

My dad's death still hurt so bad, so her words and the look on her face hit me too hard. I held her close to me, so she wouldn't see the tear that just rolled down my cheek, and said, "Yes baby…Grandpa died."

Bonnie's face turned red, her eyes filled with tears, then she started crying. I sat down on the floor, holding her in my arms, and laid the side of my face on her head. I rocked her, and kept saying, "It's okay, baby…it's okay."

Still in my arms, Bonnie kept crying, "I miss my grandpa, I miss my grandpa, I miss my grandpa."

Bonnie had such a close relationship with her grandpa. I really believe my dad loved her more than anyone else in the world. Maybe it had something to do with that day at the swimming pool when he held her lifeless body in his hands for thirty minutes and never stopped breathing into her tiny mouth. Maybe it's because grandparents can give all the love without worrying about any of the discipline. Maybe my dad loved being a grandpa even more than he loved being a father. Maybe Bonnie's love was the only love he knew that was pure and unconditional.

Lying in bed, I thought I knew hurt; I thought I knew tears; I thought I knew pain. I was so consumed with my own hurt that I didn't realize just how hard this was going to be on my four-year-old little girl.

It never occurred to me how many other people my father touched through the years until the day I returned to my dad's house and saw so many flowers, and cards, and letters. They began in the entry, filled the living room, and now were covering the front yard. People just stopped by and dropped off flowers.

My father may not have wanted a funeral or memorial, but he couldn't stop his church from holding a service to recognize all the good he'd done. One couple after another, stood at the front of the church wing my dad paid for to serve married couples and families. They each told their own story how my dad touched them.

Hundreds of friends, clients, and colleagues came to the house to pay their respects. The kitchen was so full of food that we started taking it to the local food shelters.

As Bonnie continued to cry, I told her, "Grandpa loved you most in the whole wide world."

It broke my heart to see her big bright eyes drowning in tears and her sweet little smile now full of pain. "I love Grandpa most in the whole world too," she said.

So, with that, I began the process of living again. As much as I'd like to lie in bed forever, it was clear my children needed me, my friends needed me, and Hope needed me. Without a doubt, my life would never be the same; but I'd find a way to live my life without my father in it.

– CHAPTER 47 –

Sitting beside the swimming pool, holding a mango strawberry daiquiri in one hand and my sunglasses in the other, I can't believe my own eyes. I drop my drink on the table and use my free hand to conceal my mouth that's open wide. My hand trembles in front of my face, showing the flood of emotions that almost cripple me. I can't talk. My mind says to move forward, but my body won't budge.

My dad's eyes are full of tears when he opens his arms and does his best to smile through his quivering lips. I slowly shake my head and whisper, "Oh my God."

When he takes a step closer, I jump up, run into his arms, and cry, "Daddy….oh my God it's you. You're alive."

It's so hard for me to believe I'm standing here with my dad holding me like he's done so many times before. I close my eyes so tight, and in a voice only I can hear, I pray: *God, please make this be real. Don't let this be a dream.*

Standing here with his arms wrapped around me, I'm overcome with emotion. I can barely talk—barely breathe. I can tell by the way he's crying against me, that he's also lost in the moment

"I….I….I love you," I get out through my tears. "I love you so much."

"I'm so sorry, baby," he says with a shaky voice. "I missed you."

"I missed you too…I missed you so much."

When I finally pull away, I can't believe how different my dad looks. Throughout my entire life, I never knew a day when he left the house before he showered, shaved, and his hair was neatly combed. Now his face has a heavy stubble, his hair is shoulder length and parted down the middle, and his white skin is replaced with a beautiful, dark tan.

He looks down at Wesley, who's sound asleep on the chair next to us. A smile spreads across his face as he reaches down, touches his head, and asks, "Is this my first grandson?"

I cover my smile and start crying again. When I try to talk, nothing comes out. I nod my head with tears pouring from my eyes.

"Can I?" he asks, reaching down. Not waiting for my answer, he lifts Wesley up and lays his tiny head on his shoulder. When he starts to stir awake, my dad says, "It's okay baby, Grandpa's got you."

I never thought I'd hear those words again. I look at my dad holding my little boy just like he once held Bonnie at that age. "He's got your name," I say, choking back tears. "I named him Wesley Ryan Kennedy."

My dad's eyes turn red, and for the first since Colt died, I hear him crying out loud. "He's beautiful. He looks just like Colt when he was a baby."

"That's what I thought," I say, looking at them both.

I reach out and hold both my dad and Wesley in one big embrace. I stay there until I gain enough courage to say the one thing I was unable to say before.

"I'm so sorry, Daddy. I should have been there for you. I was—"

"Shhhhh," my dad says, slowly bouncing Wesley up and down. After a few minutes, he asks, "Where's my Bonnie?"

"She's at the beach. She's at the beach with Hope."

My dad wipes his eyes clear, regains his composure, takes a deep breath, lets it out, and says, "Yes, Hope. I'm not sure how to approach her."

"Let me talk to her," I say.

"Does she still hate me?" he asks.

"I don't think she hates you. She was mad, but losing you has been too hard."

"I have to see her," my dad says, sitting down on the chair with Wesley. "I have to see my Bonnie. Can you talk to her for me?"

"Stay here with Wesley. I'll be right back."

I walk back down to the beach and see Hope and Bonnie building a castle in the sand. When I walk up, she turns towards me, and with a startled look, she asks, "Grace, where's Wesley?"

I bend over and put my hands over my face. I'm not sure how I'm going to say this.

"What?" Hope says, afraid of the answer. "What happened to him?"

I'm so overwhelmed I start crying again. She jumps to her feet, holds my shoulders, and asks, "Oh my God, Grace. What happened to Wesley?"

Still covering my face, I continue to cry. "He….he….he's here."

"Who? Who's here?"

There's no easy way to say this. "Dad….Dad's here."

Hope looks at me like she's just seen a ghost—or she's looking into the eyes of God. She starts shaking, and looks like she's going to cry. For a moment, I fear she might faint, so I hold her in my arms. Still shaking, she says, "It….it can't….he can't be here. He's dead."

I hold her to me and say, "He's not dead."

Hope holds on to me, doing her best to stay on her feet, and asks, "How? How can he be alive?"

"I don't know, but he's here. He wants to see you. He wants to see Bonnie."

"I can't," she says, falling to her knees, still crying. "I can't see him. I was so mean to him. I told him I hated him. I said I never wanted to see him again. How can he ever forgive me?"

"Hope, he loves you. He just wants to see you and talk to you."

"Is he angry?" she asks.

"He's not angry at all." I lift her back to her feet and say, "Come on, just talk to him."

I pick up Bonnie and hold her in my arms as we walk back to the hotel pool. Halfway there, Bonnie looks at me and says, "Grandpa's here?"

When I open the door to the indoor pool, our dad is sitting on a chair, holding Wesley in his arms, and kissing the side of his face.

Hope stops and says, "I can't do this."

I turn to Bonnie and start to say, "It's Grandpa," but before I can get the words out, her whole face lights up and she pulls out of my arms. She runs as fast as she can, yelling, "Grandpa, Grandpa, Grandpa." She jumps into Dad's arms, and he kisses her again and again with tears running down his cheeks. "My Bonnie….oh my Bonnie," my dad sobs.

"Why are you crying, Grandpa?" she asks with a puzzled look.

"I love you, baby. I love you so much."

"I love you too, Grandpa," she says, with such a big smile. "I missed you."

Hope starts crying all over again, as we slowly walk a little closer. It's plain to see how visibly shaken she is. When we're almost in front of him, Dad rests Bonnie on his hip, and reaches out for Hope. Saying nothing more, Hope puts both her arms around his neck and cries in his arms.

Standing here holding each other, Hope says, "I'm sorry, Dad. I love you. I love you so much."

Dad looks towards me and says, "None of you have anything to be sorry about. It's my fault. It's all my fault. I'm so sorry I put you through everything."

Once things die down, Hope looks at Dad and asks, "What happened? How are you here?"

Dad sits down on the chair and says, "I'll explain it all, but not here. I have a place not too far from here. Why don't we get your bags? I think you'll be more at home at my place."

We go up to our room, get our bags, and check out of our hotel. Parked out front of the hotel is a brand-new, bright yellow Jeep. It's so unlike anything my dad would ever drive back home.

We ride in his Jeep along this magnificent coast full of expensive homes, luxury cars, yachts, sailboats, and people walking or jogging. The road continues along this breathtaking view until we arrive at a little road on our right. The road brings us closer to the ocean, and then we stop in front of a stone wall with a gated entrance. Dad reaches up and clicks the remote clipped to the Jeep's driver side sun visor.

"What a nice neighborhood," I say.

"No neighborhood," Dad replies. "I found something a little more private."

"This is all yours?" Hope asks.

"It's all *ours*," he says as the cast iron gates with "GHC" written in the middle, slowly open.

Once inside, we continue driving down this little road with white flowering trees on each side. I can see the ocean shining through the trees, as we get closer to his house. We come to a stop in front of this gorgeous stone villa with a red clay roof. It has an amazing front entrance with pillars on each side of the front steps. Another click of the remote, and the garage door slides open. Parked to our left is a brand-new white Maserati.

We grab our bags and walk into a large, beautiful kitchen. It looks spotless, with granite countertops, stainless steel appliances, and a large refrigerator. He opens the refrigerator and then the pantry that's full of everything we could ever want and says, "Help yourself."

Anyone walking into this house has to be struck by the large living room. The whole place is modern and elegant. There's a sectional couch facing a large television hanging on the wall. Cool paintings are everywhere. The ceilings are high, and the back wall is completely made of glass. It gives an unobstructed view of an outside waterfall pouring into a magnificent swimming pool. The ocean sparkles behind the pool as far as you can see.

"This doesn't seem like you," Hope says.

"Nah…this is exactly me. I never bought the house I wanted. This is my kind of home."

Bonnie runs through the living room and goes right up to the back door. She jumps up and down, full of excitement. "A swimming pool, Grandpa. I want to go swimming."

"Let's get you into a bathing suit," my dad says, lifting her off the floor.

Dad leads us upstairs with Bonnie draped across his shoulder. He shows each of us the room where we'll be sleeping. Two of the bedrooms are fully furnished for an adult. As soon as we look around, we can tell these aren't just randomly decorated bedrooms. My room is prepared specifically for me in my favorite color. It's decorated with my old high school pictures on the dresser, my college flags on the wall, a volleyball in the corner, and a crib for Wesley. Hope's room is decorated for her with her high school photos and Stanford on the wall.

My dad looks at Bonnie in his arms and says, "What about you? You want a room too?"

Bonnie nods with a big smile.

My dad opens another bedroom door and shows us a little girl's bedroom with light pink paint, pink curtains, and a large canopy bed covered in stuffed animals. There's a little kitchen with a tiny table next to it. The table has four chairs and a baby doll in each chair. Next to the window, looking out over the ocean, there's a large three-story dollhouse full of Barbies.

"Is this my room?" Bonnie smiles.

"This is your room," he says, sitting her down.

She goes right up to the dollhouse, but my dad asks, "You still want to go swimming?"

Bonnie looks at him with another giant smile and says, "I love swimming, Grandpa."

My dad smiles back and says, "I know you do."

Once we change into our bathing suits, we walk back down to the back door. Dad releases the lock on the doorknob, the deadbolt lock, and the third lock at the top of the door. "Let's go outside," he says. "It's my favorite part of the house."

We walk outside and pause for a moment on the stone balcony. To our left, there's a wide stairway leading down to the pool with statutes spaced out every few steps. The ocean behind the pool is bright blue with giant yachts and sailboats scattered around that take my breath away. We walk along the pool, until we reach a gate at the back.

"You'll appreciate this," he says, opening the gate for us to walk through.

We walk down a little path to a circular stone area. There's a round fireplace sitting in the middle. Five chairs are scattered around the fireplace. The whole gorgeous area is sitting at the edge of a small cliff, looking out over the ocean. Hope and I glance at each other and mime "WOW" at exactly the same time.

After we all sit back in a chair, Hope can't take her eyes off dad. "I still can't believe it's real—that you're here."

"I can't believe you're here either. It's so good to have everyone back together again."

The air feels fresh and crisp. "This is amazing," I say. "How did you know about this place?"

Staring out at the ocean in his Hawaiian shirt, white bathing suit, dark sunglasses, and tan skin, my dad says, "Montenegro offers citizenship if you invest a little money in the country. They're not a part of the EU, so they have no extradition agreement with the US. Everyone's moving here. They call it the new French Riviera."

"There's yachts everywhere," I say.

"There's a lot of money here."

"I don't get it," Hope says, looking out. "How did you pull this off?"

"Pull this off?" he asks.

"The wreck…..everything."

My dad brushes his long hair back with both hands and says, "It wasn't so hard. You just have to know what you're doing."

After a brief pause, he shakes his head, and says, "It didn't have to be like this. I was willing to give Kate enough money to take care of her for the rest of her life—but that wasn't enough for her. She had to have it all. All I asked for was the house."

"Why?" I ask. "Why the house?"

"It wasn't really the house I was concerned about. It's what was in the house I wanted. I had a private safe inside the guesthouse, that no one knew anything about. It had enough money to take care of us. I wanted her to stay; but no matter how much I tried, she was done. The way I saw it, Kate could go her way, and I'd go mine."

I shake my head in disgust.

"Well, I went back to the house when she was gone. I wanted to get my things and go, but she changed the locks on the doors and the alarm code on the house—*our* house. I couldn't even get into my own house. So now you know why I offered to give her everything else, if she just gave me the house."

"So, you faked your death?" Hope asks.

"No, I just disappeared for a while."

"How?"

"It's not so difficult, really. A full tank of gas, let it burn for a while, and it's pretty difficult for anyone to know what just happened."

"What about the will?" I ask. "Don't you have to go to court or something?"

"The will? The will was one hundred percent real. Of course, I changed it once Kate locked me out of the house and started making threats. A couple days after the wreck, I had my probate attorney send a courtesy copy of my will to Kate and her lawyer. I don't know why she hired that guy. He never was the sharpest knife in the drawer. Did you know that SOB recorded me?"

Hope knows all about it. She was so angry when she met Kate's lawyer, that she told him everything she knew. Well, victory has many fathers, but defeat is often an orphan. Hope is back on the winning team for good now, so she sits there without saying a word.

"Anyway, there was no court. The will was never probated. I simply set up a trust to take care of you kids until this was all behind us, and we could be together again. It was all completely legal."

"What now?" Hope asks. "Are you in trouble or anything?"

"Not at all. It's not against the law to *disappear* for a while."

"To fake your death?"

"Fake my death? There was no funeral, no memorial, no newspaper announcement…nothing. I wasn't wanted by the law. I didn't take a bunch of insurance money. I broke no laws. The police had no reason to investigate."

"So that's it?" I ask.

"Pretty much," he answers, sitting back in his chair. "You know, one thing I've learned is that the human mind is an incredible thing. People believe what they want to believe. Sometimes all they need is a little nudge."

"Then why'd you leave? Why are you living so far away?" Hope asks.

Laying his head on the back of his chair, my dad says, "I had to get away for a while. For me…for you…we needed some time apart. I also wanted to spend some time in reflection—do a little soul searching—and I didn't like everything I saw. I want you girls to know how much I wish I could go back and change everything; but I can't. All I can do now is ask the Lord for forgiveness and live the best life I can."

I reach over and put my hand in his. We sit there as the cool air blows in and watch as the tip of the sun sizzles against the ocean way out on the horizon.

"Do you remember Tom Flint?" Hope asks. "He was arrested. He was arrested for murder."

Dad closes his eyes and shakes his head in disgust. "Tom Flint was evil––pure evil. Right after you went to his office, he called me. He threatened you. At that point, I knew he was capable of anything. That's when we all had that talk, and I begged you to let things go."

"So, what about Zach?" Hope asks.

"Flint started following Zach. He put a tracker on his car and his phone and was eavesdropping on his calls. He found out Zach was going to California to meet with you and tell you everything, so he put a hit out on Zach's life."

"I knew Zach didn't kill himself," Hope says. "I just knew it."

"Girls, I've made mistakes in my life. Let me correct that," he says, looking down. He looks back up, and continues, "Not mistakes but terrible, terrible decisions. I have only myself to blame. I'd already done enough that I couldn't take back. I had to make things right, no matter what it cost me. So, I tried to stop him. I warned him not to do it, but he didn't care what I said. I tried to save Zach."

Hope and I sit as our dad wipes his eyes. He puts his head back down and continues. "I tried. I swear to God I tried. I called him and warned him to get out of town—just leave Austin and don't come back. I guess Flint's man got there before he could leave."

Looking back up, he says, "Well, Flint found out I was the one who tipped off Zach, so he came after me. I have a good friend in Houston—he helps people with passports—who called me after Flint left his office. He was looking for me, and I'm sure he would have killed me."

"I can't believe this," Hope says.

"I made an anonymous call to the police and told them it was Flint who killed Zach. I gave them everything they needed to get a search warrant and put him away for the rest of his life."

"So, that's why they arrested him?" I ask.

"Flint had this way about him. He was the kind of guy who made enemies everywhere he went. He had this sweet little secretary who hated him. She came to my office one day wanting to sue him for sexual harassment. She said he was always making inappropriate comments, touching her, once pinned her against the wall, and…." My dad pauses for a moment. "Well, I called her to let her know the police were coming with a search warrant, so she would be gone. I knew she'd be out of a job, so I helped her out a little. I asked for just one little favor in return. She went upstairs and brought down the box that you saw when you were there. She took everything out of the box except for the file on Zach."

When you're a child growing up, you don't know your parents—not really. All you know is he's my dad and she's my mom. You don't give any thought to their lives—their struggles, their hurts, their needs. I always knew my dad was smart, but this is the first time I realize just how smart he really is. This is all just brilliant.

"You know, he killed himself," Hope says.

"I know," my dad says. "I followed the whole thing. Flint caused so much hurt in his life. Now he'll never hurt anyone again."

Bonnie walks over to Dad, and says, "Are we going swimming, Grandpa."

My dad gets up and says, "Sure, baby."

We walk back up to the swimming pool. I sit with Wesley while Bonnie, Hope, and Dad jump in the pool. My dad spends all his time playing with Bonnie—tossing her up and down, splashing back and forth, and watching her swim to the side. Then he takes Wesley.

"He can't swim," I say.

He holds Wesley in the pool and bounces him up and down. Everything picks up right where we left off. This all continues until the sun disappears completely. When the sky turns dark, all the lights around us turn on and illuminate the pool and the deck.

Hope gets out of the pool and says, "I told Blake I'd call him. If you want, I'll bring the kids inside and lay them down."

After Hope goes inside the house, my dad takes my hand, and says, "Come on….let's talk."

We walk together back down to the fire pit where he puts a few logs on the fire. Sitting by the fire with the sound of the waves crashing down below, feels like the rest of the world is far away. The stars are shining brightly above our heads. When my dad turns back to me, I ask, "So, who's the girl in the picture?"

"The picture?"

"Dad," I say with a grin. "I saw the picture on the fridge. Who is she?"

"Oh, that picture—she put that on the fridge. I'm sorry, I should have taken it down."

"So?" I ask again.

"Her? Oh, she's just a friend."

"Well, somebody better tell her," I laugh. "She sure looks all in love hanging all over you in her tiny little bathing suit."

"Nah…she's sweet. We have fun together. That's what it's all about for me now. Just enjoy life."

I always thought Kate and Mom had a similar look. This woman, however, looks completely different. She has dark hair, dark skin, long legs, and she's almost as tall as dad. "How old is she?" I ask.

"You know, I'm not really sure," my dad says. "I think she has a little boy, but I haven't met him."

"How long have you been dating?" I ask.

"Boy, you sound like the parent here. I don't know—four or five months, I guess. Like I said, we're just friends. I'm out of the love business."

I take a deep breath and say, "Me too."

"Don't say that, Grace," my dad says. "My better days are behind me now. You….you still have your whole life in front of you. I once felt just like you do, but all men aren't bad; just like all women aren't bad."

We pause a minute taking in the cool breeze. It's absolutely gorgeous.

"So, was it you the whole time? Was it you approving all the money?"

"Was I looking out for both of you? Of course. I'm sorry I had to put you through all that."

"What about the paper—the receipt in the vase in Thailand?"

"You're a smart girl. I wanted to leave something to let you know I was here. I knew you were coming to visit your mother's grave, so I took out the flowers and left that receipt for you to find. I figured you'd understand."

"I thought it was you," I say. "I knew it had to be."

"You know, I saw you. I saw you at the funeral."

I can't believe what I just heard. "What are you talking about?"

"It was killing me being away from you kids. I knew you, and Hope, and Bonnie, would be at the funeral. I wanted to see my new grandbaby. I came back, got a limousine, and stopped at the funeral."

"That was you?" I ask.

"It was me. You walked right up…maybe five feet from my window. I was sure you knew."

I lean forward, slap my leg, and with a laugh, say, "I'll be damned."

"I looked right at you before driving away. Leaving was so hard."

We sit a little longer with the cool air blowing in our faces and the wood from the warm fire popping in front of us. "It's so peaceful here," I say.

"Yes, it is," my dad agrees. "I spent my whole life full of stress. It's a wicked thing to have everyone's problems on your shoulders. Every call, every letter, every hearing, every conversation, was confrontational. Now I want peace. This is just what the doctor ordered."

I was the oldest child, so I remember everything with my mom and dad. I remember the good times, and I remember the bad times. Now that I'm grown, and I've been through everything with Jackson cheating on me, I finally ask the question on my mind.

"So, tell me, dad, how did it happen?"

"How did what happen?" he asks.

"With mom….how did it happen?"

My dad sits back in his chair and stares at the fire. He brushes his hair from his face and gives a strong exhale before answering.

"I've spent so many hours out here pondering that very question. I'm still not sure I have the answer. It still haunts me." He puts his hands in front of his face like he's praying. "I loved your mom…as much as any man can love a woman. She was the love of my life, and I've never loved that way again. When she left, I lost my love, my kids, and my home. Mostly, I lost the life I loved. Then…then I lost myself. I'm done making excuses. I know I only have myself to blame. Somewhere along the way, I lost the man I was."

My dad looks out at the ocean with such a sad look I think he might cry. Still looking away, he says, "What good is a man if he gains the world but loses his soul? Well, I lost my soul—plain and simple. It's a sad, sad thing to lose your soul. One day I'll meet my maker." A tear falls down my dad's cheek. "When I do—when I meet the Lord—all I can do is beg for forgiveness. It's something I must live with for the rest of my life."

With the moon now hanging in the distance, the temperature drops. My dad walks back to the woodpile, grabs a couple more logs, and throws them on the fire. Probably wanting to change the subject, my dad says, "You know, she haunts me. There's not a day that goes by, that I don't think about her and what I did to her. I guess I deserve as much."

Listening to my dad, it sounds so awful. I want to say something, but I don't know what to say. He turns to me and says, "So tell me about this Blake guy."

"You know, he's a nice guy. I've spent a lot of time with him. He's smart, he's kind, and he's sweet to Bonnie and Wesley."

"Does he love my baby?" Dad asks.

"God yes," I say, rolling my eyes. "It's pretty pathetic. He's nuts about her."

"That's the most important thing. If you approve, then I approve."

"I like him, and for me to say that's saying a lot. I'm not real high on guys right now, if you know what I mean."

He reaches over, puts his hand on my leg, and asks, "Jackson?"

"You know about it?" I ask, a little teary-eyed.

He tightens his lips, closes his eyes, and nods his head. While he holds my hand in both of his hands, I lay my head against his fingers without saying anything. Dad moves his chair next to mine and kneels down beside me. He puts his arm across my back and asks, "What is it, sweetie?"

I shrug just a little and say, "I don't know. Jackson wasn't the man I thought he was. I was spending all my time trying to make our marriage work, but he had this whole other life. He had another wife, another house…he even had another baby with this woman."

"I know," he says, holding me. "I heard all about it."

"It's only because of the kids that I was able to get through it all."

"You're like me," he says. "Your kids mean everything to you."

I look up and say, "You know, everyone thought he was in Paris or something. Then I find out he was right there the whole time….just a few miles from our home in Aspen."

My dad stares right into my eyes and asks, "Do you want to talk about it?"

"Talk about it?" I ask.

Still comforting me, he says, "You know, Grace, I get the American news stations here."

"You saw it over here?"

"The whole thing. I watched it again and again."

I wipe my teary eyes on my shirt and ask, "Watched what?"

Still kneeling beside me, he looks right at me and says, "The news when that guy found Jackson."

I shake my head and say, "Yeah, that was pretty rough."

"Sean….Sean Campbell."

I put my hands over my face and close my eyes, not sure what to say next. He raises his eyebrows and looks at me sideways. He sits back in his chair, puts his hands behind his head, and says, "Tell me about it."

I slowly lower my hands from my face, look over at him, and say, "Oh, my God." I've never been able to fool my dad. At this point, there's no reason to pretend any longer. I shake my head and ask, "So you know? You've known all along?"

My dad nods his head, showing no judgment whatsoever. "It's been a while, but you know me. I never forget a face. I remember him. You were what…nineteen or twenty?"

"Nineteen," I confirm.

"He spent spring break with us….nice kid."

I close my eyes, waiting for his next words.

"I didn't really understand it at first. Why? Why not just leave well enough alone? Why didn't you just leave Jackson down there? Then I figured it out. The insurance company wouldn't pay on Jackson's life insurance policy until someone found his body. So, you got your old boyfriend to go down there and find him."

I look up and say, "We waited and waited…thinking someone would eventually discover him, but it never happened."

"*We* waited," he repeats. "So, he's the one—he's the one who killed him?"

I nod my head and sit here for a moment before answering. "He loves me—even after all these years—he still loves me. He moved back to Austin after college. We'd talk now and then, but nothing more. When I told him everything Jackson did to me….well."

"So, tell me how you found out about Jackson."

"Honestly, I was already suspicious. Do you remember when we talked about it a long time ago?"

My dad looks at the fire without speaking.

"It's like I told you; he was never home. Every time I said anything, he made me feel like I was jealous, or imagining things, or...or…I was crazy. I was the one who was ruining our marriage. He was so convincing, I started wondering if I was going crazy."

Looking out over the ocean like I just spotted something far away, and with my lips trembling, I say, "Then he told me he wanted a divorce. I begged him not to leave me. By that time, I was so low—I had no pride. I got on my knees in front of him and begged him to stay. The more he said he was leaving, the more I begged. I told him I was sorry. I kept asking *him* to forgive *me*."

As I'm reliving it all, a tear shoots down my right eye. My dad's eyes also fill with tears. "You know, I've always thought I was strong. I'd never dream one day I'd be on my knees begging someone not to leave me. But I'd already lost so much, and I was so broken. I didn't want to lose my husband, too."

My dad looks out with teary eyes. I get the feeling he's thinking about his own past. "I understand completely," he says, holding back his emotions.

"So, all my begging and pleading worked—or at least I thought it worked. He agreed to stay."

As I talk about Jackson again after all this time, my hurt is replaced by the same stone-cold anger I've learned to live with. I continue staring into the fire and wait a few minutes before continuing.

"Then Hope made all these plans to go to Thailand to see Mom's grave. By now, Jackson and I hadn't been spending much time together, so I thought...*great!* I planned everything and made this great vacation out of it. I wanted to rekindle the fire we once had for each other."

With the first hint of a smile, I say, "You know, I was actually excited about it all. I even bought him this stupid watch. I went to the grocery store and bought him a card and everything I needed to make this great meal. I wanted to show him how much I loved him—how much the kids loved him. With this beautiful spread, I waited for him to come home from work. He came home two hours later than he said he'd be home. By then, the food was cold. Still…still I met him at the door and went to kiss him. He walked right past me without saying a word.

When he saw everything sitting on the table, he said he already ate and wasn't hungry. He went straight to our bedroom and got in the shower. I sat on our bed waiting for him to finish. It felt like forever. When he finally came out, he walked right past me, turned around, and said he wasn't going to Thailand."

My dad shakes his head and gives me a look of sympathy and disgust as I continue.

"He said he couldn't go because he had to work. He kept saying the same," I press my lips together and shake my head as the anger wells up inside me, "the same *shit*." Calming down just a little, I say, "That was it. I knew something wasn't right. I knew there was something he wasn't telling me, and I had to find out what it was. After he left for work the next day, I started looking around the house like some crazy woman. I dumped out drawers, shelves…everything. I looked all over the house for something…anything…but I found nothing. Then that night—after he fell asleep—I got out of bed, went to the garage, and searched his car. That's where I found it. I found this cell phone—a cell phone I'd never seen before—hidden in his trunk. The next day, I took the phone to someone who broke into it. It was all there. I learned everything——the whole damn, disgusting, truth."

"I'm so sorry, Grace," my dad says, taking my hand.

I look down and cry again. "Now, for the first time, it all made sense. That asshole was fucking another woman. He even brought her to our home…the vacation home we bought together. He got her pregnant and married her. He called her 'honey' and 'babe'. I felt like such a fool," I say wiping my tears away. I shake my head and say, "You won't believe what he did."

"What is it?" Dad asks.

"He even took her on *our* vacations. He set her up in a room at the same hotel…right next to ours!"

This whole time my dad has remained so calm. Now I see this anger on his face. as he clenches his teeth. He takes me in his arms and pulls me onto his lap. He holds me like he did when I was five-years-old, and I fell off my bike. "Look at me Grace," he says.

I turn to look at him.

"I will never know what you've been through…no one can tell you how you should feel inside, or how you should react."

I start to cry a little while he holds me. "I know it wasn't right. I know I did an evil thing. I'm not sure who I am anymore."

My dad rocks me in his arms and says, "Grace, there isn't some big line between good and evil—it's not always one side or the other. Betrayal is brutal. The hurt and anger can eat you up inside. It can cause you to lose your mind."

"I know," I say, wiping my eyes clear again. "I should have just walked out years ago, but you urged me to stay. I didn't want to be divorced. I didn't want to let you down. Then….then when I found out, I just lost it."

Dad kisses my head and whispers, "It's not your fault, Grace. It's my fault. It's all my fault."

I understand exactly what he's saying. "I don't know if it was because of what you did, or if I would have done it anyway. I really think the anger blinded me. I was so depressed. I never knew how depression can cripple you. I think I was having a nervous…or mental breakdown or something."

My dad continues to rock me in his arms.

"I'm sorry, Daddy," I sob. "I'm so sorry."

"Shhhh," he says, stroking my hair. "What's done is done."

As the fire burns out, I sit up and return to my chair.

"What about Sean?" my dad asks.

"What about him?" I ask, rubbing my nose with my palm.

"Did you agree to pay him?"

I nod again and say, "He's going to get two hundred thousand dollars from the life insurance policy."

"Have you paid him yet?" he asks.

"No, I just got the money right before we left."

"Thank God," my dad says. "Grace, you can't pay him. With that much money, you'll be under a lot of suspicion. The insurance company will be watching your every move. They've probably already hired an investigator. If you pay him, it will lead right back to you."

"Then what do I do?" I ask.

"Let me think," he says, looking up. "As far as anyone knows, he was just another hiker. No one has any idea he's connected to Jackson's death. I'll take care of it. Give me his information and I'll send the money myself. You can't talk to him…at least not for a good while."

My dad looks out at the reflection of the moon on the ocean. "The problem is," he says, "you can never know how this will all play out. You can't understand sitting here today all the consequences of something like this."

I shake my head and say, "Oh, I know…I already know."

My dad gives me this look, like he doesn't understand what I'm saying.

 "There's this one thing," I continue.

"What one thing?"

I close my eyes shut and take a deep breath and let it out before looking back at my dad. "It's Hannah—Jackson's new wife. She had nothing to do with this. She knew nothing. Well…"

"Well, what?" my dad asks.

"Well, they arrested her for Jackson's murder right before I left to come here."

My dad falls back in his chair, looks up at the sky, and says, "Oh no."

"I don't know what to do, Dad. She's in jail, and she has no money to hire an attorney."

"There's nothing you can do," my dad says.

I look down at my lap and say, "I have to. I have to do something."

"Grace, you need to stay out of it," he warns.

I close my eyes, shake my head, and whisper. "It's not so simple." My dad sits in silence, so I put my hand over my mouth while building up the courage to tell him. "It was me. I'm the reason she got arrested."

"You're the reason?"

I just sit here, unsure how to say it. Then I take another deep breath and say, "I set her up…"

"You what?"

"You have to understand. I didn't know her back then. As far as I knew, she stole my husband and broke up my family. Right before I left for Thailand, I saw Hannah's text to Jackson and knew they were planning to meet at our Aspen house as soon as I left. Sean followed him to this little store by the airport. I knew Jackson would have his other wedding ring— the ring Hannah gave him—on him somewhere. The ring was in his center console. After it was all done, I told Sean to find that ring and put it on his finger. Sean took off my wedding ring and put the other ring on his finger."

"Shit," my dad says.

"I know," I say, shaking my head. "I wasn't really trying to get her arrested….or maybe I was. Mostly, I was trying to take any suspicion away from me. I figured they'd think he made it to Denver before he died if he was wearing her wedding ring. When Sean got to Aspen, he text Hannah from Jackson's phone, "I'm here.""

"Wow," my dad says.

"Hannah says they tracked her phone to the vacation house on the night he disappeared—very close to where Jackson was found."

"What have you done?" My dad asks, looking right at me.

"I don't know," I answer, burying my face in my hands.

"Well, that explains it," my dad says. "They have the text from Hannah asking to meet; the text that he arrived; they know she was at the vacation house on the day he disappeared; and he was wearing her wedding ring. That's enough. That's enough right there to convict Hannah."

I shake my head and say, "I didn't know her back then. She's a nice girl. She's so sweet. She had no idea Jackson was married."

"This is unbelievable," Dad says, rubbing his forehead like he has a headache or something.

"I messed up, Dad. I messed up bad."

"Yeah, you messed up real bad," he says.

"Just tell me, Daddy—tell me what to do, and I'll do it."

"Grace, you've got to stay out of it," he says.

"I can't. I have to make it right. I can't let her go to prison for something I did. I'll turn myself in before I let that happen."

"Grace, no!" he says like he's shocked I'd even suggest such a thing. "Family always comes first. You have kids who need you. Without you, they have no one."

"I know, but she has family, too. She has a little girl."

"Grace, you're playing with fire. You're gonna fool around and wind up in prison."

I stand up, kneel in front of him, and say, "Please help me, Daddy."

Seeing me kneeling in front of him so helpless, my dad closes his eyes and says, "I cannot believe this."

I lay my head on his knees and beg, "I need you, Daddy. You've got to get Hannah out of jail. I could never live with myself if she goes to prison."

"I can't baby. I can't go back to the States—not for a while."

"Please," I beg. "You said you want to make things right. Well, this is your chance. Please do this for me. Do it for your family."

"We'll find her a good lawyer," he says.

I look up, shake my head, and say, "No..._you_ have to do it. Only you can get her off. If anyone can do it, you can."

"You have no idea what you're asking me to do. Plus, you're putting me in a terrible position. If I get her off, it could convict you. Then I could never live with myself."

"You have to. You have to find a way."

"Grace—"

"Please, Dad...do it for me. You have to do it for me."

Dad looks up, and says, "Let me think about it."

Right then, we hear Hope opening the gate and walking down the path to where we're sitting. As she gets a little closer, I stand up and return to my chair. I lean over to Dad and whisper, "Hope doesn't know about any of this. Please don't tell her."

Hope comes down the path looking so giddy she's practically skipping. She has the kind of smile on her face you only see on a child or a young girl in love. "Hey guys," she says.

"How was your talk with Blake?" my dad asks.

"It was great, Dad. I know you'll really like him."

"I can't wait to meet him," Dad says.

"Daddy," she says with the same smile across her face, "we're getting married."

"Married? Well, I better meet him soon."

Hope sits in the open chair to my right, looking out over the cliff, and says, "God, it's beautiful here." She catches Dad and me looking at each other and asks, "So, what have you two been talking about?"

I look away, not sure what to say. Dad gets up to grab a couple of logs for the fire. "Nothing really," he says with a smile when he returns. "Just catching up.

Don't miss the next book in the series, *The Rise & Fall of Ryan*.

SIGN UP FOR MY READER GROUP

Thanks for reading the third book in my *Killing of Faith* series. The series continues with the final book, *Ryan Brunick (Book 4)*.
I hope you enjoyed it. Please be so kind as to leave a review on Amazon and tell your friends and family. Support from readers like you can make or break a book. I hope you join me for the ride.

Want more? Click this link and join my reader group. I'll notify you when my next book is released., provide the background on each book, sign your book, and give you the lowest price on the internet.

https://readergroup.williamholms.com/

Notice any errors in the book? Email me and I'll email you the next book for free! Feel free to buy my books directly from me and I'll send you a signed copy. You can buy it for less than the retail price. Want me to speak at your event or book club, or just want to talk? Email me:

Email me: author@williamholms.com

— ACKNOWLEDGMENT —

Having an idea and turning it into a book can be quite challenging. Continuing the series has been a joy. I want to thank everyone who helped make this happen.

I am so thankful for the readers who have read, left reviews, told their friends and family, and emailed me personally and let me know how much they enjoy *The Killing of Faith* series. Your words are so encouraging and inspire me to continue the series. If not for you, I would have only written one book. Thanks for helping me grow as a writer, and for joining me on this journey.

Thanks so much to all those on my advance reader team for taking the time and making the effort to not just read my draft book, but also provide me comments and feedback, and check the book for errors. This book is far better thanks to you. Special thanks to Ted Wood, Karen Silver, Verena Rozanski, Christie Schneider, Ellen Aish, Patricia Montalvo, Kay Painter, Heather Gelato, Kate Cycyota, and Sarah Bloonfield.

I want to give a big shout-out to Deborah Jesensek for proofreading my entire book, giving feedback, and helping with the book cover.

Finally, I want to give a heartfelt thanks to Kara Kissinger who has been a great sounding board and offered wonderful ideas and thoughts to help the book along the way. Thank you.